Daniel, Luke, and John

Daniel, Luke, and John

by Karen Sloan-Brown

BROWN REFLECTIONS

Daniel, Luke, and John

Copyright © 2014 by Karen Sloan-Brown

This book is printed on acid-free paper.

ISBN: 978-0-991551798
Library of Congress Cataloging-in-Publication Data on file.

Editor: Cornelius Brown

Daniel, Luke, and John

KAREN SLOAN-BROWN

Daniel, Luke, and John

I Found My Manliness

Manhood, you are my flaming, glowing love.
I found you when I was old,
You have made me come alive
Your success overshadows past failures.
You are what I am and can be,
You are what I want them to know and see,
I love being a man, oh, how I love it.
---Cordell H. Sloan

Prologue

Daniel's lip stung and buzzed like a bee as it swelled around his mouthpiece. His forehead throbbed to an unknown beat where the last set of right-hand jabs landed. His opponent was packing every single pound of his hulking figure behind every one of his punches. Daniel needed to land at least one solid shot to get him to back off or he wasn't going to make it through this round.

Daniel had always wanted to box. He loved the sport long before he climbed into the ring for the first time. It was something about being in a roped square, having to duke it out, and may the best man win. The first time he stood toe-to-toe with another guy he found his manliness. He felt indomitable, fearless, powerful, and unique. He was his own man and his own boss. That's when he knew there was no way he was going to carry a briefcase or a broom. His two fists were all he needed to make his way in the world.

In the beginning it was the fame and glory that had him enamored, but in his first amateur fight he discovered that when he took a punch, instead of it simply hurting him, his inner pain was released. It was the physics of two masses colliding together and creating forces in opposite directions. It didn't matter whether he delivered the hit or whether he received it; the force from the impact between him and his opponent released the pent-up energy of his anger and pain.

"Dammit, where's your defense," Wendell, his trainer and coach yelled from outside the ring, stunning him more than the hit. "Don't stand in there taking his punches."

Daniel didn't know what was wrong but he couldn't find his target. It had been a cakewalk to the quarterfinals taking out the others in the first round. The semifinals proved more of a challenge but he had plowed on. He was using the same strategy he had used to beat his other competitors but this guy kept coming forward. He knew this matchup was going to be the roughest but he had earned his place in the tournament one match at a time. "You've got to win to stay in," Wendell said to encourage him before each match. "If you lose you're out of the tournament."

Now he was in the final, and it was proving to be the hardest fight he had ever had. This guy was a straight-up brawler swinging fast and wild, a total contrast to Daniel's style of a tactical boxer, and it was taking him out of his game. The other guy glared at him and snarled, "You're going down," as he threw another flurry of punches. Daniel winced from the tingling stings on his arms where he had done his best to block the attack.

Finally he got lucky with a straight right to the jaw that shocked the other guy. Except it didn't hurt him. It only made him mad and he swung back with a low blow that the ref missed or ignored, and then followed it with an uppercut that hit Daniel right under his headgear. Daniel clinched the guy to buy time but the thin gaunt referee squeezed between them and pushed him off. Saved by the bell, Daniel ambled to his corner. A drop of blood fell from his nose and disappeared on the red cushion along the top rope of the ring.

"Sit down, catch your breath," Wendell said, putting Daniel's stool down in the corner before he stepped inside the ring. Then he took the water bottle, squirted it over the top of Daniel's head and in his mouth, and held the bucket for him to spit. "You've got to come alive or you're dead," he said forcefully.

"He's tough," Daniel said through short breaths as he got to his feet.

"So are you," Wendell said, pushing him back out for round two.

Daniel backpedaled, blocked most of the punches, and countered when he could but for some reason Daniel was distracted. It might have been the too bright lights in the stadium or the extra commotion outside of the ring. People were constantly walking back and forth and in and out of the room, and some fat loud-mouth was shouting insults at him and rooting for his opponent.

A large group stood on one side of the ring chanting, "Ricky, Ricky, Ricky." At that moment Daniel wished he had his family there to yell out his name. He hadn't told them he was in the competition. He wanted to do this by himself. Mainly he wanted to prove to his Dad that he was his own boss, that he had skills, and that he could be a champion. The bell sounded again and he retreated back to his corner.

Wendell put out the stool again but Daniel shook his head.

"This one is for all the marbles, man," Wendell said, wiping his face with a towel, "There's no tomorrow."

"I refuse to lose," Daniel assured him as he shuffled his feet in the corner.

Even so, Wendell was worried, he couldn't figure out why Daniel was fighting like his hands were tied together.

The bell sounded for round three. Both fighters rushed out from their corners to the center of the ring staring into the other's eyes as they moved counterclockwise in a circle. For the first minute they traded hard punches with neither giving up an inch. Then Ricky hammered Daniel with a combination of body shots and followed them with a left hand to the side of his head. Daniel went numb and his instincts took over. After that it seemed as if his opponent's movements shifted into slow motion.

"I got him now," Daniel thought. Bouncing and weaving in front of him as his left jab connected again and again. It was like they were dancing to music and Daniel had found his rhythm. He anticipated when the other guy would throw a punch and what hand he would use. When Ricky's left hand dropped for less than a second, Daniel loaded his right hook and fired. It landed square on his chin with a force that knocked him off his feet.

"Pay dirt," Wendell hollered happily.

The slow motion ended and the room took on its normal speed. Daniel's confidence ebbed and his apprehension returned. He had given up on God when he saw his momma hurting but now he was praying that this guy would stay down on the canvas. He didn't want to hurt him, and more than that he didn't want to get hurt. He was sure that if the guy got up, his ass would be the next one to go down. He watched as Ricky pulled himself up onto the ropes and his heart started to beat fast as it filled with panic. Then the referee waved his hand. It was over. Daniel's chest collapsed down with relief as he exhaled.

The ringside announcer spoke into his microphone. "In the red corner from Philadelphia, out of Joe Frazier's Gym, is the 1991 Pennsylvania Golden Gloves Heavyweight Champion."

Cheers and claps filled the air around him and Daniel took a bow before he left the ring. He was proud and satisfied. He had done it. He had come there every week for a month and fought whoever they put in front of him and won.

"Congratulations," Wendell said when they were back in the dressing room. "You're officially the big dog on the playground."

Daniel smiled. He had believed it and now he had proved it. He was a winner.

Chapter One

Luke stood solemnly beside the grave of the only person on God's creation who truly loved him without condition. He had mourned his wife Ruth's death uninterrupted for seven years. Not merely the loss of her presence but more for the promises that were left unfulfilled and the unpaid debt that burdened his soul. He wanted to give her everything her heart could desire as recompense for all she had given him but time had short-changed them both. Cancer was the nasty-ass thief that stole her away. He couldn't see a future for himself without her so he spent the bulk of his time living in the past. His motivation for waking up every morning was to see the business they built together be carried on in their name by their son Daniel and to see their daughter Rebecca happily married to an honorable man.

He kneeled and laid the bouquet of crimson roses and white carnations, for love and remembrance, at the foot of the monument with the angel in her likeness. Then he started to speak to her as he did on the 22th day of every month.

"Ruthie, honey, I'm still here. I don't have the words to tell you how much I love you and how much I miss you. Things are falling apart for me and it seems like there's nothing I can do to bring it all back together. I've made some big mistakes, pretty girl. All I wanted to do was expand the business so Daniel would be proud to step in my shoes but he don't give a shit about it. Now I'm in debt up to my eyeballs and I could lose everything. Becca is smart and she's been working her ass off but that's not what I want for her. She's got it in her mind that she don't want no man, she don't have

no feelings for them.

I don't understand either one of them, sugar. The boy wants to fight in the boxing ring for a living and the girl wants to fight these cheating suckers in the business world. When I think about what you went through it pains me that these children can't appreciate what we've done for them. I don't want all of your hard work to be in vain."

***

Luke Randolph Clements came into this world on November 17, 1950, born the color of hot cocoa, and the youngest of five children. The two oldest siblings were his brothers, Matthew and Mark, then his sisters, Mary and Martha. His family could have been described as dirt poor except that in the rundown community of Ludlow there was no dirt or soil to speak of. It was more like concrete, asphalt, and broken glass that lined the streets where they lived.

Luke took after his daddy, John Clements, the son of a sharecropper, who was most certainly dirt poor. His folks couldn't even call the meager harvests they dragged from the ground their own. That's pretty much how it was if you were born black in Gainesville, Georgia back in 1921. Every pair of hands, no matter how small, had to work and still it was never enough. Being a child only lasted until you were big enough to go work in the field. For John, that was nine years old. He was one of the fortunate ones. He'd gone to school through the third grade. He could read, write, and decipher his numbers. That's where he got his ideas about things in the North. He figured a black man could be somebody up there.

***

John was tall, strapping, and almost twenty years old near the end of the Great Depression and full of high hopes for the plot of land he was working for himself. His body had been built by plowing the field and his skin was darkened by the sun. With a direct and no-nonsense manner, he wasn't one to struggle with battles he couldn't win. His best buddy, Charles Winfrey, a couple of years older than him and too lazy to farm, made his money running his poppa's bootleg whiskey. He was always talking about taking off for New York to make some big bucks. John thought it was a pipe dream and never paid him no mind until his first crop came in and sold. He had damn near broken his back and he still owed Deke Masters $5.93.

When the next planting season rolled around, he decided there was no sense in staying around getting deeper in debt. What was the use of picking cotton till your fingers bled down to the white meat when one pound wasn't worth a thin dime? He wanted more than a stiff back, a plate of fatback, molasses, and cornbread at the end of the day. With his knapsack and his trusty dog beside him, John stood in his dusty overalls on the edge of the road watching out for the faded sky blue pickup truck to hitch a ride with Charles to Harlem.

"I know you don't think you're bringing that stinkin' ass dog in my car," Charles said, turning up his nose at the old basset hound.

"What you talking 'bout? Jimbo is the best friend I got. He been with me for nine years."

"Well kiss him goodbye 'cause we ain't got enough food or money to take care of ourselves much less a damn dog."

"There were days I didn't have nothing to eat and he brought me a rabbit," John protested, "I can't just leave him."

"Either you can go or stay here with him."

Reluctantly, John got in the truck. His nose burned and his eyes twitched as the sight of Jimbo sitting on the side of the road blurred and faded in the distance through the back window. Aside from that dog he wasn't leaving much. His folks were dead, dying, or already gone. That's how it was in Gainesville.

They rode a while in silence before John asked Charles, "What you want to do when we get up there in Harlem?"

"First thing I'm gonna do is get me a job singing with a band in one of them high-falooting night clubs full of pretty women. They'll all be screaming my name."

"You might be needing to think about something else besides that," John said wistfully, "That place probably already got too many singers. I ain't never known a nigga who can't sang."

"Since you so smart, what you gonna do in New York City?" Charles asked in a huff.

"I'm gonna get me a job in Grand Central Station where I can wear me a crisp uniform to work every day," John said proudly.

"You don't need no uniform to shine shoes," Charles laughed.

"I ain't gon shine no shoes. I might be a doorman at a fine hotel."

John didn't know nothing else but working the fields. The only book he had opened in the last ten years was the Bible, and the only black man he knew that had anything was the preacher.

Charles howled. "You just might at that."

By the time they rolled out into Charlotte, North Carolina they had eaten all the pig ears and cornbread John had brought along. When it got dark they pulled off the road and slept. On the way to Richmond they were both encouraged by their meal of boiled peanuts, a bottle of hootch, and the future that lied ahead. The trouble was the money for gasoline and the broken-down engine of the Ford pick-up ran out just outside of Baltimore. Buoyed on by the stories that a black man wasn't a boy in the North they walked the rest of the way to Philadelphia. That's where John gave out.

"Man, my shoes are about to fall off my feet and the acid in my empty stomach is eating me up," he said, stopping in his tracks. "I can't go another mile if I wanted to."

"All right, quit your whining and complaining," Charles grumbled, "It's Sunday. All we got to do is find us a church. Church folks always got some food. We'll get something to eat and maybe some soles for these shoes."

They found a church, a hot meal, and a shed to call home. Road weary they decided to cool their heels for a while. John got lucky and was hired as a janitor down at the ship yard. He came home after his second day at work and Charles was gone. Without a dime in his pocket, John planned to work a few weeks, make some money, and then trail Charles to Harlem.

With each passing day, he got lost in the delusion that his destiny, his good life, his pot of gold, was just 200 miles up Route 1. His disappointment at Charles for leaving without him began to turn into bitterness. He celebrated his first wages with a drink and made an unfortunate discovery. Alcohol diluted his dissatisfaction and he felt happy, even if it was temporary.

***

John met Gloria, Luke's momma, in a corner bar on 8th and Master Streets on his second payday. She was sitting on a stool with a side slit in her dress that revealed her well-greased thighs. John licked his lips. They reminded him of a fresh barbecue basted chicken.

"Hey, beautiful," he said with a heavy southern drawl, "Let Big John buy you a drink."

She smiled a wide and toothy grin that was framed in bright red lipstick.

"As long as you buying, sugar, I'm drinking."

There wasn't any other place that Gloria would rather spend her time. In the bar with a glass in her hand she could escape the drudge of cooking and cleaning for her mama while she worked as a domestic for some other woman. That's how it had been since her father, a construction worker, was accidentally killed working on the subway expansion. Gloria had made up her mind that until she found a man of her own to take care of her she was going to have some fun.

It tickled John that she could hold her liquor as good as he could. They met there every Friday for six months until they got married and rented a house a block away from the bar, three doors down from the corner of Franklin and Thompson Street. Fourteen years and five children later, you could still find John and Gloria there on payday. It was only imaginings, but somehow John felt like if he just could have made it to New York his life would have been so different.

The breakdown in the family happened when Luke was five years old after his dad lost his job. That broom that John carried on his job gave him his dignity, it kept his back strong and tall, and without it he was bent. After the family got on welfare he preferred to do his drinking at the bar alone. Gloria drowned her troubles privately behind her bedroom door.

All Luke could remember from those years was being hungry all the time. They ate cold food straight out of the damaged cans his mom bought for change out of the General Sales store when the electricity was cut off. Trying to make it in the Clements household was an individual sport. Each of them went their own way, probably because each was preoccupied with their own survival. One after another his older sisters and brothers found their way off of Franklin Street.

There was a big argument the day the oldest child stormed out. John had come home drunk again to a house full of empty bellies. Matthew, seventeen, with everything he owned in a brown paper grocery sack had waited for him. He wasn't going without leaving a piece of his mind. Gloria stood helplessly by the window and listened. She knew she bore half the blame. She should have never had all these kids. She didn't know how to take care of anybody but herself.

"Where do you get the nerve to come back here every day after leaving your last nickel at that damn bar?" Matthew griped, staring his pop in the eye when he walked in. "It would be more decent if you never showed your face here again."

"Boy, I know you ain't raring up at me in my own house, you must think you a man now," John roared back.

"I ain't never had the chance to be a boy in this house," Matthew shouted, "I've been fending for myself for as long as I could walk. The bartender at Nipsey's can depend on you better that we can."

John glared at him outraged. "I'll snatch a knot in you, boy. You ain't got no idea what it's like to be on your own. You in here whining cause you hungry one day. I can't count the days my stomach gnawed at me or the years I didn't have a roof over my head or the comfort of a bed to lie in."

Scared of what was next, Mary ran up the stairs. Martha grabbed Luke by the hand and ran up behind her. Mark sat on the raggedy sofa expressionless with the toothpick he always kept in his mouth. Matthew wouldn't back down. He was built like his father having inherited his same strength without having to work for it.

"So you think that gives you an excuse to sit on your ass while your kids go hungry," Matthew said, challenging him.

"A nigga don't get many chances to make it in this white man's world. I love every one of y'all kids and I want to give you everything but I can't do what they won't let me do. At least I'm here."

"Maybe you can do better with one less mouth to feed," Matthew replied, picking up his bag.

Gloria couldn't take it anymore and turned around. "Show some respect, Matthew, he's still your daddy."

"If you woulda cared more about your children than a bitch who dropped a litter of mongrels we might have had a chance to be something in this world," Matthew bellowed at her.

"You jackass, if I had a gun right now I'd blow your head off," John roared.

"Too bad you had other things to spend your money on," Matthew said, walking out the door and slamming it behind him.

"Keep living and this life will give you something that'll make you drink," John hollered out after him at the door.

Matthew never came back after that day. He joined the Nation of Islam. They discovered he was a gifted and passionate speaker and made him an assistant minister.

Mark, who seemed shorter from walking with his shoulders hunched over like he was hiding something, left less than a year later without a word. He had been roaming the streets all night and hanging with some rough thugs in a gang for a while. Then one morning he never came home. Whether he was born a hustler or his life demanded he become one, there was no doubt he had his own code of ethics. He mission was to get money, the means didn't matter. The last they heard, Mark was a runner collecting numbers.

Mary was the quiet one, like a tender flower in the midst of thick vines in an unruly jungle. She got a job working as a bank clerk at the Citizens & Southern Bank on 19th and South Street after she graduated from high school. She hadn't worked ninety days before she came home and packed up her things in a file box from the bank. She didn't say where she was going but they heard she was living with an older man in West Philly as his wife.

Martha was like her momma inside and out, always chasing a good time. Unfortunately, she ran into the wrong one. She started turning tricks up near Broad and Girard for some pimp she fell in love with. That left Luke with his steady companions, the rats and roaches, as they competed for the few crumbs of stale bread in the kitchen cabinets.

***

As a teenager, Luke matched the height of his father and brothers even though he looked taller with less meat on his bones. He was shy and insecure, not a part of his temperament but because of his skin. His cocoa color had darkened to a strong cup of coffee and a severe bout of chicken pox and acne had left his face bumpy and scarred. He loved the pretty girls who jumped double-dutch and played hopscotch in the streets, but the only place he had the confidence to talk or tease the cute ones around the neighborhood was in the darkness of the Astor Theatre up on Girard Avenue. He learned how to hustle early from his older brother Mark and he would shoot dice under the bridge for change to make sure he had candy and movie money in his pocket.

The day he started to dream that maybe something good might happen to him was when he walked across the stage at John Wanamaker Junior High School and got his diploma. He had done something that no other male in his family had done. Possibly there was a way off of Franklin Street that didn't lead to someplace worse, like doing dope in the gutter, turning tricks on the corner, or rotting in prison.

He felt like Superman when his pop took him out with him later that afternoon. For so many years he had gawked at the neon signs outside the bar and wondered what was behind that closed door. His eyes stretched wide as he walked in the smoky dimly lit room and when he slid onto the red cushioned bar stool he thought he was a man among men. At last, he was inside the mysterious magical place that attracted his mama and pop like a powerful magnet.

"You ain't nobody's dummy, boy," his daddy said proudly with a slap on his back, sitting on the bar stool beside him.

"Thanks, Pop," Luke said, timidly touching his lip to the foam floating above the beer his pop bought him to celebrate.

"This kid here has a damn good head on his shoulders," he bragged to his drinking buddies. "He done graduated today."

Luke flashed a toothy grin when the bar patrons lifted their glasses to him. He took a sip with them and the bitter bubbles turned his smile to a frown. He listened to the dirty jokes and laughter that spread in the narrow bar, he watched a couple gyrating to a song on the juke box, but he wasn't impressed. What was the big deal? When they lifted their glasses again he joined them and took a big gulp of the sour liquid, eager to feel the thrill that engulfed the room.

By the time he had finished the glass, Luke felt dizzy and sick to his stomach. He belched and the bitter taste filled his mouth again. He held his breath to stop himself from gagging. Why couldn't they have just gone to Gino's on Broad and Columbia and bought him the Kentucky Fried Chicken dinner that he wanted.

"I'm going home, Pop," he said, sliding off the bar stool.

"You go on, son. I'll be there after while."

Luke walked slowly to the door, back out into the sunlight of the day. He belched again and when the sourness rose in his throat he didn't try to hold it down. He bowed his head and retched from the pit of his gut. He didn't want the poison running through his body. It had to be toxic. How else could it have spoiled everything? All these years he suspected that it was something wonderful, something fantastical behind that door, something his momma and pop couldn't live without. It had taken food off of their table, run all his brothers and sisters away, and now it had come between his momma and pop. He watched it flow down the sidewalk with disgust. As far as he was concerned it didn't deserve to be piss.

***

"Is that you, Luke?" his mama called out from the kitchen when he got home.

"Yeah, Mama, it's me."

"Come on in, I made you something to eat."

Luke's stomach grumbled when he saw the plate of fried tripe, rice, lima beans, and cornbread. This was unusual, more than he was used to eating but he didn't want any more of the scraps from the slaughter house.

"I was proud of you today," she said, sitting across from him.

He nodded his head and kept his eyes on his plate. "Thank you,

Mama."

"Go on and eat your food, Luke. I'll be in my bedroom."

Gloria didn't talk much when she was feeling her blues. When Luke heard her door shut, he went in the cabinet and reached for the ketchup bottle that stood by the vinegar and the can of lard. He poured some over the tripe and ate his modest but well-meant congratulatory meal. With every bite he swore he would never be a prisoner to liquor, shut up in a dark room like a slave to its power. He wouldn't be weak to anything. He was determined to be like his hero, Cassius Clay, no, it was Muhammad Ali now, strong, bold, fearless, and pretty.

Chapter Two

The next three years were miserable for Luke. If it wasn't for pinto beans, lima beans, red beans, green beans, and white beans, he would have starved. He had eaten so many dried, canned, boiled, and baked beans that he swore that once he got out on his own he wouldn't eat another bean to save his life.

He looked forward to the days that Mark would visit. He would drop by the house every now and then to check on him when he was on the street collecting numbers. He would always take the top off the steaming pot on the stove and shake his head. Then he'd laugh and say, "Beans, beans, good for your heart, the more you eat the more you fart. Here's a ten spot, little brother, get yourself a hoagie." Luke would high tail it to Cook's, get himself a hoagie, a grape soda, and two cookies out of the cookie jar.

He thought things were looking up when his pop got a job as a custodian at Harrison Elementary School. They got off of welfare and his mama was back to drinking at the corner bar with him on payday. Luke was working too, part-time at the A&P grocery store in Progress Plaza stocking shelves, and was about to graduate from Thomas Edison High School in a few months. As always, whenever things start to look bright, somebody cuts out the light. It got real dark and black people across the country were about to fall apart when Martin Luther King, Jr. got shot on the evening of April 4, 1968.

When Luke heard the news he walked out of the grocery store around to the corner of Broad and Oxford and looked up towards Columbia Avenue. The normally crowded sidewalk of vendors who couldn't afford a storefront hustling for a dollar was empty. Security bars had been drawn over the windows. He was sure that the hell and heat from the riots of three years ago was about to be rekindled and rock North Philly to the core. Yet, it was eerily quiet. He waited to hear the blaring sirens of police cars and fire engines. He waited for the sounds of breaking glass of store fronts and the sight of dark smoke rising in the air. He waited for feverish looters to run down the block with handfuls of liquor bottles, TVs, and sofas on their backs. He waited for bricks to be hurled from the rooftops. Except none of it happened. Rev. Leon Sullivan was on the streets urging black folks to stay calm. Georgie Woods was on the radio asking the brothers and sisters to be cool.

There were marches and memorials but they were peaceful and subdued. When Luke got home he could hear the gospel songs floating out the open windows from the gathering at the church across the street. The united voices seemed to beckon him to come and join them. He crossed the street diagonally and went inside. For all the years he had lived there he had never ventured through the open door.

The depth of sorrow in the singing inside the sanctuary moved him. They were all on their feet, holding hands in the pews, and swaying to the words of *We Shall Overcome*. Someone grabbed his hand tightly. For Luke it felt strange to be touched and he wanted to pull away. He looked at the sad faces to the left and right of him and that's when he saw her. It was like an alarm went off, his heart starting thumping, and he began to sweat. Her head leaned back as she sang and he watched a single tear roll down the side of her face. All of a sudden he believed in God and she was an angel. He couldn't help but lift his voice and sing.

He thought she looked just like Tammi Terrell. She was light-skinned with big brown eyes, dimples, and full lips. Her hair was straight and hung long on one side. She was wearing a peace medallion that hung in the center of her round breasts. Luke excused himself as he moved closer and then closer, easing by one person at a time. Thirty minutes later, after the room was emotionally spent from the songs, recordings of speeches, and personal testimonies, he finally stood beside her. A half hour ago all he could think about was getting next to her. Now he searched his mind for something to say before it was time to go. Then they sang the last song, *God Be with You Till We Meet Again.*

"Hi, I'm Luke, what's your name?" he asked when she turned to leave.

"Hi, my name is Ruth, but everybody calls me Ruthie."

"Nice to meet you, Ruthie. Do you go to this church?"

"Yeah, I do."

"This is my first time coming in. I heard the singing from my house."

"Yeah, everybody was upset about Dr. King getting killed so they called a special service."

"So, do you live around here?" Luke asked, wanting to know all about her.

"Straight up Thompson to 10th Street. I walk down here every Sunday."

Luke looked surprised, that was barely three blocks away in the projects.

"I live across the street and I've never seen you around here before."

She shrugged her shoulders.

"What school do you go to?" he asked, trying to keep the conversation going.

"I go to Dobbins."

He nodded. "I'm graduating from Edison."

"I graduate next year, I'm a junior."

"Can I walk you home?" he asked hopefully.

"I don't think so. I came with my momma."

Luke's disappointment was written all over his face. "Can I get your phone number?"

"Why don't you come to church on Sunday?" she suggested, looking over her shoulder for her momma.

"What time?"

"Service starts at 11:00," she said, walking away.

Luke left and walked back across the street to his house feeling like he had got a blessing.

On their way out, Ruth's mom, Mrs. Huntley, frowned at the young man trotting up his stairs. She was high-yellow with disdain for anybody who couldn't pass the paper bag test.

"Ruthie, who was that boy?" she asked disapprovingly.

"His name is Luke, I just met him."

"He sure is black and ugly too."

Ruthie glanced over towards his house. "He seemed nice to me."

"You can do a whole lot better than that, child," Mrs. Huntley said, tuning up her nose.

***

It was even hard for him to believe it himself but Luke couldn't wait to get to church on Sunday. He hadn't stopped thinking about Ruthie and how pretty she was. Every morning and every night for three days he had washed his face with Noxzema to clear up his skin. He wished he could have gotten the suit he had on layaway for his graduation out but his money was short.

"What the hell is all this noise in the house?" John grumbled, angry at being awakened. "Why can't a man get some sleep on the day the Lord said to rest?"

"Luke is getting ready for church," Gloria said, rolling over in the bed away from the stale liquor on his breath.

"Church, since when?" he asked, rising up in the bed and pulling the covers off Gloria, "Did the boy get the calling?"

"No, fool," she said, snatching the covers back over her, "He likes a girl that goes over there."

"Oh shit," John laughed, lying back down, "The boy done got his nose open."

Luke rushed out, crossed the street and went inside the church. He sat in the back of the sanctuary wearing his best shirt, freshly ironed. Ruth walked in with her mom just as the service was called to worship. She motioned for him to follow them closer to the front of the sanctuary. Luke couldn't have recalled anything that was said or done during the church service. His head was filled with the sweet scent of her perfume and the vision of her legs through her sheer pantyhose when her mini-skirt slid back.

From that first day when he slowly walked Ruth home behind her mother giving him side eyes, Luke already knew that he didn't want to be with anybody else. He called Ruth every night. Most nights he didn't have much to say, he just wanted to hold the phone and know she was on the other end of the line. On their first date he took her to see *For the Love of Ivy* and it was the first time he wasn't jealous of Sidney Poitier. He was the lucky one. He wanted more than anything to take her on his senior prom but her momma said she didn't have time to get her a dress. When he walked across the stage, the second of his brothers and sisters to graduate from high school, it was her smile, not his mama's that he looked for.

When her bright eyes twinkled as she looked at him he wondered what she saw, because whenever he looked at her he saw something wonderful and precious. He thought Ruth was like a beautiful black pearl, the rarest gem on earth, dredged from the cold, dark, and hard stinking shell of North Philly. What Ruth saw when she looked at Luke was something that he didn't see and probably no one else saw, she saw devotion, someone she could love, trust, and rely on. She thought he was like a wounded bird trapped in a cage of his circumstances who needed to be nurtured and cared for so he could fly.

Their future was sealed on the night when Ruth and some of her friends came to a house party on 7th near Berks Street. Music blared in the dark basement lit with only a single blue light bulb and filled with the smoke of cigarettes and weed. A big record player in the corner was stacked with forty-fives. Luke leaned against the wall watching his friend and some girl do the 'tighten up' to the Archie Bell and the Drells song. He was thinking about cutting out when he saw Ruth come down the narrow stairway. She looked so fine his mouth watered. He took a big swallow of the punch spiked with Yago Sangria and edged through the midst of sweating bodies to ask her to dance. Before he could get to her, the record changed and another guy pulled her to the center of the floor just in front of him. He backed up and watched her move and shake to the beat while James Brown sang, *I Got the Feeling*.

Luke wasn't about to let some other dude step to her again. He pushed his way out on the floor as the song was ending. When Ruth turned around to look for her girlfriends he was standing there in front of her. She smiled and he wrapped her up in his arms as the Dells record played, *Stay in my Corner*. He pulled her closer loving the feeling of her breasts pressed against his chest. She was all he wanted. He put one arm around her waist and pressed his firm manhood against her belly. When she locked her arms around him, he held her tighter and pushed one knee between her thighs and pulled her down against it. She didn't resist and their bodies rubbed sensually to the rhythm of the music as if they were in a room all by themselves. That's when he knew she belonged to him.

Luke didn't go to church on Sunday mornings anymore. He didn't need to. God had given him all that he could have ever asked for. Ruth was his girl. His favorite thing for the rest of the summer was sitting between her legs listening to the radio while she oiled his scalp and corn-rowed his hair. She had tamed his stubborn kinks and he was wearing a nice afro. When the sun went down they would cross the street to the schoolyard where they would kiss and grind their bodies together until both their underclothes were wet.

An even greater thing happened when the days grew shorter and evenings got colder. His mom and pop's ritual of drinking until sun up after payday, the thing he most resented as a young boy, became his most anticipated event of the week. Every Friday he brought Ruth up to his room where they laid in bed under the posters of their zodiac signs, Scorpio and Leo, and the place he once thought was his private hell became his heaven on earth. Ruthie was soft and sweeter than pancakes soaked in maple syrup.

***

One year after they met, Luke and Ruth were sitting in the Astor Theater watching Sidney Poitier's *The Lost Man*. Neither was caught up in the suspense of the movie, both were preoccupied with news that would change everything between them.

"You hungry?" Luke asked, looking at the ground as they walked up Girard Avenue.

"If you are," Ruth answered, subdued.

They walked up to Lou's and got a ham hoagie and were on their way back to her house. They were about a block away when Luke suddenly stopped.

"Ruthie, I got a draft letter, my number came up. I go for a physical in two weeks."

Then Ruth blurted out her news. "I'm pregnant, Luke."

Luke shook his right hand like he had just thrown snakes eyes with a pair of dice. "Damn. I'm sorry, Ruthie, I pulled out every time."

"It don't always work," she said sadly. "What do you want to do?"

"I'm going to marry you like I said I would."

Ruthie turned away. "How you gonna marry me and you about to go to Vietnam."

"We can get married before I go," Luke said to console her.

"I don't want to be nobody's widow. I just turned eighteen."

"You not going to be no widow. I won't let nobody kill me."

"You don't know that. In a war every man has a gun and every man can die."

"I can take care of myself, I swear."

"I'm going to have to find a job because my momma ain't going to take care of no babies. She's been telling me that ever since I turned 12 years old."

"You're the best thing that ever happened to me, Ruthie. I'll take care of you and the baby. If you don't want me to go, I won't go. I'll go to jail with my man, Muhammad Ali."

"Stop talking crazy, Luke."

"I'm for real. Either I can do eighteen months in Nam or three years in jail. Make your choice and I'll do it. Time is time."

"I don't want nothing to eat," Ruth said when they got to her back door.

She dropped down on the back stoop under the weight of her world and Luke sat down beside her. He was determined to prove to her that he was a man and he would provide for her, he didn't give a damn what her momma thought. They sat quietly with their eyes fixed on the tan bricks of the next building. Lost in the hopelessness of their predicament they were oblivious to the orchestra of ghetto life that played all around them, the steady thump of a basketball bouncing in the school yard up the street, rows of clothes on a line rising and falling in the breeze, a baby crying, a dog on his chain chasing flies, and the sound of a TV from an open window.

Ruth stood up after the sun gave way to the moon and turned to go inside.

"I can leave you half," Luke said, holding up the hoagie.

"No, that's all right. I'm going to lay down and do some thinking," she said, disappearing behind the screen door.

The door slammed and Luke got up and walked home.

***

There wasn't any way around it and no reason to put off the evitable. Ruth went straight in the kitchen where her mother was snapping green beans in the sink. She gripped the back of the vinyl chair and leaned against it to brace herself for the barrage she knew was coming.

"Mommy, I'm pregnant," she said boldly.

"I'll be damned," Mrs. Huntley hollered, stomping her foot and shaking her head without turning around. "I told you I didn't want no babies brought in here. Who is the daddy?"

"Luke is the only boy I've been with."

"This is a sin and shame, Ruthie. I thought you were too smart to throw your life away."

"I haven't thrown nothing away," Ruthie protested.

"You're so pretty, child, you could have gotten yourself a decent man who had something going for himself."

"Luke is the only man I want, and he loves me."

"That dumb-ass don't know nothing about love. He's just like all the other niggas out here, they love making babies and then they leave you alone to raise them."

Ruth held her tongue out of respect. Her mother wasn't talking about Luke; she was talking about her daddy. She had heard about him from her aunts enough times. Her daddy, Jimmy Huntley, was tall and good-looking, a pretty yellow man who thought he was born to spread himself around to all the ladies. He never could hold down a job and didn't want to. He was smooth as satin. He could talk a woman out of her drawers and then her last dime. Ruby was independent and making money as a hairdresser when they met, but by the time she divorced him she was on welfare with two children.

"We're getting married, Mommy."

"Aww, hell, how are you going to eat, where are you going to live? Neither of you have a pot to piss in. That penny-ante job he got won't pay no bills."

"I can get a job after I graduate."

"Where you going to work with a baby? I told you, I'm not nobody's babysitter."

"Luke's number came up. They gonna send him to Vietnam," Ruth cried with her strong façade falling apart.

"Lord have mercy," Ruby said, "They killing those boys left and right over there. You don't have to go through with this, Ruthie. I know somebody who can fix it."

"I told you we're going to be a family. I'm not going to hurt our baby."

"You've seen how hard it was on me to raise you and your older sister by myself. We can make this right. You can start fresh and make something out of yourself."

"Luke and me, we're going to get married before he leaves and he's coming back to me."

"All right, go ahead, be a fool. You think you grown cause you carrying a baby. For your sake I hope he don't come back in a box."

***

So instead of going on her senior prom, Ruth and Luke got married in the church sanctuary where they met. Luke wore the suit he got for his high school graduation and Ruth wore the peach colored dress her momma bought her for the prom. Ruth's best friend Laverne stood up with her and Matthew stood up for Luke. Both of their mothers sat behind them teary-eyed. Ruby was broken-hearted that her daughter had ruined her life and Gloria was filled with joy that her son had found someone to love him. John thought his son was being a fool and didn't come.

The happy couple spent their wedding night at the Divine Lorraine Hotel courtesy of his brother, Mark. Then they stayed at Luke's house in his room until he was scheduled to report back on North Broad Street and be inducted into the army. Ruth was going back to her mom's house after he left but she swore it wouldn't be for long. She was not about to live there with her talking bad about Luke all the time. She was going to get a job after graduation so she could get a place for her husband to come home to.

Chapter Three

Luke and three hundred other guys passed their physicals on the day he went to the U.S. Army Induction Center on North Broad Street. The word was if you were strong enough to hold a pen you were fit to serve. Three weeks later Luke boarded a bus off to Fort Dix in New Jersey for basic training. It was his first time out of Philly and it was courtesy of the U.S. Army. On the bus ride he glanced around at all the other guys making the trip to the unknown. They were all different but none of them were unique. It was just a busload of black, white, country, city-slick, poor, middleclass, smart, ignorant, young men, only a few years past being boys. Most were draftees but several had volunteered willingly.

At Fort Dix, Luke stepped off the bus where he and the rest of the busloads of new inductees surrendered their civilian clothes and were measured and fitted with uniforms. Luke was treated to a haircut that removed the afro that Ruth had painstakingly grown out. Next they were given an 8-digit personal ID number and issued rifles and a load of military equipment. He wasn't sure if he was relieved or more leery to meet the two black drill sergeants that were assigned to turn them all into soldiers. They were both huge muscular men, intimidating to say the least. The older one, Sgt. Marshall, had on dark sunglasses that hid his eyes. The other, Sgt. Overton held a baton in his hand. The new recruits stood in front of them at attention.

"My job is to get you numbskulls mentally and physically ready to meet Charlie, the Viet Cong," Sgt. Marshall yelled at them.

"And it don't matter whether you like it or not," Overton barked, holding the baton.

"One thing you need to remember is that they're less than human," Marshall instructed, "Show them no mercy."

"Call them gooks and dinks," Overton spat, twisting his mouth.

"The good thing is, if you ever get dropped by Charlie over there you won't even know it," Marshall told them, "You'll be dead before you hear the shot."

If the two of them ever let their guard down and smiled, Luke had never witnessed it.

Boot camp in July was blistering hot, most days the temperature in Jersey was above 90 degrees. Luke's tongue stuck to the roof of his mouth as they marched in the sand during their exercises and no one was allowed to drink from their canteens until they were told. More than a few guys threw up during training, a couple even passed out. For Luke, the mile run and the swinging on monkey bars were nothing compared to a summer day of playing basketball on Schwartz playground.

Most hated KP duty but Luke was fascinated by the mere sight of all the food they had to prepare. His primary complaint was living in the barracks. It wasn't the noise or snoring, he'd slept by the screeching of police and ambulance sirens since he was a baby. What he despised was the lack of privacy. He wasn't used to people being around him all the time. Showering and taking a shit with an audience.

Every waking hour of the long days were filled and the eight weeks went by quickly. Things got serious in the Advanced Individual Training in Infantry. They got to fire heavy weapons, learned how to use a flame thrower, and ran everywhere they went. Luke bulked up, casting aside his boyhood physique, mostly from eating three square meals per day. He got even stronger lifting and carrying guns and ammunition. He never complained because he knew that when his second eight weeks of training were done he would get two weeks leave to go home. He planned to spend every minute of it with Ruth.

***

After her high school graduation, Ruby made no attempt to hide her disappointment in her daughter. Ruth ignored it, concealed her pregnancy, and got a job at the TastyKakes factory up on Hunting Park Ave. She was strong-willed and determined to have her own place by the time Luke finished boot camp.

Of all the directions she'd dreamed her life would take after high school, she never imagined that she would be standing in the production line where the butterscotch krimpets she loved to eat so much were rolled out fresh from the oven. The unexpected worst part of the job was the sweet smell of cakes baking that had made her salivate when she first walked in the door was now making her sick to her stomach. After her second day she knew she would never buy another krimpet or peanut butter tandy cake for the rest of her life.

It was always warm on the production lines but in the summer it was hot as hell in there with the ovens fired up at 600 degrees twenty-four hours a day. The white cap Ruth wore to cover her hair made the heat feel worse and her feet were starting to swell from standing up all day. She dealt with the high temperatures and her sore feet every day by thinking how each hour brought her closer to getting her own place. She thanked the stars above for the days when she got off the trolley and the fire hydrant on the corner of 10th Street was open. It was the ghetto equivalent of a swimming pool with gushing cool water that she could walk through and comfort her feet.

She made a few extra dollars babysitting and running errands for women in the neighborhood on the weekends. It kept her busy and her mind occupied while Luke was in Basic Training.

At the end of July her savings had grown enough to put in for an apartment of her own. One that was one block up and around the corner from her mom. For so many years she prayed for the day when she could get out of the projects but now her prayer had changed. Now she asked the Lord to help find her a unit as soon as possible.

She was seven months pregnant in September when her prayer was answered. She got the notice saying she could finally move in. Her mom still wasn't happy but she let her take her bed with her until she could get some furniture of her own. Ruth only had two weeks to make it into a home before Luke got leave. Most of what she bought was second-hand and the end tables were milk crates decorated with scarves thrown over them. After she put up some shelves and hung some pictures, her place looked nice. On payday she filled up the fridge and waited.

***

Luke was sitting on the steps outside the address she had sent to him when she got home on the last Tuesday of the month. It threw him for a loop when he saw her at the end of the block. She had been his fantasy girl and now the weight of their reality crashed down on him. This was his wife and her full and rounded belly screamed that he was about to be a father. When she saw him she wanted to run to him but her tired feet refused to cooperate. Luke's confused emotions kept him from moving toward her. He felt good and bad at the same time. He was so happy to see her but he felt like he had let her down. He stood up as she reached their stoop.

"You look good in your uniform," Ruth said, holding back her tears and smiling.

"Aww, baby, you look cute and you smell sweet," he said, wrapping her in a tight hug.

Ruth unlocked the door and he followed her in. The house smelled as sweet as she did. Luke shut the door and grabbed her back in his arms, squeezing her behind and French kissing her.

"That's all we gonna be able to do," she said when he let her go.

"You jiving me, baby. I been missing you like crazy."

"Me too, Luke, but I don't want to go in labor early."

She made him a dinner of pork chops, mashed potatoes, and peas. She asked questions and he answered them while they ate. Later she played some music and he slow-danced with her to *Going in Circles* by the Friends of Distinction just like they did at that house party. Then they went to bed. Luke wanted her so bad that he couldn't sleep. He lay awake listening to her breathing until daylight. He rolled over in the bed when Ruth got up.

"Baby, you're going to work today?" he asked, frustrated.

"I don't have a choice. I don't have no vacation built up and I need the few sick days I have for when the baby comes."

Hearing her say those words, he didn't think he was worth a dime.

"I'm sorry, Ruthie. I wish you didn't have to be on your feet. I want to take care of you."

"Don't worry about me, Luke. You're the one going over to Nam to dodge bullets. I can handle things around here. I just need you to come back in one piece with nothing missing."

"This isn't how I wanted things to be for you," he said, staring down at the white sheet.

"This is only how it is for now, but it'll get better," she said on her way to the bathroom.

Luke felt even lower watching her put on her white uniform that stretched tight around her middle. She looked tired and swollen. When they got married he promised her that he would provide for her and take care of her. She was his princess but nothing had turned out right. It wasn't that he gave a damn what her momma thought, he was disappointed in himself. All he wanted was to show Ruth he was the man and here she was going to work with her belly stuck out leading the way.

"Ruthie, I love you," he hollered just before she shut the door.

***

The day before his leave was over they went up on Columbia Avenue to do some shopping for the baby. Laverne wanted to give her a baby shower but she wasn't in the mood. Her mother had run her mouth so much about Luke that a lot of the people on her street were sorry for her.

"My momma says you're not coming back," Ruthie said to Luke with her voice filled with worry. "She says that if they don't kill you over there you won't remember your way home."

"Don't listen to her, baby doll, I'm coming back," Luke assured her. "We both have to fight for what we want, and that's us being together."

They were passing a street vendor who was selling her wares when a silver chain with a cross hanging on it caught Ruth's eye. She stopped and picked it up.

"How much?" she asked the woman sitting there.

"Five dollars, but I'll give it to you for three," she answered, nodding toward her belly.

Ruthie pulled out three dollars and paid her.

"Put this on," she insisted, handing it to Luke. "It'll keep you safe over there.

***

Luke boarded an airplane for the first time in his life on a flight headed to Oakland, California. The sound of the engine roaring as the plane ascended into the clouds at more than 400 miles an hour scared and fascinated him at the same time. In the aisle seat, he ate the sparse meal the stewardess served and closed his eyes drifting in and out of sleep. As soon as they landed, he and several other soldiers walked across the airfield and climbed aboard a chartered commercial airliner destined for Vietnam. With nothing else to do, he stared out the window down at the Pacific Ocean below for nearly

24 hours minus the brief stops in Alaska and Japan where his feet could touch the ground. Flying over Vietnam he marveled at how beautiful this place they said was hell on earth looked from afar.

The heat of it smacked him in the face when he stepped off the air-conditioned plane into the humidity of Bien Hoa on October 17th, twenty miles from Saigon. It was like walking off into a steam oven that sucked out his breath. The air had a pungent and unfamiliar smell. Reluctantly he moved past the jubilant group of fortunate soldiers on the other side of the terminal who were eager to board the same plane he'd gotten off to return to the United States. Luke silently wished he would soon be one of them. He trailed in the line of fresh soldiers, also known as cherries, as they tread like sheep going out to be slaughtered. A bus completely covered in chicken wire waited for them. It would block grenade attacks on the way to the Army base.

Sounds of mortar rockets and machine gun fire in the distance reverberated in Luke's head and heart heightening his greatest fear, not getting back home to sweet Ruthie. After being processed into the 29th Infantry Regiment and 1st Infantry Division, he was given his summer fatigues, a poncho for monsoon season, and issued his M-16. The warnings of his drill sergeants, Marshall and Overton, echoed in his mind.

He didn't take long for him to learn that black dudes were cut no slack and were still treated like second class citizens way over in Vietnam. White officers looked for any reason they could to send black soldiers out in the field to get shot while they ignored the Southern hoogies riding around with confederate flags on their jeeps. It was just like home, the white dudes were getting over with the cushy jobs while the blacks got the shitty ones. The only impartial thing over there was "Charley" in the bush, he didn't make no difference between Americans. They could all catch a bullet as good as anybody else.

New arrivals were advised not to get too close to other soldiers because casualties were real, but Luke bonded with three guys in his hootch. Teddy Ferguson was from Baltimore, he was a smooth dude, well over six feet and lean. He told them that he had worked at the phone company for a couple of years, working five days and partying forty-eight hours of the other two. When he got fired for showing up late one time too many it didn't take long for him to run out of cash. He volunteered when he ran out of places to go.

James Tyler was from Columbus, Ohio even though he reminded Luke of a country boy. He worked as a painter for his uncle who was a handyman. When his number came up he got engaged to a girl he grew up with at his mama's church. They had never dated but he figured he needed another person praying for him to come back alive.

Mike Cooper was from Los Angeles. He grew up the only child in a middleclass family, his father was a longshoreman. He didn't know the meaning of hard times or how good he had it because he was always popping some pill, dropping some acid, or smoking something to take him to another state of consciousness.

The four of them talked for hours drinking and playing cassette tapes. Luke broke his rule about alcohol and drank his share. It was easier to get beer than water. They became close friends built on a common goal to live through this hell and the trust they had that each would defend the life of the other.

Luke wrote Ruth a letter at the end of his first week in Nam with no complaints about the heat remembering how she suffered on the production line at the TastyKake factory.

Dear Ruthie, I'm thinking that maybe going to jail might not have been any more terrible than this place, at least there I could see your pretty face every once in a while. I don't want to ask you for anything cause I know how hard you're hustling to hold things together but I'm dying for some Kool-Aid and Butternut candy bars. If you could send some of the pre-sweetened kind it would be right on time. I love you and miss your sweet lips. Luke

***

The first letter Luke wrote Ruth sat inside the mailbox while she labored at Hahnemann Hospital in a room with her momma and her best friend.

"I can't believe you're about to have this baby on Halloween night," Ruby complained. "It's probably going to be as black as the ace of spades."

Ruth screamed at the top of her lungs, although it wasn't from the pain of a contraction. She loved her momma but she hated her old-timey ideas about color. Silently she hoped her baby would be coal black just to spite her.

"Little girl, if I could take the pain away I would, but I can't," Ruby chided, sitting beside her. "I tried to tell you where this would lead but you were hardheaded."

"Momma, you're getting on my nerves," Ruth said between her pains. "Maybe you should go on home. Laverne is here. She can call you when the baby gets here."

"Oh no, you're my child and I'm going to be here for you."

"This is your grandbaby that I'm trying to push out, don't you care about that?" Ruth asked, wondering why her momma was being so unbearable.

"I'm not ready to be a grandmamma but nobody asked me," Ruby said, folding her arms. "Lord only knows what this baby is going to look like."

Ruth rolled her eyes and ignored her. She didn't have the energy or the wherewithal to argue with her momma. Her head was starting to hurt and she felt dizzy. She was breathed a sigh of relief when her doctor came and asked her mother to leave while he examined her.

"Mrs. Clements, your blood pressure is going up and down erratically. It can affect the amount of oxygen getting to your baby. I want to do a cesarean section as soon as possible."

"Do whatever you have to do," Ruth said, too tired to be scared. "I don't want anything to happen to my baby."

"Don't worry, everything will be fine," he said, patting her on the arm as he left.

Ruth's baby boy came into the world about an hour later.

Back in her hospital room, Ruth held her son. Ruby cried tears of joy to see he was pale with a smooth shadow of black hair.

"He's beautiful, Ruthie, he looks just like you," her momma exclaimed.

"What are you going to name him?" Laverne asked, rubbing his cheek.

Ruby held her breath, quietly begging her not to say that trifling boy's name.

"I'm going to call him Daniel for his daddy who's in a lion's den. We both need him and I pray that he gets out of that place without a scratch."

Ruby's smile flat-lined, the thought of Luke coming back dampened her spirits.

***

Ruth watched the news about the war on the TV and it had her so confused. Holding Daniel in her arms and feeding him while she watched the other babies over there in Nam being killed, she didn't know who was right or who was wrong. She wanted Luke to be safe but she couldn't imagine him over there killing babies. Every night for a week she watched the horrors on the news until she couldn't take it anymore. She turned it off.

Ruth went back to work as soon as her doctors said it was okay. TastyKake had held her job for her but she hadn't been there long enough to accumulate any off time. Luke sent her most of his pay but it was barely enough to hold onto their apartment. Fortunately, she could press and curl hair as good as her momma. When Ruby got really busy she sent a few heads her way that paid for diapers and formula for Daniel. Surprisingly, her momma was helping out more than Ruth had thought she would. She kept Daniel for her while she worked, even when she had a double shift. Ruby was crazy about her cute little grandson and spoiled him with toys and outfits.

It had been rough for the first three months before Daniel started sleeping through the night. Ruth was barely able to stay awake at work. The extra experience she got babysitting ahead of him being born prepared her well. It still wasn't easy but her little son brought so much joy to her day when his smiles turned to giggles. So many things were happening that she wanted to share with Luke, when Daniel got his first shoes, sitting up by himself, and his first tooth. She tried her best to let her baby know he had a father, she showed him pictures of Luke every day. "That's your daddy," she would say. "He'll be home soon."

Chapter Four

Going out into the field was surreal. You walked unceremoniously through the camp past the other guys who were smoking, drinking and carousing, some sleeping, some on a groovy vibe listening to music. It was just another day in Nam. You and your platoon might come back and you might not. Looking somebody in the face only made it harder to pretend this wasn't real. You looked straight ahead and followed your sergeant's orders, *get it on and move it out.* When their turn came, Luke's platoon hopped out of the UH-1 helicopter into another world at a clearing on the edge of the bush.

The jungle was more miserable than hell could possibly be with more vermin than hell could contain. Deep swamps reached halfway up Luke's neck and thick wild bushes grew well above his head. The heat was scorching, the rainstorms were torrential, and the bugs and rats feeding on the filth and garbage were bigger than any he had ever seen in Ludlow. The lizards and snakes freaked him out. Some stared at him like they would speak at any moment. There were so many mosquitoes. He was just as scared of them sucking all his blood as he was of taking a hit and bleeding to death. Since they weren't able to bathe for weeks at a time, none of them wore underwear under their clothes because it caused jungle rot. Not to mention, the more than seventy pounds of essential equipment they carried in their field packs that felt like another man sitting on their shoulders.

After his first five days in the field of running with his company through the high grass and bamboo hedges, dodging booby traps, shooting at anything that moved in their path, and firing mortars off into the distance into unseen targets, Luke was grateful for stand-down at the base. He could shower, get a new uniform to replace the one torn to shreds from darting through the bush, eat some hot food, and watch a movie on an outdoor screen. The best part was the mail waiting for him. When he saw the picture of Ruthie and Daniel and four packs of sweetened grape Kool-Aid in his care package he was on cloud nine. He kept the picture with him everywhere he went, either in his pants pocket or tucked deep in his field pack.

On the rotations when his platoon was out in the field there were many times when Luke thought he wouldn't live through the night. Times when the guerilla fighters had them surrounded. Times when he and his buddies, Teddy, James, and Mike were too petrified to look each other in the eye. That's when he would pull out his photo and touch Ruth's and Daniel's faces to remind himself that he couldn't die now. He had a son and a wife waiting for him.

Luke didn't know the exact day that he turned into a killer. It was probably the same day that he came under heavy enemy fire. He had stopped counting the search and destroy missions that he had gone out on. Nobody seemed to care. They were all living in an arrested reality that made no sense. He thought he had seen more blood and guts and smelled more rotting flesh than a butcher would see in a lifetime, certainly more than somebody trying to hold on to their sanity ever needed to see. It turned boys into men as they killed to survive, and it turned men into boys who screamed for their momma to come to their rescue. Death came so easy that Luke was beginning to believe that life was nothing but air in your body. When they blow a hole in you, your life seeps out and you die.

***

Halfway through his tour, Luke thought his hearing was damaged by all the mortar fire, machine guns, and missiles that exploded around him without ceasing. Most of the time when he sat on watch duty for a sight or sound of Charley it was like listening under water. He had become disgusted and hardened to the daily doses of death and quite a number of the killings were not by the foreign enemy but by fellow soldiers. There was a lot of talk about the black soldiers that refused patrol duty saying it was nothing but a death sentence from racist officers. The nights were alive with mischief from all sides.

Whenever they had leave time in the rear, Teddy would make his announcement, "Soldiers, it's time to get funky." Then Luke and his buddies would go to the Khanh Hoi District to relax down on Trinh Minh or better known as "Soul Alley" where they catered to black soldiers.

They could hear Aretha's voice singing "Call me" wafting out of their favorite bar.

"Now that's hip," Teddy said, "Shit, I been dying to hear my baby humming. I'm tired of all that rock and country music that Chuck likes to play. I need me some rhythm and blues."

"I need that and something else to go with it," Mike said, giving Teddy the brotherman handshake.

"It ain't home but they got it all here," James said wistfully.

"Let's get this party started, brothers," Luke said, getting out of the three-wheeled bike taxi he got a kick out of riding in.

"Right on, man, I'm going to get drunk and get me some pussy," Teddy shouted.

"I'm not fucking around with none of those nasty-ass prostitutes," Luke said. "Dude, your dick is going to rot off."

Teddy chuckled. "I don't know why you worried about that, man, we could die tomorrow. I'm gonna live tonight, you best believe that."

"Go ahead, ain't no pussy worth me losing my dick," Luke said.

"I can dig it, Luke, you been jacking off for six months now," Mike laughed, "You only got six more to go."

"That's cool," Luke said, "Laugh if you want to. I got a sweet wife waiting on me and I ain't taking no poison home to her."

"They ain't got nothing a shot in the ass won't cure," Teddy said, "Shit, if I can run around here dodging shots to my head for who in the hell knows why, I damn sure ain't scared to take my chances on getting laid."

"Let's get some real food to eat at the L&M," James said, "I need to flush them c-rations out of my system."

"I can dig it, man," Mike said, leading them down a half block.

Inside the L&M they found a table and ordered a round of beers. Luke ordered the ribs and James wanted the chitterlings, they reminded him of his mama and her down-home cooking. When the waitress brought the beers out they poured some on the floor for their fallen brothers and raised their glasses for staying alive.

Luke thought about his father when he swallowed the cool ale. Being in Nam had taught him to appreciate the numbing effects of alcohol. For the first time he wondered what horrors his daddy had seen that he needed to wash away at Nipsey's bar.

"They sure can fry some chicken over here, believe that," Teddy said, gobbling it down and licking his fingers.

"Ain't no guarantee that's chicken, my man," Mike joked, standing up. "I'm gonna split. I'll catch up with you grunts in a few."

"Later, man," James said, giving him some dap.

They all knew he was going out for a hit. Mike was halfway strung out on dope and he was losing his edge.

"Come on, brother, why you have to fuck with that shit, it'll kill you?" Luke asked.

"Every damn thing over here can kill me. I'd rather choose my own way to go," Mike said as he walked away, "That is to be totally fucked up."

James looked up at him. "I thought our plan was to survive."

"I'm outta here too, man," Teddy said, getting up, "I'm, ready to get taken down by a boom-boom girl."

James ordered another plate of food and ate it before he cut out about 20 minutes later.

Luke sat alone in the bar for hours drinking and tripping on the tiny bubbles floating up to the top of his glass until the beer was nearly flat. He was grooving to Sly and the Family Stone's *Thank You for Letting Me Be Myself*, Stevie Wonder's *Heaven Help Us All*, and Wilson Pickett's *Sugar, Sugar*. He drained his glass when he heard, "*War, what is it good for, absolutely nothing*" because he had learned that was straight up truth. He got homesick listening to *Ball of Confusion*, and his eyes burned when he heard the Jackson 5 singing *I'll be There*.

When the crew got reunited in the early hours of the morning they were all torn up in one way or another. They got two pedicabs and rode back to the base.

***

Choppers took Luke and the rest of his platoon out to a hillside where they were divided into teams to search for ambushes in the field. Orders were to push forward, clear the area, hold it and claim it. During the night they hid in the bushes. Luke rubbed the silver cross that hung around his neck for comfort. It was so dark you couldn't see your own hand in front of your face.

Suddenly Luke was attacked from behind, pounced on from out of nowhere. He yelled as he struggled to free himself from the thin arms that scratched and pulled at him. He felt the short course hair just before he was gripped by a mouth full of teeth on his shoulder. James woke up from all the commotion and with one slice of his knife Luke's attacker went limp. They all got a good laugh afterwards. It was a monkey.

The next night they weren't so lucky. The squad ran into enemy fire. Luke fired his rifle in the direction of where the NVA were encamped. They kept firing until they didn't hear any return fire. They moved forward looking for enemy bodies, except there weren't any. Out in the open they were easy targets for the rocket that shot in blowing up with a burst of red fire and black smoke. Luke felt a strong kick to his thigh. Rounds of artillery followed the explosion and everything shifted into slow motion. Mike was barely two steps ahead of Luke when a string of shots ripped through his body tearing him apart. Luke's leg began to burn and he realized he had been shot too. He went limp praying for his body to drop and hit the ground before it was filled with bullets like his fallen buddy.

A medivac helicopter flew down about fort-five minutes later and picked up the wounded and dead. Back at the field hospital the extent of Luke's injury was encouraging and disheartening. The good news was he had been hit with shrapnel from the rocket and the damage was minor. The bad news was it wouldn't be the ticket home that two other survivors in his team had received. He was out of service for only two days.

***

James was just one of the dudes in his hootch who got a Dear John letter and he was taking it pretty hard. His mood was contagious since Luke hadn't got a letter from Ruth in over two weeks. She was so fine. He knew other guys were trying to beat his time while he was gone and the thought of her leaving him was more frightening than anything he had encountered in Nam. Without Ruthie he didn't feel like he had much to go home to. Halfway through the next week when he got a letter without a care package he was scared to open it. His mind was put at ease with pictures of Ruthie smiling and Daniel in his Easter suit.

It was the dry season, hot like fire during the day, and the morale in their company was plummeting as the war had no end in sight. Yet Luke was revitalized. Ruthie was still waiting for him. He did whatever he had to do to live and counted the days. He had a reason to celebrate on July 4th when it was time for his week of R&R from his tour of combat. He turned in his gear, cleaned himself up and changed into his khakis. When he got to Vung Tau he rented civilian clothes and boarded a plane for Bangkok. He hooked up with two other brothers on the plane. They checked into the same hotel but after that they didn't see each other until they were climbing the stairs of the plane on the way back.

Luke hired a guide and filled his days with sight-seeing on land and water through the traffic jams filled with bicycles, motor scooters, and trucks. His guide offered to take him to the massage parlors where pussy was as cheap as a good meal but he told him no thanks. He had made it this long and he had less than three months left in his tour. He opted to go shopping instead. He bought a camera to take some pictures and a watch to keep track of the time. He had his guide take him to a tailor where he could get two suits made. Back in the quiet of his hotel room he couldn't sleep, he kept listening for the sound of enemy fire that wasn't there. He sat up in the night writing on a letter to Ruth.

Dear Ruthie, I'm here in Bangkok and it's a relief to be out of the line of fire for a while. I'm sorry we didn't have the money for you to fly out to meet me in Hawaii like some of the other wives. I'm so lonely in this room. I spend most of the day visiting a lot of the temples in the city and the countryside that they have here reaching high in the sky and shining like they were dipped in gold. There are Buddha statues everywhere here in all colors and sizes. They say there are more than 100 poses for Buddha and they all mean something different. I wish I could take you shopping here. The prices are a lot cheaper than at home. I went to a floating market on the river that was outta sight. I met a tailor who's going to make me some new threads so I can look good for you when I get home. It won't be much longer. Hug Daniel for me. I love you both more than anything in the world. Your husband forever, Luke.

***

Ruth read Luke's letter about his leave in Bangkok. She looked at the postcards he had sent with all the pictures of the exotic places he had visited. It made her feel envious sometimes and then she felt guilty about it. She knew he was fighting for his life most days and not away on a fun vacation. The only thing was she felt like she was fighting too. Her life had changed so much in such a short time. She had gone from being a high school senior to being married with a baby and she was only nineteen years old. She worked her ass off at work and then had to wash dishes, wash clothes, and take care of Daniel when she got home. There were days when she'd give her last dime if only she could get a few days leave from her frenzied life. Things had moved too fast and there was no way she could go back and slow them down.

She had just put Daniel to bed when she heard a knock on the backdoor.

"What's happening, sister?" Laverne called out, walking in and finding her in the living room.

"Nothing, I'm tripping," Ruthie said. "All this stuff is starting to get to me."

Laverne sat down on the sofa. "I don't know why you won't give yourself a break from cleaning dirty diapers all the time. All work and no play makes Jill a dull girl plus gives her a nervous breakdown."

Ruthie smiled and shook her head. "You got that right."

"Well you can kick those blues to the curb because I've got the cure for you, girl."

"Oh yeah, what's that?"

"Guess who's coming to the Spectrum on August 22nd, the same day as your birthday?"

"I don't know, tell me," Ruth said, too tired to guess.

"Soul Brother Number 1, James Brown of course, and I've got us some tickets."

Ruthie scooted forward on the sofa and her face lit up with excitement she hadn't felt in a long time. "You better not say psyche or I'll kill you."

"I'm for real."

"That sounds good to me. I need to get out of this house and go somewhere else besides the TastyKake factory."

"Girl, you can go anywhere you want and you know it."

"What are you talking about?" Ruth asked, squinting her eyes, puzzled.

"I heard Eddie Speller was trying to rap to you."

Ruth waved her hand like she was fanning a fly. "I ain't thinking about that pimp, Laverne, you know he's in the Black Mafia."

"That's why he pulling all that bread, girlfriend. If I were you I'd talk to him. Busting your ass at the crack of dawn every morning is for the birds."

"You must have lost your mind. I'm married and I wouldn't do Luke wrong like that."

"You sure Luke's not messing with them Viet chicks over there?"

"You don't know my man like I do."

"That's true, but you might not know him as well as you think. He's been gone ten months."

Ruth asked her angrily, "Are you my friend, because right now you talking like my mother?"

"Take a chill pill, Ruthie, I'm your best friend. I just don't want you to be hurt if things don't turn out right."

"Don't worry about me, I'm cool. If you want to help me out, fold those diapers over there."

Laverne laughed, grabbed the laundry basket, and got busy.

***

Ruth looked at the calendar hanging on the wall in her kitchen. She had scratched off the days, the weeks, and the months that Luke had been gone. He had been gone for almost a year and Daniel's birthday was coming up. It had been a tough year. She had never worked this hard in her life. She had only gone out one time when Laverne took her to the James Brown concert. Soul Brother had turned up the heat so hot in the Spectrum with his band and his moves that they were all sweating when it was over. It was the first time she'd felt like she was a teenager since she'd graduated and gotten married.

That was two months ago and the time between the letters she got from Luke had spread out longer and longer as he became a short-timer. The foot of her crossed leg bounced up and down with her thoughts as she watched Daniel stumble around the room playing with his yellow Tonka truck. His first birthday was coming up and Ruth had wished Luke would have gotten back to celebrate it with them. She had even bought two tickets for them to see The Dells and Isaac Hayes at the Spectrum hoping he would be home. Her mind flashed back to the night at that house party when he held her like he would never let her go to the tune of *Stay in my Corner*.

A car horn beeping outside brought her back from her musings.

"I'm coming," she shouted, scooping up Daniel and a bag full of everything he might need.

She frowned when she saw Eddie Speller was driving.

"What's happening, sweet mama?" Eddie said, grinning. "You looking fine tonight."

Ruthie got in the back seat of the car rolling her eyes. She didn't feel like being bothered with him trying to get next to her all night.

"Eddie offered to drop us off," Laverne said happily.

"You should have called me," Ruth said with no enthusiasm.

She would have walked to her momma's house, dropped Daniel off, and then come back. She didn't want her son around any riffraff. She didn't blame Laverne, who was up front with Eddie singing to the radio with a cigarette in one hand and a bottle of Boone's Farm apple wine in the other, she didn't know how it was to have a baby.

"I don't know how you do it, Ruthie, that boy is getting big," Laverne said, watching her struggle to get Daniel and his stuff out of the car when they stopped at her momma's. "Hurry up. I don't want to get there late."

Ruth shut the car door. "I won't be but a minute."

Eddie lustily watched her through his window as she walked in.

"Forget it, Eddie," Laverne chuckled, "You're not getting none of that."

"You never know," he said, smiling.

Ruby was there in the doorway waiting for her grandbaby.

"There's my handsome boy," she said, picking him up. "Give Grandma some sugar."

"Everything should be in the bag, Momma," Ruth said, rushing to leave.

"I raised you, remember," she said to Ruth's back.

Ruth didn't have any doubts that her momma loved Daniel but whenever they were in a room together she could feel she still hadn't forgiven her for getting pregnant and marrying Luke.

"Take a swig off this bottle, sweet mama, it'll take the edge off," Eddie said, passing it to her over the back of the seat after she got back in the car.

Ruth took the bottle, brought it to her lips, and poured herself a mouthful. Her throat hurt as she forced it all down at once in a big round gulp. She relaxed as the warmth spread through her insides and joined Laverne singing *Stop the Love You Save* with the radio.

"All of Philly is down here tonight," Laverne said excitedly as they approached the Spectrum.

Eddie pulled over near the steps to the entrance to drop them off.

"I'll be out here waiting when the shows over," he said to Ruthie with a wink.

"Cool," Laverne said, grabbing Ruthie's arm.

Laverne pushed through the crowd making a path for Ruth behind her until they found their seats on the second level.

"It feels good to be out," Ruthie said, looking around the stadium.

Laverne laughed. "You act like you been locked up."

"Between work, doing hair, and taking care of Daniel, I don't have no time for myself."

"Not tonight," Laverne said as the music started, "These bad brothers are getting ready to blow your mind."

"I can dig it," Ruthie said, standing on her feet.

The atmosphere in the room was electric. The Dells were smooth, soulful, and unforgettable. When they sang Ruthie and Luke's song she shed a few tears in the dark. Isaac Hayes took over once he got on stage. He was a master on the piano and the mic. When he sang *I Just Don't Know What to Do With Myself*, Ruthie thought he had written it especially for her. By the time the show was over, both of them had clapped until their hands tingled, screamed until their voices were hoarse, and jumped until their legs muscles burned.

"That was outta sight," Laverne said on their way out.

"I didn't want it to end," Ruthie said.

They made their way outside where the spirits of the swarm of concert goers were still high.

Laverne strained to see through the heavy traffic. "Do you see Eddie's car?"

"Let's just catch the subway," Ruthie urged, not wanting to be bothered with Eddie.

"No way, my feet are killing me. Anyway, I see him over there."

"Make sure he drops me off first."

"Don't worry, I know the deal. Besides, I don't have a problem with him spending some of that cold cash of his on me."

"More power to you, sister."

Laverne talked nonstop to Eddie about the show all the way to Ruth's house. When they got there Ruthie thanked him and hopped out. The exhilaration of the evening had ebbed and the night had turned cold. Ruthie felt alone as she approached her darkened house. Inside the door she checked the time on the wall clock and it was after 1:00, too late to pick up Daniel. She closed the door and bolted the lock.

***

James, Teddy, and Luke parted ways similar to the day they met, like strangers. Few words were spoken. No addresses or phone numbers were exchanged. Most of their experiences would be locked away in a vault, deep in their memory banks with no plans to retrieve them.

Luke didn't tell Ruth when he was coming home. He didn't want to jinx it. Besides that he didn't want her going to a lot of trouble trying to pick him up at the airport with the baby. Discharged GIs had been warned about anti-war demonstrations stateside and some hostile attitudes they might encounter. Luke had heard that protesters were harassing soldiers around the airports, cursing them, calling them names, and some had even been spit on.

When Luke got off the plane at Fort Lewis, Washington, the anti-war protesters were there to greet them. He had to see it with his own eyes to feel the betrayal. "They drafted me, why am I the bad guy?" he asked himself. He ate his courtesy steak dinner and got his ticket home to Philly. He was beyond ready to take the uniform off and put it all behind him. He went in a bathroom and changed into one of the new suits he'd bought in Bangkok before he boarded his flight. It was close to midnight when he got off the plane and caught a taxi.

The city seemed peaceful compared to Saigon as he looked out from the rolling cab. Not much had changed from what he could see in the dark. He couldn't help feeling he had been gone for a long time. His heart began to beat fast and hard in his chest when the car stopped in front of his address. He paid the fare, got out with his bags, and walked to the door. He could see a light inside. He knocked but Ruthie didn't answer. He thought she might be asleep. He used his key and went inside.

The house smelled sweet like he remembered. There was more furniture and a playpen in the living room filled with toys. Quietly he eased up the stairs; he didn't want to scare Ruthie. He looked in the bedroom that was for the baby, eager to lay eyes on him, but the baby bed was empty. He hurried to the room he shared with Ruthie and saw their bed was empty as well. He didn't know what to think, he was too exhausted to think, he had been traveling for two days. He laid down on top of the covers and closed his eyes.

The click of the lock turning sounded like a gun being cocked and Luke was on his feet before he remembered where he was. He listened to the footsteps moving below and moved to the top of the stairs. Then he saw her.

"Ruthie," he called out.

She screamed, frightened at first, then she collapsed down to the floor overwhelmed when she saw him coming down towards her. Luke jumped to the bottom of the stairs and picked her up.

"Why didn't you call me and tell me you were coming home," she said, getting her bearings.

"I didn't want you to go to no trouble. I wanted to get here so bad for so long it wouldn't be real until I walked in here and saw you and our son. I flipped out when the house was empty. I thought you got tired of waiting for me."

"No way, I went to the show at the Spectrum with Laverne."

"You look so good, Ruthie. I kept thinking some other guys

would be around here trying to get next to you."

"I never wanted nobody but you, Luke, and I never will," she said, looking in his eyes.

He kissed her long and hard on the mouth, then he held her tight as he cried tears into her hair. "Thank you, baby," he said sincerely.

"What are you thanking me for?" Ruthie asked.

"I don't know, everything," he said, still holding her.

"Let's sit down on the couch, my legs are shaking."

Luke picked her up and sat down with her in his lap.

"I missed you so much," he said. "Where's Daniel? I want to see my son."

"I missed you too. My momma is watching Daniel but it's late. We can pick him up as soon as it gets light outside."

"I'm never going to leave you again, baby. I don't care what happens."

They sat on the couch for a while absorbing the presence of each other.

"We can stretch out upstairs and get some rest," Ruthie said, "It's been a long day."

Luke watched Ruthie undress and all the desires he held down for so long rose up. She was dead on her feet but she welcomed him and the evidence that he was still alive. The sight, touch, and the smell of her skin were like a drug to him and he was too high to come down. He made love to her not like a man who hadn't been with his wife in a year but like a man who believed this might be his last time. He had lived life tentatively for so long, it would take an even longer time to behave like tomorrow was a certainty.

***

Ruby frowned when she answered the door and saw Luke standing behind her daughter.

"I see you made it back in one piece," she said without any sentiment.

"Yeah, I'm home to stay," Luke answered obstinately.

"Did it make a man out of you?" she asked mockingly.

"It wasted my time, but I'm glad it didn't waste my life like it did for some other good brothers over there."

"Daniel is still sleep," Ruby said, still standing in the doorway, "Y'all are up with the birds."

"That's okay, momma," Ruthie said, pushing her way in, "We'll carry him home and let him sleep in his own bed."

Ruby and Luke stared at each other in silence while Ruthie went up to get Daniel. He had stared down death on so many occasions that Miss Ruby's hard eyes had no effect on him. When Ruthie came back with the boy on her shoulders, Luke was overwhelmed inside but he steeled his emotions in front of his mother-in-law.

"I'll carry him," Luke said, taking him out of her arms.

He held his boy close to his chest, feeling his own flesh and blood for the first time. It was supernatural, a miracle, this wonderful thing that had happened to him. He had a family all his own. It was love like he had never known existed. He turned and walked out with his right arm around Ruthie and Daniel wrapped tightly in his left.

Chapter Five

Luke sat at the kitchen table scouring over the want ads in the Inquirer while Ruthie cut his hair shorter around the sides and gave his afro a blow out with the pressing comb to look like Jim Kelly.

"It ain't nothing out here for me right now, baby," he said, discouraged.

"Something will come, honey, be patient. You only been home for a few months."

"It's been six months and I still can't put food on the table. I can't deal with that."

"We're not hungry, Luke, and we got a roof over our head."

"Watching you go out to the factory everyday and watching you stand on your feet doing hair when you're here is killing me. I want to take care of you and Daniel. I'm sick of your momma looking at me sideways."

"You will," she said, rubbing his head, "After you get your break I won't lift my finger except to tell my maid what to do."

"That's the way it will be, Ruthie, I promise," he said, picturing it in his head.

"I know it, I'm not worried," she said, blowing the hot comb to cool it.

"Right now I'm thinking about hooking up with Mark and doing a little business. It could keep some cash in my hands until something else comes through."

Ruthie stopped with the hot comb hanging in her hand. "I didn't sit up nights for a whole year praying for you to come home just so you could get in these streets with your brother and get locked up or shot up. I bet if you go up to the Plaza you could probably get hired back at the A&P."

"I need to make some real dough, baby, not some change jiggling in my pocket."

"Take what you can get until you can do better."

Luke took Ruthie's advice and went to put in an application at the A & P. His old manager hired him without hesitation but he only needed him part-time for the time being. To Luke it seemed like he was running backwards. How was he going to get ahead being a stock boy again?

The days turned into weeks and into months and before Luke knew it he had been home for more than a year and hadn't taken one step forward. Mr. Price at the store was giving him a few more hours but Ruthie was still holding things together with overtime at the factory and paying most of the bills.

The track for Luke's train of thought was on one thing. He needed to make some money to move them out of the projects. Ruby was always coming around their house unannounced and uninvited, and she always had a snide remark in her mouth to tear him down. He had quite a few things in his craw that he could have spat back at her but out of respect for his wife he didn't let them cross his lips.

For their first wedding anniversary he was in Vietnam, for their second he was too broke to buy her anything. Her birthday was coming up and he wanted to treat her special. She had already dropped Daniel at her momma's house. Watching her get dressed in her gold and brown sizzler dress and hot pants it still amazed him that she belonged to him. She worked so hard that sometimes he didn't think he deserved to have her. She was still the prettiest girl he had ever seen.

"Come on, Ruthie, I don't want to miss the next trolley," he said as she slid on her lipstick.

"All right, you want me to look sexy for you don't you?"

He smiled at her and said, "You always do."

He took her to Jim Kelly's restaurant on 12th Street for dinner and then they stepped high in their platform shoes up to 15th and Chestnut where the movie *Superfly* was playing. After they watched the movie, Luke bought them some water ice from a guy on the corner to keep cool while they walked down to the trolley on 11th Street.

"I'm going to have to get you to do my hair like that Youngblood's," Luke said, joking. "I'll be the smoothest cat on the block."

"I don't think it's long enough for all of that," Ruthie laughed, "But I'll cut you a slick style you'll like."

"As long as you don't have me looking like somebody's pimp," he laughed.

It was a short ride to Thompson Street. Luke held her hand tightly as they stepped down to the street.

"Let's leave Daniel at my momma's until tomorrow," Ruthie said, at the corner towards her momma's house. "I want a little more time with just us."

"Since it's your birthday I'll do whatever you want," Luke said, grinning back at her.

It was a muggy night and half the neighborhood was still sitting outside while the project bricks released the heat they absorbed during the day. Luke and Ruthie spoke to some of them and waved to a few others as they walked the half block to their house.

"Thanks for taking me out," Ruthie said once they were inside. "I miss having fun like we used to before you left."

"Things are going to get easier, baby," Luke said, opening a window to let some air in. "Hang in there with me for a little longer."

Ruthie pursed her lips. "I don't know, Luke. There's something serious I need to tell you."

From the look on her face, Luke knew it was something heavy. He plopped down on the couch to hear what she had to say.

She hesitated so he asked, "Are they cutting your hours again at TastyKake?"

"No, I wish they would sometimes."

"Then what is it?"

She sat down beside him and stared at the rug on the floor. "I'm having another baby."

Luke's heart rushed. He was happy and distressed at the same time.

"Wow, Ruthie, I don't know what to say. I love you and I want our family to grow but I'm barely pulling my own weight. I feel like I'm wearing you down."

"I got faith in you, Luke. You just haven't found your way yet. You're real smart. I was thinking it might be a good idea for you to go to college. You could get a big time job and then I could stay home and take care of our babies."

"How am I going to go to school now? I gotta find myself a second job."

"You can use that GI Bill you got from going to Nam."

"What in the world am I going to go to school for?" he asked, perplexed.

"You can study business, get you a big time job in an office downtown."

"I can dig it, but that don't happen overnight. How are we going to live in the meantime?"

"We gonna live like we been living. I know it seems like we're old folks most of the time but we're young. We got all the time in the world."

"Tell that to another hungry mouth to feed."

Ruthie knew what to say to get Luke to say yes.

"I'm counting on you and I know you won't disappoint me."

"No, I won't," he said, putting his arms around her. "I can't disappoint my lady."

The next day went Luke went to Drexel University and applied for admission. Six weeks later he got a letter that said he had been accepted for the spring semester.

***

Ruthie didn't say anything to her momma until she noticed it for herself. It was a week past Thanksgiving when she went to pick up Daniel after work.

"Child, you look like you're pregnant again," Ruby said, watching Ruthie zip up Daniel in his snow suit on the sofa.

"That's because I am, Momma."

"Lawd, lawd, lawd, you know they have birth control pills out here for free now."

"Luke and I are married. We can have another baby if we want to."

"That baby is only two years old. I was praying that you might go on and go to college after he got old enough to go to Get Set."

"Luke is the one going to college. He got accepted to Drexel and he's going to start classes after the holidays in January."

"I don't know why you let that boy make a fool out of you. He ain't good for nothing except for making babies. I don't know what you see in him. He don't have nothing and he don't look like nothing."

"I see somebody who loves me and only me, and I love that. Instead of running around like Daddy, thinking he's God's gift to women, he thinks that I'm God's gift to him."

"Oh no, wait a minute. As long as you live you better respect your father."

"You sit around here worshipping a man who left you and never did anything for us because he looked good, you hate Luke because you think he's ugly."

"Look here, little girl, I'm your momma and I loved you before you met that sorry nigger you married. Am I wrong for wanting the best for my daughter?"

"No, Momma, you're just too blind to see I already have it."

"We'll see, you think you're so smart. Trust me you have got a lot to learn about men. When he gets through using you, I'll be here."

"Luke is not Daddy, he's good to me," Ruthie shouted back.

Daniel hugged his momma tight around her neck and buried his head under her chin. He didn't like to see her upset.

"I ready to go, mommy," he whined.

"Okay, Pooh bear, let's go see Daddy."

***

Luke started his first semester in January. He was able to keep working part-time at the A & P and still have time to study and make good grades. The hard part was seeing Ruthie working so hard as her belly grew bigger and bigger. There were days when she was so tired she didn't have the energy to speak. Daniel was the joy that kept both of them laughing and smiling through the times when they were worn-out and irritated with each other.

On April 3rd they had a baby girl and named her Rebecca. She had big brown eyes that sparkled like her momma's, dimples that framed a smile that lifted your heart, and she was born the color of cocoa just like her daddy.

"Lord have mercy, this child is gonna be black as hell," Ruby said, when she first saw her in the hospital.

"Do you want to hold your granddaughter?" Ruthie asked, ignoring her comment.

Ruby frowned. "No, she's laying there quiet now. I don't want to get her riled up."

Ruthie hated that her momma was color struck. After all it was 1973, when was she going to get over that old-timey slave thinking. Hadn't she got the message that in any shade 'Black is Beautiful?' Besides, her baby girl was the most beautiful thing she had ever seen.

***

Things got tight while Ruthie was on maternity leave. Mr. Price gave Luke some extra hours but Ruthie kept the bills paid by fixing hair. She'd taught herself how to use the chemical straighteners and bought herself a used hair dryer. More customers wanted the permanents in their hair and once she got going she had more heads than she could handle.

She was just taking out the rollers of Cookie's hair, one of her co-workers from TastyKake, when her momma walked in the back door with Daniel.

"Mommy," he squealed, running up and hugging her leg.

"There's my boy," Ruthie said, leaning down and giving him a kiss.

"I don't know how you stand the smell of those chemicals all day," Ruby said, fanning the air in front of her.

"It's not any worse than the smell of hair burning," Ruthie remarked.

Ruby watched as Ruthie combed Cookie's curls out.

"That looks good," Ruby said. "How long does it hold?"

"About a week and a half," Cookie replied.

"This summer has been so hot my hair sweats back after three days," Ruby complained.

"I can give you a perm if you want, Momma."

"I guess I'm going to have to try it and see if it can keep my edges smooth in all this heat."

"How's it look, Cookie?" Ruthie asked, holding a mirror for her to see.

"It's shining like silk, thanks, girl."

She paid Ruthie fifteen dollars and left out of the back door. The slam of the screen door woke up Rebecca and she start to cry.

"I'll feed her and then I can start on you," she told her momma, rushing to see about the baby.

Ruthie walked back in the kitchen with Rebecca on her hip and warmed a bottle of formula. She shook a drop on the back of her hand and then sat down at the kitchen table across from her momma. Rebecca stared up at her momma's face while she sucked and slurped from the bottle.

"She's a greedy little thing," Ruby said, watching her.

"She's my real live doll baby. She's no trouble at all."

Ruby stood up abruptly and said, "Daniel has had his lunch already. I'll put him in the playpen with his toys."

"Okay, Rebecca is usually asleep by the time she finishes her bottle."

Once both the kids were napping, Ruthie combed out her momma's hair. It felt awkward touching her hair, it was so personal. They hadn't been close like this since she met Luke. It was the perfect time to bring up something she had been thinking about.

"You know I'll be going back to work in a couple of weeks," Ruthie said carefully, "And Luke goes back to school in a month."

"The summer sure has flown by," Ruby commented.

Ruthie parted her hair and began to apply the perm. When she got it all on she sat down to talk some more.

"We are going to need some help with the kids."

"I can probably help you with Daniel since he's potty trained and can walk but my back is giving me all kinds of problems and I just can't handle a baby."

"It would only be for a few months until she got old enough to put in daycare."

"Maybe Luke should drop this school thing for a while and get a decent job where he can help you take care of these children. Anyway, rinse this stuff out of my head it's starting to burn."

"Never mind, Momma, we'll work it out. Come on over to the sink."

Ruthie washed out the perm and put on a conditioner that she had mixed up herself. She rolled up her momma's hair and put her under the dryer. She hated that her momma was making a difference between Daniel and Rebecca but she knew there was nothing she could say or do to change her mind.

After her hair was styled Ruby checked it in the mirror and admired her reflection.

"You missed your calling, child, you laid my hair down." On her way out she turned around and said, "Sorry I can't help you with that baby but anytime you need me to watch Daniel just give me a buzz."

Against Luke's wishes, Ruthie switched her work schedule and went in on the second shift. It was the only solution they could think of and it paid Ruthie a little bit more on the hour. Luke had to give up his few hours at the A & P to be at home with the children since his job paid less money. She didn't care if she had to work her fingers to the bone, clean houses, work in a restaurant, or be a maid, she was going to see all his dreams and potential come to reality.

Luke studied tirelessly and made good grades in all his classes. There was no way he could fail with his wife breaking her neck to keep a roof over their heads and food on the table. He waited up for her every night so he could rub her feet. She kept telling him they were a team but not bringing any money in made him feel like he wasn't doing his part. In his mind he was less than a man if he didn't contribute to the finances.

***

They were so busy trying to make it that the years sped by without them realizing it. In what seemed like a blink of an eye it was May of 1977 and Luke was graduating from college. Daniel and Rebecca were seven and four years old by then. They played hide and seek behind Luke's blue graduation gown.

"Our dreams are coming true, Luke," Ruthie said, taking his

picture after the commencement ceremony, "I'm so proud of you."

"You should be proud of yourself, you're the one who pushed me and held us down."

"We both worked our asses off and it was worth it. Now you've got an interview next week at Smith Kline & French and I know you're going to get the job."

"I have to, Ruthie, I just have to," he said intently, "It's time for me to take care of you."

"Don't worry," she laughed, "You'll have the rest of your life to do that."

"It will be my pleasure," he said, smiling.

When they reach the bus stop on the corner Ruth said, "In honor of this special day we are taking a cab home."

Luke figured she was tired and flagged down a taxi on 33rd and Market Street. Daniel sat between them and Rebecca bounced on her momma's lap gazing out of the window.

"One day soon we're going to have our own car," Luke said. "I think you would look good in a Chevrolet Monte Carlo."

"Yeah, Daddy, let's get a red one," Daniel chimed in.

Ruthie closed her eyes. "Yes, I can see myself cruising around town in that."

"I'm hungry, Mommy," Rebecca said, seeing a hot dog stand on the corner when they stopped at a light.

"We'll be home in a few minutes, baby, we're having a graduation party for your daddy." She paused for a moment. "Don't be mad, Luke, I invited you family to come and celebrate."

"Gimme a break," Luke griped, "Why did you do that, Ruthie? I don't feel like being bothered with them today. All they're going to do is drink up everything and then raise hell."

Ruth felt Luke deserved to be congratulated and her momma never had anything good to say about him. Sometimes being close to people doesn't guarantee respect. Even if his folks fought among themselves, they still had love for each other.

"Give them a chance, they're happy for you. They're still your family."

"The only family I need is in this car," Luke grumbled.

Smoke rising up from the grill and the smell of meat cooking greeted them when the cab dropped them off by the side of their row. They were all there except for Mark. Ruthie led the way, and the kids seeing unfamiliar faces held on tight to Luke's pants leg and jacket.

"There he is, I can't believe it, my son is a college graduate," Gloria said, standing over the grill as they approached.

"I told you that boy was a genius," John said, raising up his half empty can of Schlitz.

"Thank y'all for coming," Ruthie said.

His sister Mary walked up to Luke and hugged him. "I can't stay but I wanted to come by and say congratulations and give you this," she said, handing him an envelope.

"Thanks," Luke said, slightly taken aback.

They all watched her hurry down the walkway where a man was waiting in a silver sedan.

"That nigga is old as I am," John said with his nose turned up.

"Leave it alone," Gloria said, "Don't spoil Luke's party."

Luke's brother, Matthew, who had been sitting quietly, got up from his folding chair and gave him the black power handshake.

"As-salamu alaykum?" Luke said warily.

"It's all about you, brother man, congrats," Matthew answered pleasantly.

"It's good to see you, it's been a while," Luke said.

"Yes it has," he agreed. "You have a lovely lady and a beautiful family."

Luke's edge softened. "Thank you, man."

Daniel saw some of his friends playing wall ball at the end of the row just as his Aunt Martha walked up. "Mommy, can I go over there and play?"

"Change your clothes first," Ruth replied.

"Okay," he said, running in the house.

"Congratulations, little brother," Martha said, handing Luke a card before she got a beer out of the cooler.

"Thanks," Luke told her, "Glad you could make it by."

"You know I had to be here for my baby brother."

"I can't believe that loser let you out of his sight," John said snidely.

"I'm grown and out on my own," Martha said without looking his way. "I don't have to answer to anybody."

"Who are you kidding?" John laughed, "You have to answer to everybody."

Gloria punched him in the arm. "Hush your mouth, J.C., that's your daughter you're talking to."

"Well excuse me," John said in a huff.

"Have you ever thought that maybe you had something to do with that?" Matthew asked sarcastically, agitated by his father's attitude.

"Y'all are all grown now," John said, "How long you gonna keep blaming me before you get your own shit together."

Martha went to the table and made herself a hefty plate. "Can I have some aluminum foil to wrap this up, I can't stay."

"Yeah, I'll get you some," Ruthie said moving towards the back door.

"No, no, sit on down and relax," Gloria said, "I'll get it and make some plates for you and Luke. Get them something to drink, Matthew. You both have worked so hard for this day."

Gloria rushed back with the foil, handed it to Martha, and fixed plates for Ruthie and Luke. When Martha had wrapped up her plate, she reached for another cold beer to take with her.

"Later, everybody. I'll call you, Mama," she said as she casually walked away.

"Take care, child," Gloria said behind her.

There was an awkward silence before John called out to

Rebecca, "Come here, little one. Say hello to your grandpa."

Rebecca looked at Luke for his approval.

Luke nodded. "Go ahead, baby girl, it's okay."

"So what is your next move now that you've got all that education?" Matthew asked, sitting back down across from Luke.

"Get a job and make some bread," Luke answered with his mouth full.

Matthew nodded his head. "Right on, man, I can dig it."

"He's got a job interview on Monday," Ruthie said, smiling with pride.

"Where's it at?" John asked curiously.

Luke said, "Down at that pharmaceutical company on Spring Garden Street."

"What are you going to be doing down there?" Gloria asked.

"Hopefully I'll be a manager in their marketing department," Luke said.

"Vietnam vets are supposed to get preferred hiring so that job should have your name on it, my man," Matthew added.

"He should get something for risking his life in that hell hole over there," John said.

"The real deal is that we need to focus on our own businesses in our own communities so we don't have to go to the white man for handouts," Matthew argued.

Ruthie raised her hand. "Uh-Uh, cool it, baby, no more militant talk, this is Luke's day."

"No, sweetheart," Luke corrected her, "It's our day."

They sat outside until it got dark listening to John talk about how hard life was down south when he was growing up and the things he might have done if only he'd made it up to Harlem. Luke didn't mention it after they left but despite all the fussing and talking trash it felt good to have his family there. They made him feel like Captain Marvel while Miss Ruby always made him feel like Wile E. Coyote.

Chapter Six

"I'm ready to fix your hair for your interview," Ruthie said, running her hands through Luke's thick afro. "I want you to blow their minds when you walk in."

"I guess I should get a haircut," Luke said.

"Not tonight, I'm going to do something different on you. It's something I've been trying out. If it works you're going to look like Billy Dee Williams."

"I'm game as long as you don't have me looking like the guy talking about 'uncola' in the sprite commercial."

Ruthie laughed thinking about his bald head. "He is kind of cute."

Luke followed her into the kitchen and watched her stir up the mixtures. She had been experimenting with perms and treatments on her customers. She made some adjustments to one of the mild perms so that it could be left on for longer times. She combed the concoction through his hair until it began to straighten.

"I hope you not giving me a process, baby, because they went out twenty years ago."

"What are you talking about? Sammy Davis Jr. is still sporting his."

"Have you done this before?" Luke asked, getting a little nervous.

"Nope, you're my guinea pig."

"Aw hell, Ruthie, this ain't the time for you to be doing experiments on me."

"Don't worry," she said nonchalantly, rolling his hair on small hard rollers.

"I don't want to look like I'm a faggot or something."

"Have I ever messed up your hair?"

"Not yet."

"Trust me then."

"I do, if I didn't I wouldn't be sitting here."

It took a lot of time. She had to wash one mixture off and put on another blend for him to sit under the dryer. After a while she washed the blend out with the rollers still on. She put him back under the dryer for another half hour. She smiled to herself as she put on a conditioner that she had mixed from a combination of oils. It had worked. His hair looked like naturally curly hair. She held the mirror in front of him to see.

"What did you do?" he asked, touching his hair. "This isn't my hair."

"Yes it is. It's a technique I've been working on for a few weeks."

"How did you come up with this?" Luke asked, still feeling his hair and staring at it in amazement.

"I've been diluting the chemicals for the perm because they were burning some of my customers too fast and damaging their hair. Then I mixed up my own moisturizer and conditioner to keep the hair from breaking. I wanted to do something special for you since you didn't want to wear a big fro anymore and I know you don't want to look like somebody's pimp."

Luke gazed at his reflection. "If I didn't know better I would think I had some good hair."

Ruthie had to laugh. "The only difference in hair is the curl pattern and the texture."

"I don't know what you're talking about but you got me looking fly."

"I'm glad you like it. Now let's go to bed, I'm exhausted."

"Do we have to put the rollers back on or can I sleep on this?"

"I'll give you one of my bonnets and you can go to sleep like you usually do."

"Thanks, baby," he said, playfully slapping her on the behind, "You are my angel."

***

Luke got up the next morning, showered, shaved, and put on the blue three-piece suit he bought in Bangkok. After a light breakfast, Ruthie ran her hands through his curls with a touch of moisturizer and he was ready to go. There wasn't a more confident man stepping out in Philly that day. Luke was ahead of schedule and could have walked to his interview but he didn't want to sweat up his suit. He caught the trolley on 12th Street to Spring Garden and took his time to walk the three blocks to 15th Street.

Cars and buses were rushing by and he could hear the rumble of the subway underground while streams of people were moving briskly in every direction trying to get to work. He smiled to himself as he took it all in. None of them knew his life was about to change.

He opened the heavy glass door of the brown and yellow building and walked into another world. He saw an information desk and went over to find out where he needed to go.

"Hello, ma'am, my name is Luke Clements. I have an interview this morning."

"Good morning, Mr. Clements, please sign in and have a seat," the receptionist said politely. "I'll call Mr. Tetti and let him know that you are here."

"Thank you, ma'am," Luke said before taking a seat on a colorful couch in the lobby.

About two minutes later a short man with a tanned round face greeted him enthusiastically.

"Hello, hello, I'm Dennis Tetti. Please call me Dennis. Do you mind if I call you Luke?"

"By all means, please do," Luke said, shaking his hand.

They caught the elevator to the fifth floor and Luke followed him through a complex maze of cubicles until they reached his office. He motioned for Luke to take a seat in front of his desk as he sat down.

"All right, Luke, first off, we have a copy of your resume that you filed with the Career Resource office at Drexel as well as a copy of your transcripts. Your qualifications for this position are not in question. So why don't we just talk a bit and give me an opportunity to learn some more about you and what you can bring to this company."

"All right," Luke said, beginning to speak, "I was born and raised in North Philadelphia. I graduated from Edison High School. I worked for a year at a grocery store and got married right after I was drafted. After I finished my tour I came home, worked for a while, and then went to school on my GI Bill."

"I'm blind as a bat in one eye so I didn't pass the physical, one of my cousins wasn't so lucky, he died over there."

"Sorry to hear that," Luke said, thinking about all the soldiers he saw get wasted.

The interview was relaxed and went smoothly. They talked some more about his year in Vietnam and if he had any lasting effects from being over there. They even talked about him working at the A & P.

After about forty-five minutes, Dennis stood up and said, "If you want the job it's yours."

"No doubt about it, I want the job," Luke said, standing up and thanking him.

It was an incredible feeling of relief and exhilaration. It was finally a dream come true.

"If you have time today, I'd like to take you around and give you a feel of the company."

"Absolutely, I'd like that," Luke said eagerly.

Dennis showed him the managerial and administrative floors on the eleventh and twelfth floors and Luke was visibly impressed. He was fascinated by the eighth and ninth floors where the research and development was conducted by busy scientists in long white coats. It amazed him to see the actual manufacturing of medications and pills in the huge vats before they were packaged on the third and fourth floors.

"The marketing division for Sea & Ski is located on the sixth floor," Dennis said, pushing the button for the elevator again.

Luke was stunned when the elevator door opened. There was a huge wall poster with a blonde-haired blue-eyed young woman in a bikini beside a line of suntan lotions. He had assumed he would be working on the cold medication, Contac. All of sudden he was puzzled. "Why were they hiring a dark-skinned black man to help them sell tanning products?" he asked himself. A small section of his brain wondered if the whole thing was a joke.

Dennis read his facial expression as they walked.

"Don't be thrown by the products that you'll be working on here. We're looking for a fresh outlook on marketing this brand. It's an image of beauty and vitality that we're selling more than the suntan lotion."

Luke understood that and forced the reservations out of his mind. At the end of the tour, Dennis instructed him to report to work on the following Monday. He caught the elevator down to the lobby, exited through the heavy double doors, and high-stepped his way up Broad Street with long strides fueled by the excitement of his new gig. He didn't even think about sweating up his blue suit.

Ruthie was beside herself with pride after he told her the news.

"I knew you had it in you," she said, throwing her arms around his neck.

"Now you can finally quit that job at the factory and let me take care of my wife."

"I will eventually, honey, but I don't think we need to rush it."

Thrown for a loop, Luke asked. "What are you talking about, baby, that was the plan from the beginning."

"It still is the plan," she reassured him, "But we can move to a bigger place where the kids can have their own rooms or even think about buying a house if we hold out a little longer."

Luke was disappointed, he was ready to show her how much he appreciated her love and support all this time, but what she was saying made sense. He wanted to get his family out of the projects and away from her momma as quick as possible. She spoiled and fussed over Daniel but she barely paid Rebecca any attention.

"We can put it off for a little longer, Ruthie, but you have to come off the second shift. Then as soon as we get settled in another place you will be unemployed. The only job you'll have will be loving your husband."

"That's cool with me," she said, kissing him on the lips. "That's the only job I want."

***

It took longer than they both thought it would, two years longer, but Luke and Ruthie had accomplished their goal of moving out of the projects. They bought a house in Yorktown. It was only four blocks away in Dondill Place, but they felt like they had come a million miles. On Valentine's Day, Luke used his Christmas bonus for a down payment and got her the red Monte Carlo she wanted.

Ruthie had finally agreed to quit her job at TastyKake. She had put it off over and over again. It wasn't easy to say goodbye to the relationships she had formed during the last ten years. The comforting thing was she would still get to see quite a few of them when they came by the new house to get their hair fixed. She had talked Luke into finishing the basement and she turned it into a hair salon. The irony was that Ruthie was already making more money than she did at the bakery and had more people wanting what she called 'the Ruthie confidence curl.'

They had been living there about four months when Ruby called to say she needed her hair fixed. She had only been there once before, shortly after they moved in. What she really wanted was to come by and see her grandson. As Rebecca had gotten older, Ruthie had cut off the time she spent with Daniel. There was no way she was going to allow her baby girl to feel slighted by anyone, not even her mother.

Ruth answered the door. "Come on down, I don't have anybody else until after lunch."

"Looks like you're still putting in more hours than your sorry ass husband."

"I don't have to work, Momma, my husband can take care of his family. It's just that I don't mind helping out."

"Anyway, I came to take Daniel to the movies. You don't bring him over to see me anymore. It's like you think you're too good now that you moved over here."

"I don't mind you spending time with the kids but you can't take Daniel if you don't want to take Rebeca too.

"I miss my grandson."

"You have two grandchildren."

"I'm not that close to her. I kept Daniel from the time he was a baby."

"That was your choice. You didn't want to keep Rebecca."

"I guess you're going to shut me out of your life like your sister did."

"That's not what I'm doing. You're welcomed here anytime as long as you give Luke the respect he deserves."

"Hmph, maybe it's time I got somebody else to do my hair," Ruby said, standing up and reaching for her purse.
"That's your choice, Momma, not mine."

Ruthie watched her walk back up the stairs. She dropped her head when she heard the front door bang shut.

***

Luke was doing his thing at SmithKline & French. He had run two successful campaigns and the money was good. The problem was Ruthie was working more hours at home than she had at the factory. Where their house used to smell like fresh baked sugar cookies it now had the pungent odor of chemicals to strip paint or clean floors. Some evenings when he got home she was working on one head, another was under the dryer, and there were three more waiting in line. The ladies he could tolerate but the men sitting around his house were too much to take. He couldn't stand the thought of Ruthie's hands in any man's hair but his own.

To clear his head and help him relax, he walked home at least twice a week. He had only made it to Ridge Avenue when he had an epiphany. It all made sense, the perplexing puzzle pieces had fallen into place. He could have kicked himself in the ass for not figuring it out earlier. He took off his sports jacket and ran the rest of the way home.

Rebecca was playing jacks on the porch and Daniel was playing four-square with some friends on the driveway.

"Where's Mommy?" he asked breathlessly at the bottom of the steps.

"Downstairs working with Aunt Laverne," Rebecca said.

"Thanks, sweetie," he said, patting her on the head.

"Ruthie," he yelled as soon as he got in the door. He jumped down the stairs in two steps.

"What's the matter?" she asked, slightly startled.

"Nothing except I'm taking you out to dinner," he said, grabbing her up in a tight hug.

"I have one more head to finish," she said.

"Can you handle it, Laverne?" Luke asked excitedly.

"Hell yeah, I can always handle some extra cash."

"What about the kids?" Ruthie asked.

"I babysit too," Laverne said with a chuckle.

Ruthie took off her rubber gloves. "All right, I'll get changed."

A half hour later Ruthie came down in a turquoise wrap dress.

"You look so good, baby," he said, looking her up and down. "Maybe we should make a sandwich and go back upstairs."

"Oh no, sir, I'm ready to be wined and dined."

Luke drove downtown and pulled the Monte Carlo up in front of Bookbinder's Restaurant.

"What's going on, Luke? My birthday is three weeks away."

"I can't wait to tell you," he said, getting out and hurrying around to open her door. He handed the keys to the valet and looped his arm through hers and led her inside."

"Champagne, please," Luke said to the waiter after they were seated.

"You must have gotten another raise," Ruthie said, smiling.

"It's better than that, baby. We're going to start our own company."

"What are you talking about, Luke. We're doing good right now."

"Ruthie, I think we should package your curl perm and sell it. I'm sure we can make a lot more money."

"Why would we sell my mixture? I make seventy-five dollars a head and I can probably charge more. I can't even do them all even with Laverne helping me."

"That's in our neighborhood, baby. I'm thinking bigger than that. I'm talking about going national, and you don't have to be on your feet working for hours. I know how to market it, baby. I do it every day selling suntan lotion as the bronze of Greek gods and goddesses. Let's do this. I know we can build something great together."

The waiter returned with the champagne and poured it in their glasses and gave them menus.

"I have always believed in you, honey, and I always will. We can try it, but we are going to take it slow. I don't want you quitting your job."

"Not until the time is right, I promise. I won't let us go backward, angel face, we're on our way to the top."

Ruthie raised her glass. "I'll drink to that."

Chapter Seven

It was a slow process but things were coming together. They had decided to package the curl as a kit with four parts, perm, shampoo, conditioner and moisturizer. Luke had been brainstorming with one of the chemists at work and he had given them some suggestions on refining the texture and scent of each formula. Ruthie usually mixed her concoction fresh every time but she had to learn about emulsifiers so that it could be packaged without the components separating over time. Between fixing hair in her basement salon, she cataloged the ingredients and their exact measurements for the chemist to prepare a sample for them.

"I can feel it, 1980 is going to be a spectacular year for us, baby," Luke told Ruth as they sat in front of the TV waiting for the ball to drop at Times Square in New York City. "We'll be running our own business before I turn 30 years old."

Ruthie looked at the kids asleep on the carpet in front of them.

"That's your dream and I know you'll make it happen," she said, turning to look him in the eyes. "I just want you to know all my dreams have already come true. I'm happy with you, Daniel and Rebecca, and our home. There's nothing else I want in this world."

"I love you, Ruthie, and I want to take care of you like I promised. I want to get you a big house with a maid to clean it for you. I want you to have a garden where you can sit outside and relax. I want to buy you diamonds, fur coats, and ride you around in a Mercedes. Then you momma will have to eat all those nasty things she said about me."

"Why do you care? It never made any difference to me what she said about you. You don't have anything to prove to her or anybody else."

"I know I don't but I want to," he said, reflecting back.

"You've been working your behind off for the longest, babe. Why can't we slow down and take the kids on a vacation this summer."

"We will, right now I'm working with a graphic designer on the branding and packaging. What do you think about calling it the Kush Kurl?"

"Kush, is that a play on words, putting curl and bush together?"

"Some will look at it that way but it refers to the Kush African Kingdom near the Nile River Valley where the Black Pharaohs originated. Some people say it's where the Garden of Eden was located. The Kush were the tallest and handsomest people on earth."

"That's deep, I like it."

"We'll market it as the curl of the regal and majestic sisters and brothers."

"I guess that isn't a hat rack on your shoulders after all," she teased, rubbing him on the head.

"None of this could have been possible without you," he said, pulling her close.

***

The design and the packaging for the Kush Kurl was completed by the end of the year. The patents were in hand and Luke was ready to move forward. He found a low cost private label cosmetic manufacturer where they could outsource production. Their new business venture was named the Clements Cosmetic Company. The demand was already there, all they needed to do was supply the product.

The word about Ruthie's curl was all over Philly. There was no way she and Laverne could do all the male and female heads that wanted the hairstyle. They were always booked up and running a long waiting list. A week before Christmas, Luke came home to find his brother, Mark, in Ruthie's chair and two other thug looking dudes sitting in the room waiting.

"I'll be damned. What's up, Luke. It's good to see you," Mark said with a smirk on his face.

Ruthie froze as the tension between them filled the air.

"This is a surprise," Luke said.

"I can't get over it. Who knew," Mark said, "Word around town is this is the place to come and get your 'do' hooked up."

"Then you just showed up at my house," Luke said indignantly, mad about the thugs in there with his wife. "I haven't seen you in years."

"You know how it is, brother, I've been kinda busy."

"I can imagine. I can't believe you got the nerve to bring your criminal ass and your crooked friends in my house uninvited."

"Why are you insulting me, brother? I ain't never been arrested or locked up for no reason."

"Just because you haven't been caught don't mean you're legit."

"You got a nice set-up here," Mark said, ignoring his comment. "I'm sure it's not too late to say congrats. You obviously have a dynamic, sexy lady. I'm almost jealous."

"Is that right?" Luke snapped angrily.

"Relax, baby brother, I wouldn't disrespect your house."

"No doubt," Luke said, letting it go and turning to leave, "I've got some things to do."

"That's cool, later, man," Mark said.

Luke stomped up the stairs pissed off and it got him thinking. After Ruth came up several hours later and was finishing a late dinner, he sat at the table across from her to explain what was on his mind.

"I can't take all these people in the house and around my kids," he told her.

"I'm sorry, babe. Maybe we should rent a place on Girard or Columbia Avenue?"

"No way, the plan was and still is to get you off your feet, and that's what I'm going to do. Your fixing hair days are coming to an end."

"You can't think while you're upset, Luke. We agreed that we wouldn't go into debt and we need all the money we can get for advertising and distribution. When you calm down we'll talk about it."

"I was mad as hell but I'm over it now, my head is clear, and so is our next move. We're going to do a series of seminars at some nice hotels on the East Coast, starting here in Philly. We'll charge beauticians a fee to attend, you'll give a demonstration on how to do the curl, and then we'll sell them the product. It will be more profitable than what you're doing here and its promotion at the most effective level."

Ruthie thought about his plan for a minute and then a smile spread across her face

"Your daddy said you were a genius," she said, getting up and sitting on his lap."

***

Luke spent the next week making phone calls trying to get ball park numbers for his first seminar. He wanted to plan a five star event to debut their product but his pockets were saying hang up and call back when you get your hands on some real money. The manufacturer was going to charge him three dollars each per one thousand kits and the price was higher if the quantities were less.

The Sheraton downtown on 17th Street had given him the best quote on a meeting room with 200 attendees. He preferred to schedule on a Saturday but Friday was less expensive. They purchased a full one page advertisement in the Tribune, the Daily News, and the Sunday Inquirer inviting local hairstylists. Optimistically, if he could get each attendee to buy five of the Kush Kurl kits the seminar would be a success. Then they would have enough money for several more and he could tell Ruthie to shut down the shop in the basement.

Rebecca was sitting in the living room watching TV when he got home from work.

"Where's you momma?" Luke asked, rubbing her on the head.

"She went to get some stuff from the store."

"Where's Daniel?"

"He said he was going over to Grandma Ruby's."

Luke shook his head in dismay. That boy was back in the projects every chance he got. He hung up his coat and went in the kitchen to get something to drink. He grabbed two cans of black cherry soda out of the fridge and went back into the living room. He popped one can and handed it to Rebecca.

"What'd you learn in school today?" he asked, making conversation.

"Adding and subtracting," she said, still absorbed in her show.

Luke chuckled. "I could have used your help, that's all I've been doing all day."

"I'll help you, Daddy," she said, paying attention.

"Thanks, sweetheart," he said, putting his arm around her narrow shoulders.

Then Ruthie walked in the door.

"You're home early," she said, pleasantly surprised.

He stood up to give her a quick kiss. "I needed to speak with my business partner."

Ruthie took off her coat and sat on the sofa beside them.

"All right, lay it on me," she said, waiting for the update.

"I've finalized everything, the date is March 20, 1981, the first day of spring, fitting for our burgeoning business. The bottom line is we need five thousand dollars."

"Wow, babe, I think that might be a stretch, that's less than a month away. We haven't really recovered from the down payment on the house and the car."

"I know but I believe we can pull it off," he said, getting revved up. "We have about fifteen hundred in the bank. All we have to do is hold off paying the mortgage and the car notes and hold whatever we make for the seminar. We've got to have the full amount for the newspaper advertisements and the manufacturer on delivery of the kits, but the hotel will only require a 50 percent deposit."

Ruthie wasn't convinced. "That's squeezing it real tight, Luke. Too tight. We don't have any breathing room. I don't care about losing the car but we can't lose our home. We have to think about the kids."

Rebecca pretended to watch her TV show but was listening to every word.

"This is our opportunity," Luke said, trying to put her fears to rest, "When it's over we'll be back in the black."

"What if nobody comes and we're in a deeper hole than the one we came out of."

"I'd rather for that to happen than to not take our chance to blow up."

"I don't know if I'm prepared to talk in front of a lot of people."

"All you have to do is keep your eyes on me, just like we're talking now. The product is ready, production is ready, and we're ready, baby."

"I'm not going to waste my breathe trying to change your mind, go on and do your thing," she sighed, giving in.

"It's our thing, Ruthie, for our family."

"Okay, Luke," she laughed, "We still might be able to get our old place back."

"This train we're on doesn't go in reverse, angel face, its full speed ahead."

***

The Sheraton was packed. Luke and Ruthie had twice the number of attendants than they had seats. He made a quick arrangement with the hotel to give them a few more hours so that they could repeat the seminar for those who wanted to wait.

"I'm so nervous I'm shaking," Ruthie said to Luke.

"Just relax, Laverne is going to be up there with you and she'll do the demonstration. You just look out in the audience at me."

Excitement filled the meeting room. Black folks love their mama's, their babies, and their hair. Luke had learned that if you can develop a way for most people to make money and be sharp as a tack they will beat a path to your door. He opened the seminar welcoming the beauticians, barbers, salon owners, and those who were interested in doing it for themselves.

Then he began his spiel. "Everybody in here knows that hair is our crown and glory. If it's right you're royalty, baby. If it's not right, you better get it right."

Applause filled the room and Luke introduced them to the Kush Kurl and had some of Ruthie's customers model their different lengths and cuts of the curl. Then he introduced Ruthie to talk about the process of applying the products to get the style before he sat down in the reserved seat in the front row. She started off talking too fast. It took a few moments for her to slow down and the uneasiness to disappear from her voice but she did a great job. Luke was really proud of her.

They repeated the seminar for the second group that had been patiently waiting and they were all receptive even as the clock went past the eleven o' clock hour. It had been a phenomenal success. At the end of the long day they had sold-out the one thousand kits they brought with them and took orders for another fifteen hundred.

"We did it, baby," Luke said, lifting Ruthie off her feet in a big hug. "We've cleared fifteen grand tonight and we have orders for another thirty grand. When I first saw you I knew that you were my dream come true."

Ruth was overwhelmed. "I can't believe it. It's too much."

"No, Ruthie, it's just the beginning."

***

Luke pushed forward with the momentum from the first seminar and took their show on the road. He scheduled a series of seminars in Trenton, New York City, Baltimore, D.C., and each one was more profitable than the last. Luke used sick days and vacation time to get off from work so he could be there for the seminars. He bought a used truck to carry the kits with them.

It was tough traveling on the road with Daniel and Rebecca being only eleven and eight years old. Neither of them wanted to take the kids out of school and Laverne was making the tour with them. Luke still didn't trust his mama to look after them and Ruthie knew her momma made a difference between them. Miss Ruby still grinned at everything Daniel said and did and frowned at the sight of Rebecca.

Interest was spreading across the country even on the West coast where the Jheri-curl was gaining traction. With the size of the market there was room for them and the competition to do well. Six months into the promotion, Luke realized the Kush-Kurl kit had an engine that ran and made money without them having to continue with the seminars. The curl required retouches and maintenance like any other perm or color on the new hair growth. The components of the kit needed to be sold individually as well. The next step was to begin mass distribution in stores like Empire and Sally's Beauty Supply.

The money was coming in so fast that Luke hadn't had time to set up the infrastructure to handle the rapid growth of the company. He and Ruthie were up most nights trying to keep the books and process the orders.

"I'm done, babe," Ruthie said in the midst of a yawn. "I can't hold my eyes open."

"It's time to think about taking this to the next level," Luke said, staring at the pile of orders on the dining room table in front of him.

"We already have more work than we can do."

"I'm talking about going at this full blast, us getting a building or a warehouse where we can expand. We need a support staff to handle our accounting, processing the orders, and to take care of billing. I've been punching some numbers and we can save a lot of money if we manufacturer the products ourselves. We can rent the equipment and get some temporary employees until we really get it rolling. The Clements Cosmetic Company is growing and we have to grow with it."

"You know I support whatever ideas that you have for the business. It's just that I don't want to gamble with everything we've work so hard to get."

"It takes money to make money, baby. We have gotten this far by investing in ourselves."

"It also takes money to live. Our family comes first before the business."

"This is for our family. Our children will always be taken care of if we do this right."

"I need to get a cup of caffeine if we're going to have this conversation."

Ruthie went in the kitchen and made a fresh pot of coffee. At least she didn't have to get up and go to a job in the morning. She brought two mugs back to the table.

"I'm ready to give this all I got, Ruthie. I don't know how you'll feel about this but it's time for me to quit my job at Smith

Kline.”

Ruthie sighed, she knew that was coming. How much money do we have?” she asked.

“Our personal account is around $14 thousand, the business account has about $390 thousand after all the bills are paid.”

“How much do you think you’ll need to do this expansion?”

“It will run about $200 thousand for six months.”

“That’s half of what we have, in a year we could be broke again.”

“No way, baby, the money won’t stop. We can capitalize on the demand as it grows. This is how Johnson Products did their thing.”

“There’s something you’re not thinking about, hairstyles change. What happens when nobody wants their hair curled anymore? Then we’re out of business and you don’t have a job.”

“Companies evolve, we can add to our line. This is not something I’m trying out. We have a thriving successful company that will make us enough money in the next few years where we will never have to work for another man in our lives.”

“I’ll compromise with you. You take half of all we have. That will give you six months. I’ll hold the other half as an insurance policy.”

“We can borrow as much as we need, we don’t have to use our money if that bothers you.”

“That’s my only objection, borrowing a bunch of money that we might not be able to pay back. Anyway, I’m going to bed,” Ruthie said, yawning again. “I’ve got to start planning for Becca’s birthday party this weekend. I can’t believe she’ll be turning nine years old.”

“All right, angel face, get some rest. I accept your compromise. I’ll use half of our money and make it work.”

***

Over the next two years, the Clements Cosmetic Company struggled to meet the demand for the Kush Kurl. Black people from coast to coast were wearing some kind of curl, politicians, entertainers, preachers, and teachers. The money was coming in so fast Luke and Ruthie didn't have time to enjoy their success. They had to manage the growing payroll of employees, insurance, shipping and receiving, and business and income taxes. They hired a chemist to formulate a Kiddie Kurl Kit that loosened the natural curl of the hair and didn't need hair rollers. They added a smooth wave as well as a conditioning relaxer to give some variety to their line. They were even discussing some skin care products they might add in the future.

Luke needed someone he could fully trust to be his right hand man. Someone he could trust with his money and his family, someone honorable with principles. Only one person came to mind. He was going to see him first thing Saturday morning.

***

Luke banged on the door like he was SWAT coming for its 'most wanted.'

"What the hell?" Matthew said, snatching the door open. Then he saw it was Luke. "Oh shit, who kicked the bucket?"

Luke laughed. "Nobody, you're crazy, man."

"You ain't darkened my doorway before so this has trouble written all over it."

"Can I come in and sit down or am I going to have to conduct my business on your stoop?"

"Negroes are all out of control these days," Matthew joked, stepping to the side for Luke to come in.

Luke looked around as he walked in, checking out the pictures that decorated the neatly kept living room.

"Where's the family?" Luke asked.

He knew that Matthew and his wife had two teenage daughters.

"Take a seat," Matthew said, pointing at the sofa. "They're in and out. We're having some issues and both of us are too stubborn to change."

"I'm sorry, I didn't know."

"I've broken with the Nation of Islam. Here in Philly it's still too corrupt, I can't deal with the drug dealing, extortion, and murders. Instead of uplifting the people they're doing the same thing the white man did, making us slaves."

"That's deep, Matt."

"Corrine remains faithful to the Nation and that's what has come between us. The girls are loyal to their mother so I'm here by myself. We still love each other and she comes back from time to time to try and convince me I'm wrong but it hasn't worked so far."

"I came here with a proposition for you too. Hopefully I'll be more successful than Corrine."

"Go for it, man, I'm listening."

"You were always riding me about working for the man and how I should do my own thing."

"I guess I'm guilty on that charge," Matthew said with some regrets.

"That's why I'm here. Ruthie and I have started our own company and its booming. We can't manage it by ourselves. I need a Chief Financial Officer who I can trust with my business. I want you for the job."

A cornucopia of emotions swirled within Matthew and for a moment he couldn't respond. He was so proud of Luke and touched that he would come to him for help.

"It would be my honor and pleasure to work with you, man. I heard about your company and I admire and respect what you're doing."

"Thanks, man, you don't know what that means to me."

"Maybe not, but I know what it means to me."

Luke stood up and the brothers looked at each other for moment. So much was unspoken, so much was understood.

Luke smiled. "Then I'll look for you in the office on Monday morning."

"I'll be there before you get there," Matthew said.

"In that case you'll need these," Luke said, tossing him a handful of keys.

Chapter Eight

Ruthie's birthday was almost a month away but Luke couldn't hold his surprise for her any longer. They had developed a weekend ritual of taking the kids to his sister Mary's house and going out to dinner. Luke loved it when Ruthie got all dressed up. He loved to show off his beautiful wife. It was Sunday so he made reservations for 5:30, he would tell her the surprise over dinner and they wouldn't be late. Luther Vandross was coming to the Spectrum on July 29th and he had tickets for the show.

"Let's make another stop before we pick up the kids," Luke said as they were leaving the restaurant.

"We can drive through Fairmount Park and catch some air," Ruthie suggested.

"Or we could go to the Luther concert," he said slyly.

Ruthie contained her reaction. "Don't play with me like that, Luke."

"I'm for real, baby," he said, pulling two tickets out of his pocket.

She grabbed him around the waist. "I would kiss you if we weren't out here in public."

"You can do a lot more than that when we get home," he said, laughing.

The concert was an enchanted performance of magnificent mesmerizing mellow music. Luther Vandross was the consummate singer as he serenaded them with his string of hits. For a few hours they were transported to a magical place where time had stopped.

"I wish I could follow that tour and listen to that man sing every night," Ruthie said in the car while they were driving.

"When things slow down some with the business I'll take you to see him wherever he goes."

Ruthie snickered. "Promises and more promises. When will that happen?"

"I don't know but it will."

Luke looked at the time on the dashboard as they got closer to home.

"It's late," he said, "We can pick up the kids in the morning."

She yawned. "They're probably sleep by now anyway."

They parked their car in the driveway and went in the front door. Ruth stopped in her tracks. The inside of the house looked like it had been hit by a tornado.

"Oh my God," Ruthie said, covering her mouth in shock.

The sofa was laying on its side and the tables had been turned over. Luke rushed by her checking all the rooms. Their office had been ransacked. The TVs and the VCRs were missing. The kids' rooms weren't bothered but Luke and Ruthie's mattress was on the floor.

"Shit," Luke yelled out, "We've been robbed."

"I can't believe it. This is our neighborhood."

"It's time to go," he said furiously. "We can't stay here. The company is doing real well and these crackheads think we got money in the house. I'm just glad we weren't here but I can't take a chance on these crazy ass niggas coming in on my family."

"I don't want the kids to know. It'll scare them."

"Call the police, after they make the report, I'll clean up."

***

It was Ruthie's birthday and they were having dinner at the Capitol Grille to celebrate. It had been less than a month since the break-in so she was nervous about going out. Both of them seemed to rush through their meal but for different reasons. Ruthie knew Luke had planned something special because he looked like he was about to burst.

"Tell me what's going on before you have a heart attack," she said, looking at him from across the table.

"Everything I ever wanted for us has happened, Ruthie. Most of it is because of you. You have worked so hard. I want to thank you for standing beside me, behind me, and in front of me to get us where we are. To show you how much that means to me, and how much you mean to me, I have these keys for you."

"Don't tell me you bought me a new car," she said, taking the keys in her hand.

"No, baby, I finally got you the house you deserve."

Ruthie was stunned. "Luke, I love our house, you didn't have to do that."

"Yes I did. I want to show how much I love and appreciate you."

"Where is this house?" she asked, totally shocked.

"It's in Chestnut Hill."

"Chestnut Hill, we don't need to be out there with all those rich and siddity people."

"That's where we belong now. We got real money, baby. We've built a multi-million dollar business. We're lucky nobody has held us up or knocked us in the head by now. We can give the house to my mama and daddy, and your momma can stay too if she wants. We'll keep the utilities paid and food in the fridge. Mary can handle it and there's space for Martha if she wants to get off the street too. Think of it as a way to help our family."

Ruthie smiled. "Okay, okay, you've made your point, when do I get to see this house."

"Tomorrow, tonight we enjoy each other and our last night in North Philly."

***

Two life changing things happened at the Clements home on November 22, 1986.

Ruthie was having a surprise party to celebrate Luke's thirty-sixth birthday. He'd been out of town on business the whole week and would be home around seven. She'd ordered the pay-per-view heavyweight championship fight between Trevor Berbick and Mike Tyson as part of the entertainment. She'd invited a few associates from his old job, a couple of their new neighbors, her momma, Laverne, his mama and daddy, Mary, and Matthew. She was having the whole thing catered by Judy B. Baker. Laverne had come early to show the caterers where to set up.

Ruthie had gone to Saks Fifth Avenue that morning and bought a new hot pink cashmere dress with dolman sleeves that hung around her curves perfectly to wear at the party. She couldn't wait for Luke to see her in it. She was in the shower smiling to herself when she found it. It was a small lump about the size of a pecan in her left breast. She shuddered with fear and a chill ran down her spine. She froze under the flow of water in shock, paralyzed, until a knock on the door with Rebecca calling her got her moving again.

"Mommy, it's almost time for Daddy to get here, I need you to fix my hair."

"Give me a minute, sweetie," Ruthie said, steeling her emotions.

She turned off the water and dried off in front of the steamed mirror. Then she wiped the mirror with her towel and stood there staring at her body. Nothing seemed wrong or out of order. She looked the same. She had panicked without reason. She was fine, like Luke always told her, she was "super fine." Quickly, she finished dressing, did her hair and make-up, and sprayed herself with her favorite cologne.

"Becca, come on, I'm ready for your hair," she called out.

"I coming," Rebecca said as she burst through the door.

"Sit down," Ruthie said, motioning towards her dressing table.

Rebecca had already taken the rollers out. Ruthie gently combed the soft curls and fluffed them in the front and pinned them up in the back. Her baby was only thirteen she didn't want her hair swinging down her back like she was grown.

"You look pretty, Mommy," Becca said, smiling at her in the mirror.

Ruthie squeezed her shoulder. "And you look prettier."

"We've got to hurry up, everybody is here and Daddy is probably about to come home."

"Okay, baby, let's go," Ruthie said, taking her hand to hold as they went downstairs.

All the guests were gathered in the great room munching on hors d'oeuvres and sipping on drinks while a Billy Ocean CD played in the background.

"What's up, good people," Ruthie said, coming into the room like a model hitting the runway.

"The lady of the manor has arrived," Matthew said, being sarcastic.

"Don't pay him no attention," Gloria said, "This is a beautiful home y'all got here. You two have worked hard and you deserve it. Isn't that right, John?" she asked, elbowing her husband.

"That is right," John said, nodding to the music. "And when you move to the next one we'll be ready to come on in here and take care of this one for you too."

"Let that go in one ear and out the other," Martha said, walking over to her. "I want to tell you how grateful I am that you let us stay at your old house. It's been so long since I had any place to call home."

"You're more than welcome, and I'm glad you all could make it," Ruthie said with a smile.

Mary walked over and greeted her with a hug, "You're looking good, girl."

"Thanks, sister," Ruthie said in a low voice, holding her an extra moment for support.

"Everything okay?" Mary asked, slightly concerned.

"Yeah, just a little tired."

Daniel hollered from across the room. "Momma, Dad just pulled up."

"All right," Ruthie answered, "Turn the music down."

She hurried out of the great room closing the doors behind her to meet Luke when he walked in. She got to the foyer just as he unlocked the front door.

"Welcome home, babe," she said when he stepped in.

He pulled her close for a hug and kiss. "I missed you. You look gorgeous."

"I missed you more," she said, squeezing him tightly.

All Ruthie wanted to do was breakdown and cry in his arms. Tell him how scared she was. Instead she kept her smile in place, determined not to spoil the party.

"There are some cars outside, do we have company?" Luke asked curiously.

"Follow me," she said, taking him by the hand.

She opened the double doors to the great room and everybody yelled, "Surprise."

Luke was overwhelmed for a few seconds remembering his birthday was earlier in the week. He looked around the room and saw a few familiar faces from his old job, a few of his business associates, then he saw Matthew, Mary, Martha, and his mama and daddy. Rebecca ran up and hugged him and he found his voice.

"Wow, this is a surprise," he said, recovering from the shock.

"Happy Birthday, son," John said, extending his hand.

Luke shook his hand. "Thanks, Pop."

The music was turned back up and Luke made his way around the room getting high-fives and well wishes. The food, the liquor, and the company were all good. At 9:00 the music was turned down again. The volume on the 40-inch TV screen was turned up. It was time for the heavyweight championship fight between Trevor Berbick and Mike Tyson.

"Now this was worth the drive out here," Matthew said, taking a seat closer to the TV.

"I know that's right," somebody else added.

Magically, the excitement from the Hilton Hotel in Las Vegas was transmitted across the airwaves and filled the room as the young challenger, Iron Mike, moved towards the ring with his body already covered in perspiration. The crowd roared with cheers, whistles, and claps.

"He looks like he's ready to fight," Matthew said.

"Yeah, he's unstoppable," Daniel said, enthused and too hyped to sit down. "He's the baddest fighter on the planet and he's only four years older than I am.

The champion, Trevor Berbick, made his entrance into the ring and took off his black robe.

"He's in shape too, it's going to be a good one," Luke remarked.

From the sound of the bell the action started with both fighters barreling out from their neutral corners surging with confidence. Within a minute it was clear, the youth and strength of Mike Tyson demonstrated why he was the number one ranked contender. He moved at a feverish pace, bobbing and weaving between his attacks. By the end of the first round his powerful punches had dominated and stunned Berbick, who was tying him up and holding on every chance he got.

"Damn, that was only the first round," Matthew said, holding his fist to his mouth, "I know Berbick wished that was the last one."

"I bet he's going down in the next round," Daniel said even more excited.

"No doubt," Luke agreed, "The kid is taking him down just like he did Muhammad Ali five years ago. There's going to be a new champ tonight."

John laughed. "That's right, what goes around comes around."

In the second round, the question was not if he would be knocked down again, it was how many times. Mercifully the referee ended it after the third time. Mike Tyson had made history, being named the youngest heavyweight champion ever to hold the title.

Daniel was mesmerized by the frenzied scene on the TV. The atmosphere was electric. He couldn't think of anything he wanted more than to be in the center of that ring.

"That's going to be me one day," he said, raising his fist in the air.

*****

After midnight the party was over and the house was quiet.

"Thanks for doing that for me, baby," Luke said, closing their bedroom door. "Everybody seemed to have a good time."

"I just want you to be happy," Ruthie said.

"You make me happy, I don't need anybody else," he said, kissing her.

He put his hand under her sweater dress and lifted it over her head. His eyes drifted down the length of her body and back up to her eyes.

"You're so sexy," he said, "I love your body."

Ruthie had always loved it when Luke gushed over her but tonight it made her feel self-conscious. Standing there she had a moment of vertigo, as if she were at a high height about to fall. She sat down on the bed to take off her heels. Luke sat down beside her. He kissed her shoulder and took off her bra. Ruthie shuddered. Luke reached behind them and pulled the comforter back.

"Slide under the covers, angel face, I'll warm you up," he said, taking off his suit.

When Luke slid next to her she closed her eyes and listened to his breathing and concentrated on the sound of his voice while they made love.

"You feel so good, baby," he whispered to her, "I love you."

"I love you too," she said, shaking with passion and fear.

***

Ruthie decided not to think about the lump in her breast until after the holidays. Except those six weeks turned into six months. She had tried her best to forget it, pretended that she never felt it. School was almost out and they were planning a family vacation to the Bahamas. She was out shopping for the trip, trying on a bathing suit in Macy's when she felt it again. She collapsed on the floor of the dressing room and cried. Then she rushed out to her car and called her OB/GYN doctor on her mobile phone. They could see her that afternoon but she was afraid to go alone. She started the car and sped over to her mother's house.

"Ruthie, what going on? Why didn't you call me and tell me you were coming by today?" Miss Ruby said, surprised to see her standing at the door.

"Momma, I have a lump in my breast. I'm scared. Will you go with me to the doctor?"

"Oh Lord, child, you know I will," she said, pulling her inside. "Come on in, let me get out of this house dress and put some clothes on real fast."

Ruthie sat down on the sofa feeling relieved. Finally telling somebody had taken away half of the burden she had been carrying.

"I'm ready, sugar," Ruby said ten minutes later. Out of the door, she ushered Ruthie back to the car. "Don't worry now, child, I'm sure it's nothing serious."

Ruby chatted nervously and nonstop during the drive to Thomas Jefferson Hospital. She didn't stop when they reach the office or while they sat in the waiting room. It was only when the nurse called Ruthie's name and she went to the examining room did she stop and begin to pray.

Dr. Hayes's physician assistant weighed Ruthie and got all of her vital information before she took her to the room where they performed the mammogram. When all of it was done she led her back to the doctor's office. Ruthie sat there looking at but not seeing the covers of the magazines on the table until he walked in with another doctor fifteen minutes later.

He shook her hand before he sat down.

"Mrs. Clements, I'm very glad that you came in today," Dr. Hayes said, taking a seat. "This is Dr. Pat Albright, she's an oncologist here with us. We are very concerned about the mass in your breast and would like to schedule a biopsy immediately. I would also like to speak with you and your husband about options for treatment. Can he come to the office this afternoon?"

Ruthie's heart was beating hard and fast with fear and her thoughts were jumbled together. She needed some time to compose herself, think about everything on her own, before she or Dr. Hayes talked to Luke.

She took a breath and said, "Dr. Hayes, my husband has a number of important meetings this week and we are going out of town on a family vacation this weekend."

Dr. Albright pulled her chair in front of Ruthie and leaned in close.

"This is very serious, Mrs. Clements," Dr. Albright said frankly, "I would prefer not to delay this procedure. It is our concern that this mass may be cancerous. In that case it may be necessary to perform a lumpectomy or mastectomy. This is something I would like to discuss with you and your husband together as soon as possible."

"Doctors, this is a lot for me to process right now. I really need some time to discuss it with my husband before we talk about treatments."

"I can understand that but this is not something we want to delay," Dr. Hayes said.

Ruthie stood up.

"I'll call the office as soon as I can," she said, turning to leave.

"Time is of the essence," Dr. Albright said, opening the door for her.

Ruthie stopped in the restroom on her way out, rinsed her face in cold water, combed her hair, and put on fresh lipstick.

"That took a long time," Ruby said when she came out into the waiting area. "I was just about to come in there looking for you. What did the doctor say?"

"He said that it wasn't anything to worry about but they'll keep an eye on it."

Ruby clasped her hands together. "Thank you, Jesus. I was praying for that."

Ruthie reached into her handbag for her sunglasses and slid them on her face.

"I'll take you home now, Momma. The kids will be home from school soon."

"Let's go, I'm so happy you're all right."

Ruthie dropped her momma at home but she wasn't ready to go home. She need some time and a place to think. She thought about driving through Fairmount Park and finding a quiet place to sit for a while, except for some reason she was scared to be alone. When she got to the edge of the park on corner of 33rd and Girard she saw the sign and pulled into the zoo parking lot.

It was the perfect place to walk and reflect on what she was going to do. Seeing the animals confined behind fences and glass she knew how they felt. She had become a prisoner of this thing in her breast. She was very much like them. They all looked powerful, beautiful, and even exquisite from the outside but she imagined they were lonely, subdued, and heartsick on the inside. She wanted to be like the birds and fly free without the weight of her secret. By the time she had walked by the big cats, still defiant and fierce, she had decided she would tell Luke when they got back from their trip to Nassau.

Chapter Nine

"**T**hey didn't lie, baby, its better in the Bahamas," Luke said, stretched out in a lounge chair on the warm beach. "The kids are having a ball down here."

"I wish we didn't have to go back home," Ruthie said wistfully as she watched the foam covered waves roll in on the sand.

"I know but I want Daniel to begin working at the company with me this summer. It's time he started learning how to run the business. He doesn't need to spend all his time at that gym."

"He's still young and being at the gym is good exercise for him. It keeps him from hanging in the projects and getting in trouble."

"That boy is playing around all the time. He's got to get his head on straight sooner or later, he's going to graduate from high school next year."

"These kids don't have to grow up so fast like we did, Luke," Ruthie said, thinking about what they had been through and the situation that was waiting for them at home when their trip was over. "Life is short. Let them enjoy themselves as long as they can."

Luke swung his legs to the side of the lounge chair. "A black man doesn't have time to waste. We don't get that many chances."

"I don't want to talk about the business or anything back in Philly," Ruthie said, pushing it all out of her head. "I just want to relax and enjoy this time with my family. If I could freeze time, I would stop it right here and now."

"You're right, sweetness," Luke said, standing up. "Let's get that sexy swim suit wet."

Ruthie took his hand and they ran out into the ocean.

***

The week in Nassau passed quickly like the tide going back out to sea. It had been a good trip. Ruthie felt like she owed her family a reprieve before they ventured into the unknown with her. When they got home, Luke opened the front door and Ruthie followed him in.

"Everything is just like we left it," Luke sighed, turning off the alarm.

"So it seems," Ruthie said, looking around.

The driver they hired at the airport brought in the rest of their suitcases filled with dirty clothes and souvenirs and dropped them inside the foyer. Daniel and Rebecca nearly knocked him over on his way back out.

"I've got to call Denise," Rebecca said, dashing up the stairs to her room. She couldn't wait to get on the telephone she had missed for a week.

"I'm going to the gym," Daniel said, running down to the garage.

"It's just you and me again, baby," Luke said to Ruthie.

"I'm going up to change," Ruthie said, "Pour me a glass of wine."

"Sounds good to me. We can deal with these suitcases later."

Ruthie needed a few moments alone before her world turned upside down. She couldn't postpone it any longer. She put on her flowing caftan in shades of light blue that made her feel light and free for the heavy conversation. Back downstairs, she found Luke out on the patio sipping on the wine. She sat down in a chair beside him.

"Here you are, sweetheart," he said handing her a glass.

She took a large gulp of wine and then another, searching for words in the glass but she couldn't find any.

"I don't know how to tell you this, Luke, so I'll just say it," she said quickly. "I went to see Dr. Hayes before we went on the trip. There's a lump in my breast and they want to do a biopsy and if it's cancer they want to remove my breast."

Luke was dumbstruck. He stared at Ruthie unable to process the words in his brain. He put down the glass in his hand thinking he was about to drop it. The look on his face as he struggled to make sense of what she told him made her want to cry. It was impossible. All he could do was get out of his chair and take her in his arms. He held on to her as tight as he could without hurting her.

After a few minutes, Luke was able to speak. "We'll go to the doctor tomorrow. Don't worry, angel face, you'll be all right."

She nodded her head into his chest holding back her tears.

***

Luke sat in the waiting room with Miss Ruby and Laverne. Needing all the moral support she could get, Ruthie had told her momma and her best friend what the doctors had said. They both insisted on being there when she had the surgery. He and Ruthie had explained to the kids that she was going to the hospital for a procedure and they were to stay in the house until he called them. It was two hours later when Luke saw a man in blue scrubs and a cap coming towards them. He pushed himself up to his feet to hear the results.

"I'm sorry, Mr. Clements, the tumor is malignant," the man said in a low voice. "Dr. Albright will proceed with the surgery as she discussed with you."

"How is my wife?" Luke asked, barely audible.

"She's doing fine."

Miss Ruby started rocking and praying and Laverne shook her

head with disappointment.

Luke nodded and his eyes followed the man as he walked back out of the door. This had to be a bad dream. Luke sat back down in the chair and dropped his head in his hands. The thought of Ruthie suffering was more painful to him than anything that could happen to him. He sat there for the next three hours in a stupor until Dr. Albright came out to the waiting area.

"Your wife is in recovery, Mr. Clements. The tumor had already spread to the lymph nodes so we'll have to begin chemotherapy immediately," Dr. Albright told him. "You can see her now."

"Thank you," Luke said, rising to his feet and following her.

Miss Ruby and Laverne trailed behind them.

When they were outside of the door Luke turned around and said, "Give me a minute alone with my wife."

Miss Ruby glared at him with narrowed eyes and didn't respond, but she took a step back.

Luke walked in the softly lit room over to the bed. The sight of Ruthie lying there looking so weak and worn out made him sick to his stomach. It was only yesterday that she looked strong and healthy. Luke rubbed the side of her face and her eyes opened.

He smiled and brushed her hair from her eyes. "Hey, beautiful, how are feeling?"

She shook her head no. "Did they take it?" she murmured.

He nodded yes. His eyes filled with tears.

"Are you in pain?" he asked.

She nodded yes.

"I'll get the doctor. Your momma and Laverne are here to see you."

Luke needed a moment to pull himself together, he didn't want her to see him cry.

"You can go in," Luke told Miss Ruby, "I'm going to find somebody to give her some more pain medication."

Miss Ruby moved to the side of her daughter's bed. Laverne

stood near her holding Ruthie's hand in her own.

"I hate this happened, baby," Ruby said with tears in her eyes.

Ruthie nodded.

"Nothing can keep us down," Laverne said, smiling to cheer her up.

Ruthie smiled half-heartedly and nodded again.

"I knew that man wouldn't be good for you," Ruby hissed, her sadness turning to anger. "It's probably because of him that you're laying here."

Alarmed at her words, Laverne interrupted, "Don't go there, Miss Ruby."

Ruthie's face frowned up with pain mixed with irritation. "I don't believe you Momma. If you can't bring love and good feelings for me and my family, don't come and see me."

"I'm the one who brought you in this world, child," Ruby said, "Ain't nobody here can take care of you better than I can."

The door opened and Ruby got quiet. Luke had returned with a nurse to lessen Ruthie's pain. He could see she was more distressed than when he left.

"What happened?" he asked, looking at Laverne and Ruby while the nurse administered the medication.

Laverne looked away. Luke guessed that Ruby had been talking against him again.

"You can go on home now, Ruby," he told her firmly.

"I'm not going anywhere," she snapped back.

"You can't do that in here," the nurse said quickly, ready to put them all out.

She was a short older black woman who looked like she would do it.

"I only need my husband," Ruthie said weakly.

Laverne did a quick wave and then the nurse ushered her and Ruby out.

***

The next few months were tough on the family. Initially Ruthie had refused to go on chemotherapy. She thought about the pride Luke had always had in her appearance and it gave her pause. She didn't want to go through all the changes and side effects of losing her hair and being sick all the time.

"It's only going to break me down and make me ugly," she argued, "How do I know if it will even work?"

Luke did his best to reassure her. "You can beat this if you fight, baby, the doctor says you need to have a more positive outlook for healing to take place."

"I'm sorry, Luke, there's no fight left in me."

She was like Samson, the Israelite warrior who was powerless without his hair. She had allowed her confidence and strength to be concentrated on her outward appearance. It had suffered and now she was shaken. The problem was that she had to battle this disease from the inside and she couldn't find her inner strength. She had surrendered it when they took her breast.

Luke pressured her and her mother pleaded with her until she eventually gave in. They tried three different cocktails but Ruthie wasn't responding as Dr. Albright had hoped. She had lost her hair, twenty pounds, and her sense of who she was. They had just come home after another round of tests at the hospital.

Ruthie got into bed and Luke laid alongside of her.

"I'm here for you, sweetheart, we can beat this together," he said to encourage her. "The children need you and I need you even more than they do."

"I'm sorry, babe, for being like this. I should have told you months ago when I first found the lump, but I was scared. I kept thinking about Minnie Ripperton and how they took both of her breasts and she still died. I didn't want you to look at me and not love me anymore."

"Baby, how could you think that? I love the way you look, I have from the first time I saw you. But I'm in love with the woman you are inside, under your hair and under your skin."

"I wish I could go back. I would tell you right away."

"When did you first feel it?" Luke asked, wondering how long she had known.

Ruthie hesitated before she answered, "It was last year, the day of your birthday party."

"Oh, Ruthie, honey, I can't believe you didn't say something to me then. It would have been easier then. We should not have let it go that long."

"There were a lot of things going on in the company and I didn't want to distract you."

"I care more about you than making some more money for the business. I'd give it all back to make you well again. I don't need anything but you."

"You're all I wanted too."

Luke wrapped his arms around her. "Don't you know I'd be happy to grow old with you in a rat and roach infested one room shack with nothing to eat. You're my heart, Ruthie. You're my everything."

"How you looked at me always made me feel so special and loved. You were so proud to have me as your wife. I didn't want you to leave me."

"I would never leave you. You should know that. How you look isn't why I wanted to marry you. The truth is you are the only one who ever gave a real shit about me in my life. I love you. I wouldn't care if you were blind, cripple, and crazy."

Ruthie laughed with relief. "Now you tell me."

***

The doctors tried everything to beat the cancer but the disease had gotten a head start. Ruthie drifted away a little more each day.

Luke spent every waking hour at her bedside praying, begging, and willing her to get better. Without his knowledge she had said her goodbyes to Laverne, Mary, and Matthew, asking them to lookout for him and the kids.

"I can't live without you, angel face," he whispered close to her ear. Trying to drown out the sound of the beeping machines and her labored breathing he kept talking. "I didn't know what it was like to be happy until I met you. Please don't leave me, Ruthie."

Ruthie opened her eyes and looked into his. She wanted to give him words but she was in too much pain to speak. He had no idea of how she struggled to hold on for him but she couldn't stand to watch him suffer another day. She closed her eyes and let go.

***

All of Luke's family, even Martha and Mark, and what looked like half of Philadelphia showed up for the funeral of Ruth Elizabeth Clements. Daniel sat on the left side of his daddy with his fists balled up, angry at the word, and Rebecca sat on the right with a hole in her heart, crying for her momma. Luke looked towards the end of the pew and wondered how they had gotten there. He'd learned in Vietnam how fleeting life can be but he had vowed to hold onto Ruthie, he didn't understand how she could have slipped through his fingers. This wasn't how their story was supposed to end. He hadn't had time to show her what she meant to him. He hadn't gotten a chance to pamper her. He hadn't let her rest or relax. He had worked her to death.

Luke grew weary of the never-ending procession of mourners and well-wishers who offered their condolences to him and the children. Some of the women were bold enough to press their bodies against him in manners inappropriate for the inside of a church and even a few of them kissed him on the lips as he sat in front of his wife. It was for the sake of the children that he didn't pitch a fit and tear the place down with his bare hands.

Miss Ruby, with her long-lost husband at her side, went up to look at their child for the last time. Jimmy barely recognized her; he hadn't seen her in more than thirty-years. Lord only knows where he found the nerve to show up. Miss Ruby screamed with agony and collapsed into his arms. Two ushers helped them back to the pew and fanned Miss Ruby. Luke and the children kept their seats. Mercifully, the casket was closed and Reverend Slocum opened the service.

Luke felt numb, the words spoken swirled around him but didn't touch him. It was only when Douglas Miller began to sing, *My Soul is Anchored in The Lord*, that he felt anything. The deep richness of the man's voice brought Luke back from the brink and the lyrics steadied him. Squeezing the hands of Daniel and Rebecca beside him, he focused on what Ruthie would have wanted him to do. He needed to make sure everything that she had created survived, their family and their company.

Chapter Ten

Daniel came down in the kitchen in his sweats and poured himself a large glass of milk. He was up early for his morning run. Wearing flannel pajamas and a robe, Luke was scrambling eggs for their breakfast. Cold and alone in his bed, he barely slept more than a few hours a night.

"Have you given your commitment to Cheyney, son?" he asked again, tired of repeating himself. "You know there are deadlines you have to meet."

"Why are you always on my back, Dad?" Daniel complained. "I don't need to go to college. I'm going to make more money boxing than you ever dreamed about."

Luke turned off the stove. Daniel's words had him as hot as the skillet.

"Boy, now you're really tripping," he said, still holding the spatula. "You sound like you need some sense knocked into your head."

"Whatever, Dad," Daniel said, blowing him off. "You don't know everything. I'm not stupid. I can make my own way."

"I been through some shit in my day, son, shit you don't know nothing about. You're too young and dumb to appreciate what your momma, may she rest in peace, and I have built for you."

"I didn't ask y'all to do that for me. You did that for you. That's your life. Give it to Becca. I want to live my own life."

"I'll be damned. That's exactly why the Asians are successful as a race of people. They respect their elders and let them guide them.

You can't accomplish anything in this life if you don't have any knowledge. I'm here trying to share mine with you until you get some of your own and you want to throw it back in my face."

"That's not what I'm doing, Dad."

"Oh yeah it is, but you're not going to make me come out of myself this morning. Your momma wanted you kids to go to college and that's what you're going to do."

"I'm eighteen years old. You can't tell me what to do."

"As long as you're spending my money, I'm the boss."

Daniel had a lot to say but he held his tongue. He wasn't ready to get out there on his own yet. He didn't have his plan in motion. Going to school would buy him some more time.

"That's cool, Dad, you're right. You're running things. If momma wanted me to go, I'll go," he said before he stormed out the back door.

Luke stood up to watch him run out of the yard and up the street. All he could do was shake his head in frustration. It was Luke's dream that he would work with him and eventually take over the family business. The problem was the boy had no interest in the company.

Daniel was tall and strong like his daddy but he took after his momma, light-brown and handsome. He was smart; everything from the day he was born had always been easy for him. His Grandma Ruby had doted on him and spoiled him. He excelled in sports, and from that night he saw Mike Tyson win the heavyweight championship he'd been on a mission to do the same.

"Good morning, Daddy," Rebecca said, greeting him with a hug when she came downstairs for breakfast.

He kissed her on the forehead and said, "Good morning, sweetheart."

She'd always stuck close to Luke and could sense his moods. Whenever she saw a shadow of sadness over his face she would always tell him a joke or a funny story to make him laugh.

"I've got a joke for you today," she said, making herself a plate of eggs.

"Oh yeah, let's hear it," he said with a forced grin.

"Why can't an elephant smile?" she asked, sitting down at the table.

"I don't know, why?" he said without guessing.

"Because he's got chapped lips," she laughed.

Luke laughed too. "That is so corny, baby girl. You need to work on your material."

"Okay, I'll tell you another one," she said, smiling.

"No, please don't, besides you need to get out of here soon or you'll be late."

He sat down with a cup of coffee beside her while she ate and chatted about last night's episode of *The Cosby Show*. After she left for school he poured himself another cup of coffee before he got started with his day, he knew something was up because Matthew had been beeping him all morning.

He showered and dressed and when he passed the mirror on the way out of his bedroom he barely recognized himself. He'd gone to a barber the day before and had him cut out all of the Kush Kurl. His hair hadn't been this short for nearly twenty years. He couldn't stand any other hands but Ruthie's on his head, definitely not another woman's.

In the garage he got into Ruthie's red Monte Carlo. Her scent still filled the car even though she hadn't driven it in years. Driving her car reminded him of the days when their lives were so much simpler. He could almost hear her singing to the radio beside him.

It was the 22nd day of March. Luke bought flowers at the florist and made his monthly drive to Mount Peace Cemetery to see Ruthie. It had broken his heart again when he had to lay his love there in the cold hard ground. Walking through the path of headstones, the signs of spring were showing themselves in the specks of green grass and buds on the trees. It made him feel better.

He saw her marker from a distance. Moving closer his grief rose to the surface.

"I love you, Ruthie. I miss you so much," he said, kneeling down to place the flowers. "These days without you are torture, and if it wasn't for the kids I wouldn't have a reason to suffer through them. Sleep well, baby."

He stood there for another minute with his eyes closed to picture her face and imagine the feel of her kiss before he left.

***

Matthew was waiting for him in the lobby when he arrived at the office.

"Luke, we need to talk, the numbers have come in and they're not looking good."

"Can I at least sit down and have a cup of coffee before you spoil my day."

Matthew nodded and followed Luke to his office. His secretary, Sherry, brought in a tray with coffee and bagels and set it on the conference table. Sherry was the secretary/mail girl/errand person for the company. Luke hired her on the spot four years ago because she looked like Dionne Warwick.

"Thank you, Sherry," Luke said as she left the room. "So what is the problem, Matt?"

"Look, Luke, I know you're going through a rough time but you've got a company to run. The Kush Kurl sales have dropped. We need to make some decisions."

"So what do you suggest, my brother?" Luke asked, edgily.

"It's not what we want to do but we don't have a choice, we're going to have to lay off at least a third of the employees."

"That option is not even on my list. All of the people working here have been loyal to the company since we started. We're a team."

"This isn't personal. I know you don't want to hurt anybody

working here but you can't afford not to. This is serious and I know you don't want to risk losing everything you and Ruthie worked to build here. Clements Cosmetic Company is a business, not a charity, we have to make a profit or we're done."

Luke looked past Matthew, out of the window into a fluffy white cloud that was breaking up the blue of the sky. What had he done to break his winning streak? Was his run in the sun over and now it was time for him to go back to a life in the dark. He'd lost Ruthie, Daniel seemed to be pulling away, and now the business was in trouble.

"You handle it, Matthew," Luke said, aggravated. "You're the Chief Financial Officer. Do whatever you feel needs to be done to keep us in the black."

"Good deal, Luke," Matthew said, patting his shoulder. "Hopefully, this is a temporary adjustment. I know how you feel about the Kush Kurl but we have other hair and skin products that can pick up the slack. I need you to get your head on straight and put together a marketing campaign to push them to the front."

"No problem, I'm on it," Luke said, turning from the window and regaining his focus.

***

Luke could feel the distance between him and his son growing and it seemed like the more he tried to connect with him the more he pulled away. The last thing he wanted to do was encourage his crazy obsession with boxing but he thought that getting tickets to the Mike Tyson and Michael Spinks fight in Atlantic City after graduation might give them the quality time they needed to bridge the gap between them. He splurged on VIP tickets and booked them a room at the Trump Plaza Casino.

"This is the bomb," Daniel said as they walked into the Atlantic City Convention Center.

"Yeah, it doesn't get any bigger than this," Luke admitted,

impressed with all the celebrities in the rows ahead of them.

The venue was filled to capacity, even Muhammad Ali was down in the ring. The crowd was pulsing with electricity from the excitement of the match even before the contenders came in. Daniel was fully plugged into it, exhilarated to the point of breathlessness. Music started playing and everyone in the room stood shoulder to shoulder. A path was made for the fighters to make their way to the ring. First Michael Spinks came in, and then Mike Tyson was escorted in by security like a superstar. He swung his body through the ropes and the crowd erupted with claps, roars, and whistles.

Daniel scooted to the edge of his chair. "He's a bad man, Dad. He's got all three belts."

"Yeah, but he's still got to win to keep them. They're both undefeated. They say Spinks might take this young boy to school."

"Ain't no way. He's going to hit the canvass like the rest of them."

Daniel could feel his idol's energy as he jumped and bounced in the ring throwing punches in the air. "He's pumped, Dad."

"We'll see, it's show time."

From the time the bell rang, Luke could see that Daniel was right. Tyson was too quick, coming for Spinks like a lion after an antelope. There was no time to run and no place to hide. The nonstop flurry of punches were packed with power and in 91 seconds of the first round Spinks was knocked out by a short right uppercut to the chin.

"I told you, Dad," Daniel shouted, throwing his fist up in the air. "The only competition out here for 'Iron Mike' is me."

"After that, I don't want to see what he'll do to you," Luke joked.

"You can laugh now but when I get my game on there won't be anything to laugh about."

"I hear you talking much shit, son. Just make sure you hit those books when you get up there at Cheyney."

There was nothing that Luke could say to bring Daniel's spirits down. There was no other place in the world he wanted to be. He was thirty yards from where he envisioned his dreams coming true. Luke was pleased to see Daniel so happy. Both father and son got a reprieve from their pain and anger and had a good time together.

***

Daniel walked through the door of Joe Frazier's gym at Broad and Glenwood Street with his duffel bag in his right hand. He took a deep breath of the mixture of sweat, menthol cigarettes, and chicken grease and a smile spread across his face. He pictured his own face in the massive painting of Joe Frazier and in the photos and posters of boxers that lined the brick walls. The sounds of punches hitting leather bags, ropes hitting the wooden floor, yelling, grunts of pain, resonated through the room. There was harmony in it, music to his ears. Working out in the YMCA gym was boring. This was the place he'd been trying to get to. This was where he would prepare for his destiny.

He went back into the locker room, changed clothes, and put on his brand new boxing gloves. He came out and walked over to the heavy bag. He stood there, hit it once and it felt good. He hit it again and it gave him a sense of relief. He was busy pummeling the heavy bag and the memory of the sadness in his momma's eyes when the guy who had been watching from across the room came over and held it still for him.

"I like that, don't show it no mercy," he said. "You've got real power in your right."

Daniel nodded and kept punching the bag.

"The name is Wendell Williams. I ain't seen you around here before."

"Uh-uh," Daniel said, annoyed at the interruption.

"I've been watching you. You look good, a natural."

"Uh-uh."

"You've been training a while?"

Daniel kept pounding the bag. "Yeah."

"There's one more thing you haven't thought of."

"What's that?" he asked, pausing for a second.

"Yoga, my man," Wendell sniggered.

Daniel went back to hitting the bag. "Is that right?"

"Hell yeah, I was messing with this white girl and she hipped me to it. Believe it or not, it helps. It gives you muscle tone without bulking up and it increased my reach and my flexibility."

"I'll try anything if it'll help me get where I'm trying to go."

"So what's your story?" Wendell asked.

"My story, what are you talking about?" Daniel replied impatiently.

"Yeah, everybody got one. What's setting you on fire?"

Daniel stopped beating the bag and inhaled deeply to catch his breath.

"Look here, man, I don't have no ghetto story to tell you. I've never been hungry, never been on the streets, never slung no drugs, and never been locked up, none of that. No molesting uncle or crazy relative who beat my ass. I had a mother and a father who loved and cared for me and I'm going to college in a month. Now can I finish what I'm doing?"

"Lucky you," Wendell said nonchalantly. "So where is all the anger coming from cause you're giving that bag holy hell?"

"My momma died. But I wanted to fight a long time before that. And why you all up in my business, why are you here?"

Wendell clasped his arms behind his back. "When I first walked in here some years back I didn't have nowhere else to go. I was hungry and I had no choice but to fight for my supper. I was damn good too."

"I never heard of you."

"I had my shot, I was about to fight Tommy Hearns for the

Light Heavyweight Championship."

"What stopped you?" Daniel asked, interested.

"I took another fight to make some extra bread. I thought it would be a good tune-up. I caught a thumb in my right eye, tore my retina. I'm damn near blind in one eye. That ended it for me. Unlike you, my fortunate friend, I ain't had nothing but bad luck."

"That's too bad, sorry to hear that," Daniel said without the edge in his tone.

"If you're serious about boxing, I wanna train you," Wendell said frankly.

Now he had said something that really had Daniel's attention.

"Yeah, I'm serious. All the top fighters want to train here."

"How far do you want to go?"

"Straight to the top. I want to wear the belt."

"It'll take some time. You need to put on about twenty pounds of muscle but if you're willing to bust your ass in the gym, I think I can get you a shot."

Daniel grinned. "That's why I'm here."

"What's your name?"

"Daniel, Daniel Clements."

"That'll work. That ring over there will be the lion's den."

***

For the most part Daniel was going along with Luke's program. He had registered at Cheyney University and was majoring in business administration. He knew his dad was hurting just like he and Rebecca were so he didn't want to add to his pain. Besides, things were working out better than he thought they would. The classes weren't that hard, the ladies were lovely, and he got a brand new white 1988 Nissan 300zx to whip around the city.

He stayed on his own game too, doing his push-ups, sit-ups, jogging twice a day, and going to the gym to train three times a week. He watched his diet, eating plenty of protein and replacing the fluids and electrolytes after his workouts. Wendell coached him through calisthenics, rounds with the heavy bag, rounds with the speed bag, and rounds with the double end bag. After that, Wendell held the hand pads for him to hit and timed him while he jumped rope. In his dorm room between classes and studying he spent hours shadow boxing.

Ten months later while they were tossing the medicine ball Wendell finally said the words he was waiting to hear.

"Your conditioning is spot on, man. I think you're ready to do some sparring."

"I've been ready. Let's take this to the next level."

"Bernard Hopkins is going to be training here this summer and he needs a couple of sparring partners. You got a job if you want it."

"Oh hell yeah. That's what I'm talking about," Daniel exclaimed.

"It pays good money and you'll get some damn good experience."

"I don't care what it pays, I'm down."

Daniel was on top of the world. The spring semester had just ended and soon he was going to climb in the ring with a major contender. He didn't even care about the shit that was going to hit the fan when he told his dad he wasn't going to work at the company during the summer. What he really had on his mind was a place of his own. He was almost 20 years old and didn't need his daddy trying to run his life.

The beeper in Daniel's gym bag went off and he knew who it was, none of the cuties he knew called him at this time of day. For the umpteenth time he wished his momma was here, she was the only person who could get him to chill out. He put on a clean shirt and jumped in his car. He pumped up the bass on his Heavy D cassette and headed up to Germantown Avenue bobbing his head to *We Got Our Own Thang.*

"What up, Dad," Daniel asked, walking into the rec room where Luke was sitting.

"Where you been all day?" Luke asked.

"Hanging, working out at the gym."

"Didn't we talk about you working at the company when school was out?" Luke asked sternly.

"Yeah, we did, but something came up and I'm not going to be able to do that."

Luke shifted on the couch and inhaled to try and hold his anger. "Something like what?"

"I got another job," Daniel answered calmly.

"Doing what, where?"

"I thought about lying to you but I'm going to tell you the truth. I'm going to be a sparring partner for Bernard Hopkins."

"Are you telling me you intend to let some big nigga bash your head in all summer? That doesn't make any sense. Your momma and I prepared a place for you. It's what you're supposed to do. I can't believe you're coming up with this muthafuckin' bullshit again. Now you're getting me all out of myself."

"It's what I want to do, Dad."

Luke tried to bring his frustration down a notch where they could have a discussion.

"Obviously you don't know what you need to do. Why do you want to use your hands to fight when you have other resources? I just don't understand that."

"I'm not the man you want me to be, I got to be who I am."

"Number one, you're not a man yet. I'm still taking care of your ass. Second, who in the hell do you think you are? What is so fascinating about getting knocked out?"

"I'm not about to be knocked out. Anyway, I don't know why you always trying to control my life. When you were my age you were married with a baby. Nobody was on your back telling you what to do."

"The hell they weren't, when I was in the service Uncle Sam was bossing my ass every night and day, and when I got home the bills told me to get my ass out there and get a job. Furthermore, they told me and your momma to work our asses off around the clock. I'm the one here trying to make sure you can be your own man."

"Chill out, Dad, it's not that serious. I promised you that I would go to college and graduate and I'm going to do that, but I'm going to be training to box. That's something you're going to have to live with."

Luke got up and walked out of the room. He knew if he stayed in the room with Daniel much longer he would be the one throwing punches. He headed straight for the kitchen looking for something to drink. He almost laughed out loud as the words his Dad said so long ago rang in his ears, "Keep living and this life will give you something to make you drink." He opened up the liquor cabinet, took out a bottle of cognac, and poured a glass. He stepped out onto the deck for some fresh air.

Rebecca had been listening to the argument between her father and brother. Since her mommy died, it seemed like they couldn't stand to be in the same room together, and neither of them noticed she was around. She figured that now was the time for all that to change.

"I want to talk to you, Daddy," she said, standing behind him.

Luke was startled. He didn't hear Rebecca come out to join him.

"Sure, sweetheart, what's on your mind?"

"There's nothing for you to worry about. You can let Daniel go do his thing. I'll be here to run the company with you."

"You don't need to be concerned about all that, honey. I want you to enjoy yourself, have fun with your friends. I'll handle the business."

"Being at the company is what I would enjoy doing. I want to work with you this summer. That's what I think will be fun. Next year when I graduate I want to go to Drexel like you did, and when I finish I want to be your partner."

Luke looked at her and smiled. Rebecca was quiet, demure like her mother, but she was smart. He had never thought of her as the choice to run the business. It wasn't that he was a male chauvinist or that he didn't think a woman should run the business. It was because he saw his wife work so hard all of her life that he didn't want that for his daughter. He wanted her to enjoy her life. He wanted to lavish her with material things, treat her the way he would have treated Ruthie if she had lived.

"You're young, Becca. The time we get to be young and carefree is so short. I feel like I just blinked and it was over. I want you to take your time and savor these years. Daniel is older, it's time for him to be a man and be responsible."

"Why do you place so much value on him? I'm not worthless, and I'm not a baby."

"You're my daughter. I love you and I'll always take care of you. Your brother can carry on the family name."

"So can I, Daddy, if that's so important to you. My children can keep the Clements name if that's all that matters."

"One day you'll meet somebody and you'll feel differently."

"I don't know if I will or not. Right now I want you to give me the job you had for Daniel. He doesn't want it and I do. If Mommy were here she'd make you give it to me."

"That's true. I can't argue with that," Luke admitted, realizing she wasn't going to take no for an answer. "When school gets out you have a job."

Chapter Eleven

Daniel looked down at his new amateur boxing license. Wendell had promised to get him a bout at the gym as soon as it came through. His time had come. He had spent more than a year sparring with boxers who were competing in professional bouts. His skills were sharp and he knew he was better than most of them. Now Wendell would have to get his foot off the brakes. Daniel was tired of being in the slow lane, he was fired up and ready to fight. The only reason he didn't bitch about it was that he still had another year and a half before he graduated.

Rebecca was a sponge absorbing every bit of knowledge about Clements Cosmetic Company, about running a business in her classes at Drexel, and about fashion and styles of the rich and famous. She had already picked up on the fact that merely a precious few set the tone for the masses to imitate. Rebecca worked part-time after school and fulltime during the summers at the company. She wanted to nurture the company and watch it grow. She felt her mommy had given birth to it as much as she did to her and Daniel. Luke had insisted she move on campus and have fun but she spent half of her time at home.

Luke was the one who was stuck. He didn't see anything left in his world to excite or encourage him to move on. Most of his thoughts were of Ruthie but he wasn't an old man. He longed for the warmth and touch of a woman. He toyed with the idea of going out to Happy Hour or Ladies Night at one of the popular spots to see what he was missing.

A few days before his fortieth birthday he went to Studio West, got a seat on the bar, bought a double cognac, and watched the women move their bodies to the rhythm of the music on the dance floor. It was his second time going there, the first time he was slightly uncomfortable and didn't stay very long. The club scene was worlds away from the house parties he and his fellas used to go to back in the day.

The DJ shouted out to them over the music, "All the ladies in the house say "Yo.'"

The ladies on the dance floor jubilantly yelled back, "Yo."

Then the DJ roared, "Now everybody scream."

Howls and screams filled the club while the DJ rocked them with Chubb Rock's *Treat 'Em Right* and then Naughty by Nature's *OPP*. The floor cleared when he slowed it down with Jodeci's *Forever my Lady*.

One woman in the center of the crowd wearing a burnt orange dress captured his attention. She was light brown-skinned, shapely, her hair hung over her left eye, and she reminded him of Ruthie. The vision of her meshed with his imagination and it made him smile. She took it as an invitation to come closer.

"Hello, my name is Tonya," she said, easing onto the seat beside him. "I've seen you here before but you never get out on the dance floor."

"I'm Luke, Luke Randolph," he said, giving her only his first and middle name while extending his hand, "I guess I'm out of practice."

"It's like riding a bike. When they play your jam you get out there and get your groove on."

"I hear you," Luke said, taking a swallow of his drink.

Tonya noticed the ring on his finger when he put down the glass.

"So what do you do, Luke?" she asked with a smile, checking out his Armani suit, Italian shoes, and gold Rolex watch.

"I have my own business," he answered casually.

"That's impressive. It's good to see a brother doing it big."

"I don't know about all that," he said modestly. "It keeps food on the table."

Tonya appraised Luke on the sly in the low lights of the club. She didn't think he was all that nice-looking in the face but he had style and class. She was damned sure he had money and plenty of it.

"Pardon me for getting in your business, but where is your wife tonight?"

Luke didn't know how to respond at first. He was pretending she was Ruthie and now she was killing the moment.

"We're not together anymore."

"She must have left you. You're still wearing the ring."

"Yes, she did," he said sadly.

A funky beat full of bass rocked the club causing a rush to the small dance floor. Keith was singing *Make You Sweat* in a low growl.

Tonya grabbed his elbow. "That's my jam, dance with me."

Luke let her pull him to the floor with his eyes fixed on her hips. She was sexy and she moved smooth like Ruthie. He couldn't take his eyes off her. He stayed out on the floor with her for three more songs. Then the DJ played a slow song, *Make It Like It Was* by Regina Belle, and Tonya moved in close to his chest. Luke put his arms around her and let his mind drift away. He hadn't held Ruthie in so long. The passion and yearning he had for her swelled in his body. Tonya felt his desire and pressed herself against him.

When the song ended she said, "You know a different crowd comes in here and gets crunked after eleven. It's about time for me to go, I'm not trying to get shot."

"Too bad, I was enjoying your company."

She smiled. "The feeling is mutual."

"We could go someplace else if you like?" Luke asked, not ready for the night to end.

"Are you asking me to go home with you?"

Luke was flustered for a moment. "Oh no, my daughter lives with me. I don't think it would be right to show up with somebody like that. You can respect that can't you?"

"I understand completely. Would you like to go to my place? I don't live far from here."

Luke had been out of the game for a long time. Things moved a lot faster than they did twenty years ago. He was hesitant, but he was turned on by her. Maybe he could have his fantasy come true for one night.

"Yeah, that sounds like a plan," he told her.

"Give me a minute, I have to get my coat."

Luke watched her hips sway as she walked over to the table where she had sat with some friends.

"I'm gone, bitches," she said playfully, taking her coat off the back of a chair, "My number came out, I hit the lotto over there."

Their eyes traveled over to where Luke was standing.

"You better go, girl," one of them laughed, "See if he has a brother for me."

Tonya grabbed Luke's elbow and he led her out of the club. She wanted to shout and praise the Lord when he unlocked the door of a forest green Jaguar XJ6.

"My apartment is a few blocks over in Cedar Park."

Luke turned on the radio so they wouldn't have to talk. It wasn't her voice that he wanted to hear. He wanted to keep pretending.

"It's the building on the corner," she said.

Luke parked and followed her inside the building and up the flight of stairs to her apartment. She opened the door and he could smell the odor of a cat. A plate with chicken wing bones sat on the coffee table beside a half-filled bottle of orange soda. He frowned.

Ruthie had always kept a neat house. He sat down amongst the crumbs despite an urge to head back towards the door.

"I'm gonna make myself a drink, my buzz is wearing off. Would you like one?" she asked, tossing her coat on the sofa.

"I'll join you," he said. "Do you have cable?"

"Uh-huh, a friend of mine got me hooked up for free."

She gave Luke the remote before she left the room. He turned on the TV and surfed the channels until he found BET, the music videos would distract him from where he was. A few minutes later Tonya walked in wearing a black satin caftan with the drinks in her hands. She handed one to Luke. He smelled it was gin before he tasted it. The bubbles were probably 7up. She sat down next to him with her legs touching his.

"Thank you," he said.

Tonya turned towards him and leaned in to look Luke in the face.

"I don't want you to think that I bring dudes to my house like this all the time. I don't get down like that but I was very attracted to you."

"I like to think I'm special," Luke said, smiling back at her.

"Oh you are," she said, pressing her lips against his.

"You're not shy," he said after the kiss.

"Not when I see something I want."

"You're not turned off by it are you?"

"Not at all," Luke lied.

He closed his eyes while Tonya unzipped his pants and put a condom on him. She had been burned before and she wasn't taking any more chances. She got busy doing everything she thought would blow his mind, except it was already in another stratosphere. She would only have his body to impress. When it was over she passed out. Luke sat back up on the couch where she was stretched out absorbing the view of her body in the light from the TV. Her hair covered her face and all he saw was his wife.

It made him feel guilty but he had to admit he felt good. He needed that physical release. He was so relaxed he was sure he would sleep all night for a change. He gathered his clothes and walked down the hallway to find the bathroom where he could clean up. He dressed and counted himself lucky that he didn't have to lie in her bed. If she kept it like the rest of her place he had dodged a bullet.

Back in the living room he tapped Tonya on the shoulder to wake her.

"I'm heading out. I wanted to tell you I enjoyed your company."

Tonya propped herself up on her shoulder. "You don't have to go, you're welcome to stay here tonight."

"Thanks, I appreciate that but I've got to check on my daughter and I have a busy day ahead of me tomorrow."

"All right, but let me get your number so I can call you," she said, sitting up and wiping her face.

"Give me yours and I'll call you," he replied.

She slipped her caftan on and went to find a pen and some paper. She wrote her number down, gave it to him, and then moved in for a kiss but Luke wrapped her up in a hug.

"Take care," he said on his way out.

"Call me," she said.

Luke wanted to burn rubber on his way home but it was after three o' clock in the morning. He didn't want to be a black man driving a Jag in the middle of the night and get stopped by the cops. He replayed the evening in his mind and he didn't know if he would call Tonya or not. Technically, he hadn't been with anyone else besides Ruthie and he wasn't sure he liked all the new freedom and aggressiveness that he saw in some women nowadays. He was comfortable being the pursuer.

***

It was the evening of Daniel's first amateur bout. It was time to start showing the world who he was and what he was about. Luke was the first one on that list. He had asked his dad to be there but it was Rebecca who convinced him to come.

"Daddy you've got to support him even if you don't agree with him," Rebecca insisted, "It's called unconditional love."

"It's because I love him that I don't want to see him ruin his life."

"We talked about family relationships in my psychology class. They say the relationship between father and son is dynamic, like forces that push and pull against each other creating friction. The father wants his son to imitate him but the son wants to be his own man. Both are coming from a good place but it causes resentment and misunderstandings that can last a lifetime. We lost Mommy and I don't want to see you two lose each other."

Luke thought about what she said for a minute before he responded.

"You're getting real smart up there at Drexel aren't you?"

Rebecca laughed. "It's about time you noticed."

Luke and Rebecca stood in the gym with a small group waiting for the fight to begin. Daniel was back in the locker room with Wendell.

"Are you sure you're ready to break your cherry?" Wendell asked, wrapping his hands and wrists. "If you need more time just say it."

Daniel stood up. He'd been waiting for this moment for as long as he could remember.

"I've been ready."

"I know you got some nerves, that's natural, but this other guy is scared too. He wants this thing to end quick. He'll be headhunting, praying he can knock you out before he gets hurt, so watch your chin, and don't start brawling, you'll gas out."

"I got this, man," Daniel said confidently.

"Don't ever underestimate what another man is bringing into

the ring," Wendell told him.

"That goes for him and me," Daniel said wistfully.

He had dreamed about his momma last night and today he was mad at the world. The picture of her lying in that hospital bed hurting so bad she couldn't speak was fresh in his mind, and since his 71 inch reach couldn't reach the chin of God, somebody sometime soon was going to suffer a beat down whether they deserved it or not.

Daniel followed Wendell out to the ring. Luke shook his head as he watched him walk in wearing white trimmed in red. Amateurs have to have a clean face, and his son looked even more like a kid with his thin mustache shaved off. Rebecca started clapping as he climbed in with the referee and his opponent. Daniel looked over and saw them and lifted his glove.

"Check him out, Daddy, he's in shape to fight for real," Rebecca said.

"So was Tyson when Buster Douglas beat his ass."

"Stop saying that or you'll jinx him."

Luke wished he could. Maybe if he got is ass whupped he would get these notions about boxing out of his head.

Wendell fastened on his protective headgear and a man on the side of the ring introduced both of the fighters, telling their weight and names. Daniel was in red the other guy in blue. The ref motioned for them to come out of their corners and told them to tap gloves. Then he sent them back into their neutral corners to wait for the bell. Daniel bounced up and down unable to contain his energy while the other fighter, standing flat-footed, stared him down. Then the bell rang.

They both charged at each other from their corners. Daniel moved in close stretching his arm out to measure the distance for his punches. The fighter in blue throws a jab and Daniel counters with a combination. The one in blue ties him up. The ref breaks them apart. Then the other fighter starts pressing him, swinging wildly with most of the punches missing. He's headhunting like Wendell said.

Feeling the tension, Rebecca balled up her fists. "Watch out," she screamed.

Shouts came from the corners of the boxers and the spectators sitting around the ring.

"Jab, jab, jab," Wendell yelled.

"Breathe man," the blue corner man hollered.

Daniel kept his guard up. There's no way he was going to let this guy take him out in front of his Dad. They traded punches for another minute and then the bell rang. Both fighters went back to their corners where stools were waiting.

"Good work," Wendell said, pouring water in his mouth. "I need you to work the body, that's where you'll take away his strength."

Daniel nodded and took deep breaths. Wendell chopped on his shoulders to keep him loose. Then the bell beckoned them to come back to center ring.

Daniel jabbed with his right and his opponent fired off a flurry of punches. Daniel blocked them and stayed on the defense, that way he could save his energy while the other fighter burned his. Daniel jabbed with his left and the one in blue tied up again. Daniel pummeled his core with two hard blows before the ref separated them. Daniel tucked in his chin and kept throwing body shots, breaking him down like a wall, brick by brick. The other fighter, weakened, drew back to fire off a power punch and left himself open. Daniel threw a right uppercut to the chin that knocked the other fighter off his feet and onto the canvas. Daniel went to his corner.

Rebecca jumped up and cheered. "Daniel is about to win this, Dad."

The ref had counted to six by the time the fighter got up. He grabbed his gloves, looked in his eyes, and waved his hand. It was over. Daniel jumped straight up in the air. Wendell held up his arm in triumph.

"He's the winner," Rebecca said, waving her arms up.

Luke frowned. "He was a winner before he got in there. He just doesn't know it."

The spectators clapped in appreciation for the fighters.

"You've got the gift man," Wendell hollered in his ear.

"What gift is that?" Daniel asked.

"The one for knocking muthafuckas out."

Daniel threw his other glove up in victory.

Chapter Twelve

L uke needed a distraction from Daniel fighting, Rebecca worrying him, and the pressure of growing the business. Being with Tonya had stirred the coals that he thought had died inside of him and he was feeling the heat. He called her and made reservations at the Waterfall restaurant inside the Wyndham Hotel and booked a room. He had no desire to go back to her apartment. He didn't want to take it too high level because she might get the wrong idea.

Luke ordered them some cocktails to relax. Tonya had gotten on his nerves talking the whole way to the restaurant. Wanting and needing her body was the only thing that kept him from making up an excuse to take her back home.

"This place is really nice," she said, scanning the restaurant.

"I thought that I owed you a proper night out on the town."

"Thank you, but I would have been happy to cook for you."

Luke winced at the thought of eating with the smell of cat litter wafting in the air.

"You deserve somebody to wait on you," he said.

Tonya gave him a sexy smile. "I like the way you think."

"Order anything you want," Luke said when the waiter returned to the table with their drinks.

"I'll have prime rib, baked potato, and a salad," she said, grinning at the waiter.

Luke handed the waiter his menu. "The same for me."

Tonya had looked for Luke Randolph in the phone book but he wasn't listed, she couldn't find any businesses in the Yellow Pages under the name of Randolph. He was tight-lipped but she was determined to find out what his deal was.

"You didn't tell me that much about yourself when we met," Tonya said, beginning her fact-finding mission. "How long have you been separated?"

"Almost three years," he replied softly.

His reaction puzzled her. She thought he was acting like it happened yesterday.

"You seem like you still have feelings for her."

"She was my wife for eighteen years and the mother of my children."

"Do I need to worry about you two getting back together?" she asked, somewhat concerned.

Luke looked down in his lap. "No, that won't happen."

"Okay, I'm sorry. I'll leave it alone," Tonya said, seeing how it bothered him. "Why don't you tell me about your business?"

"I just left the office an hour ago," Luke said, getting agitated. "Why don't we talk about you?"

Tonya decided to put her mission on hold for the time being.

"That's cool," she said, "I've never been married. I have a nine-year-old son who lives with my mama, and I work at Macy's downtown. There's not much else to tell."

"What kind of things do you like to do when you're not working?" he asked to keep the subject on her.

"I hang out at the Studio West or the Impulse and I like to go to the movies."

"I haven't been to the movies in a long time," Luke said, thinking back.

"I saw *Pretty Woman* about a month ago and it was good. I really want to see this new Spike Lee movie with Denzel Washington, *Mo' Better Blues*. I heard it was really good."

"In that case, I'll take you next weekend."

The waiter brought their food. Tonya looked at her plate and smiled again at Luke. She was tired of being used and now she had finally met somebody who could do something for her.

"Could we order some champagne?" she asked after they finished eating.

"If that's what you want, or we could have some sent to a room where we can kick back while we drink it."

"That sounds like a plan to me."

They rode the elevator to the eighth floor. Luke opened the door and they walked in. Room service brought the champagne and strawberries right behind them. Luke pulled the curtains and dimmed the lights. When he turned around Tonya was coming out of her dress.

"We have the room for the whole night," he said to slow her down. "I'll pour you some champagne."

He filled the stems almost to the top.

Tonya held her glass out for a toast. "Let's drink to you and me."

"To the night," Luke said and tapped her glass.

"Why don't you undress and come to bed?" she said.

Luke swallowed the rest of his champagne and took off his clothes, resigned that this woman wasn't going to let him seduce her. She pulled back the sheets, slid into the bed, and held them up for him to slide in beside her. She pulled a condom out of her bra and put it on him. It felt like heaven to lie down between cool sheets next to a warm body again. Luke closed his eyes to concentrate. He wanted to hear Ruthie's voice and imagine it was her touch that he was feeling.

Tonya fell right asleep after her work out on him. Luke turned off the lights to let her sleep for a half hour before he took the opportunity to get on top for a change. When he was satisfied he collapsed on the bed beside her.

"I don't want to disappoint you but I can't stay the night," Tonya said, getting out of the bed. "I've got to go to work early tomorrow. You know how it is, bills are due and I can't afford for my check to be short."

"Yeah, I know how it is."

Luke didn't know if she was dropping a hint or not, but when she went into the bathroom he reached in his pants pocket, got out his wallet, and pulled out two one hundred dollars bills. He turned on the TV to catch the late news until she came out.

"A little something to help with the bills," he said, handing her the money and grabbing his clothes from the chair.

"Thank you, but it's not necessary," she said, being polite.

"Take it, you're welcome. I'll take a quick shower and then I'll take you home."

Tonya had hoped to go through his wallet while he was in the shower to find out more about him but he had taken it with him into the bathroom. No matter, she had another idea. She put the money in her bra and sat down on the bed to wait.

Getting the release he needed and a hot shower, Luke was refreshed. He could make it a little longer. The best part was the relief that they weren't spending the night. He finished dressing and in no time they headed to the parking lot. Tonya memorized his license plate as they approached his car. If he wouldn't tell her what she needed to know she would find out on her own.

***

Tonya got up early the next morning like she had to go to work. She wasn't on Macy's schedule but she definitely had a job to do. The first thing on her agenda was to go to the police station. She told them that a car with the license plate she showed them had hit her car in a parking lot.

"I'm sorry, ma'am, we can't make reports on accidents that occurred on private property," the officer informed her.

"Oh no," she said, feigning frustration. "Is there any way you can tell me who the car is registered to?"

"That information is usually confidential."

"I'm desperate, I wouldn't tell anybody where I got it," Tonya pleaded, leaning forward and giving the officer a perfect view of her cleavage. "I don't have the money to fix my car. I just want to contact them and see if they would be willing to repair the damage. That's it."

"Hold on, let me check real quick," he said, taking the small piece of paper out of her hands.

The officer pressed several keys on the computer in front of him and in a few seconds he wrote a name on the back of the paper and handed it to her.

"That's all I can do," he said.

Tonya looked at the name and said, "Thank you, officer. This should get me what I want."

Luke had only told her his first and middle name. She rushed out of the precinct and went straight to a phone booth to look up Luke Randolph Clements. "Damn," she hissed, "He's not listed." She stood there thinking for a minute and then she rushed to her car. She was going somewhere she hadn't been since her junior year in high school. She was going to the library.

"Excuse me, please," she said, to the librarian at the front desk. "I need to look up some information on a businessman in the city. I have an interview and I want to learn about the company."

"What is the name of the company?" the librarian asked.

"I think its Clements. His name is Luke Randolph Clements."

"Let's look at the catalog for Philadelphia businesses and see if anything comes up."

Tonya tapped her foot nervously while the librarian searched for Clements.

The librarian pulled out a card. "Here's something. Clements Cosmetic Company. Now we can look up any articles that may have been printed on them that you can read."

She took the card to a drawer and pulled out a roll of film.

Tonya trailed her to the microfilm readers. The librarian put the film into the reader and forwarded it.

"You should be able to find out something here," she said with a smile before she left.

Tonya scooted her chair close to the screen and started to read. The first photo was a magazine article in Ebony Magazine. Luke and his wife, Ruthie, were the creators of the Kush Kurl and the owners of a multi-million dollar company. The second article was in Jet Magazine, it was about the passing of his wife three years ago.

"Holy shit," Tonya whispered. She couldn't believe it.

She moved further and found the obituary and wrote down the number of the funeral home. She asked to use the phone at the front desk and called the funeral home. She gave them a story about wanting to contact the family about buying one of the plots they had purchased for her grandmother and they gave her the phone number and address. She drove straight out to the house from the library running through yellow lights and rolling through stop signs.

"I knew he was a big fish," she said under her breath as she looked at his house. "I just didn't know how big. All I've got to do now is reel him in."

***

Luke called to take Tonya to the movies like he had promised and she was ready. She used almost half the money he had given her to get her hair curled up liked Whitney Houston's in the *So Emotional* video. Her make-up was perfect and she was wearing her skintight 501 Levi's and a black leather jacket. She snatched the door open when she heard him knock.

Luke was stunned when she opened the door. She had changed her hair and he hated it. As many Kush Kurls as Ruthie had put in, she never wore one. Her hair was always straight.

"You changed your hair," he said

"Oh yeah, do you like it?"

"It looks nice," Luke said, lying again.

"I've been thinking about you all day," she said, rubbing her body up against him.

"The movie starts in less than thirty minutes, we better keep moving."

"Okay, but I've got something special for you later."

Luke drove to the Ritz at Bourse building. It was near the Wyndham where he had rented a room for them. He bought popcorn and cokes and he enjoyed the movie in spite of the distraction of Tonya's hand running up and down his leg.

"I'm so hot for you right now," she said as they exited the movie.

"I got us a room two blocks from here," he said.

"I was hoping we could go to your place. I'd like to see where you live."

"You know my situation."

"Okay, this time, but I'm not going to be your secret forever."

Luke didn't comment. When they got to the hotel he picked up the room key and they went up to their room. Tonya pulled her clothes off and was tugging at Luke's belt like she was burning up and the water hose was in his pants.

"I can take my clothes off," Luke said, backing up.

When he was undressed he got in the bed beside her.

"Come to Mama," she said, straddling his legs.

"Where's the condom?" he asked.

"I forgot to bring one. We don't need it. I trust you, baby."

"We need to use protection until we both get tested."

"Are you telling me you think I have something?" she asked indignantly.

"No, it's that I haven't been tested and I need to know I'm good before we take that step."

That seemed to calm Tonya down.

"They probably have some in the hotel gift shop in the lobby," she said, sliding off of him.

"Next time," Luke said, putting his clothes back on. "It's getting late and I've got an early flight in the morning.

"I can stay at your place and you can drop me off in the morning."

"Another time," he said firmly, closing the subject.

The sixth sense he developed in Vietnam was telling him to back off. More than any worries about a STD he couldn't get rid of, he wasn't about to let a gold-digger tie herself to him and his family's business with a baby.

***

Tonya was calling Luke at work and at home. She kept wanting to see him, going on and on about wanting to cook Thanksgiving dinner for him and their children. He put her off with excuses for a few weeks and then she started talking about what her son needed for Christmas and what she wanted for herself. She didn't like the way he was acting, she thought he was being standoffish all of a sudden, and that was making her mad. He was not about to be playing her for a fool anymore. She called when he and Matthew were in the middle of a meeting.

"I know who you are Luke Randolph Clements, I know where you live, I know about your wife, and I know you own Clements Cosmetic Company."

"So, what is that supposed to mean?" he asked, annoyed with the call.

"It means you were trying to run a game on me."

"Come on, how do you figure that, Tonya? You're a grown woman and I'm a grown man. You didn't have any objections to what went down."

"You weren't honest with me. I have genuine feelings for you,

Luke, but I feel like you took advantage of me."

"What do you want, Tonya?" he said, hoping to get the whole thing over with.

"I just want you to know that if you're going to be my man, you've got to take care of some of my personal business."

Luke looked at the phone in his hands, he couldn't believe she was tripping like this. The good thing was this encounter hadn't gone any further and no harm was done to either of them.

"I'm going to be straight with you," he said with the phone back to his ear, "I'm not looking for a relationship with anybody right now. Since you feel like I owe you something, I'll send you a thousand bucks and after that lose my number. I'm done."

Tonya went into a tirade, cussing him out thoroughly until Luke slammed the phone down.

"Who was that?" Matthew asked, wondering what was going on. "Don't tell me you are finally involved with somebody?"

"No fucking way," Luke said, pissed off. "Y'all are making me get outside of myself."

Matthew laughed. "What's the deal, brother?"

"Some chick I messed with a couple of times. She's crazy, stalking me all the time. There's no way I would bring another woman in Ruthie's home."

"If you only want to get some pussy every now and then you might as well go to a pro and spare yourself all the other trouble and pretense."

Matthew reached in his pocket and pulled out a card and threw it across the table. All Luke could do was shake his head.

Chapter Thirteen

aniel looked down at his Professional Boxing License from the State Athletic Commission with optimism and anticipation. Now he was free to fulfill his destiny. It meant more to him than the diploma he had walked across the stage and received that morning at Cheyney University.

"Come on downstairs, bro, everybody's waiting to get this party started," Rebecca said, bursting into his room."

"I'm coming. It's time for me to celebrate my freedom."

"What are you talking about? Now it's time for you to go to work, son. The pressure from Daddy is about to go through the roof."

"Don't even trip, Becca, you know better than anybody that's not going to happen."

"He doesn't mean any harm. He worries about you, that's all."

"I'm a grown man. I don't need anybody worrying about me."

"Since you won the Pennsylvania Golden Gloves, you should have gone out for the regionals and the national championship, then you could have gone away to the Olympics this summer."

"That's not for me, sis. It wasn't a walk in the park winning that tournament. I'm not taking no extra punches for the glory of it. It's time for a brother to get paid. I'm going pro. My man Mike Tyson is in jail over some bullshit rape charges and I'm about to step in for him and get those belts back in the hands of a real champion."

"Daddy is going to have a heart attack."

"He can do whatever he wants, he doesn't have anything left to hold over my head. I got my degree for Momma and I'm out."

"When are you going to tell him?"

"Right after he gives me that money I need to hold me down until the dollars start flowing."

Rebecca laughed hard. "Oh shit, I want to see that. Your next fight won't be in some boxing ring, it's going to be in the rec room and I'm going to get a front row seat."

"You are truly silly," he said, walking out of his bedroom.

"All right, let's get ready to rumble," Rebecca said, running down the stairs behind him.

Daniel raised his arms in victory when he walked into the great room. They were all there, his grandmom Ruby, grandpop John and Grandma Gloria, Aunt Mary, Aunt Martha, Uncle Matthew and his family, and even his Uncle Mark.

"There he is," Luke said proudly, "Class of 1992 graduate of Cheyney University with a bachelor degree in Business Administration."

Everybody applauded.

"Thank you family for being here to celebrate this day with me." Then Daniel paused for a moment to swallow the lump in his throat. "I did this for my momma even though she's not here to see it."

"She would have been so proud of you, baby," Grandma Ruby said, giving him a hug.

"We're all proud of you, son," Luke added. "In honor of this occasion and as a graduation gift from your family I have opened up a bank account for you and deposited $25 thousand into it."

He handed Daniel the passbook and everybody cheered.

"I didn't know if you wanted another car or something else," Luke explained happily.

"Cash always works for me," John joked.

"So what are you going to do with all that bank?" Mark shouted at him from across the room.

"I've got big plans for next month," Daniel answered.

"I heard that," Grandma Gloria said, "Take some time to enjoy yourself."

"What are your plans?" Mary asked.

"I'll be out of town," he said, looking at his dad.

"Going on a trip before you have to start clocking those hours at the company?" Matthew teased. "I don't blame you."

Daniel stood tall with his legs apart and put his hands behind his back as if he were bravely preparing to face a firing squad.

"Not really, it's all business," Daniel said.

"What kind of business?" Luke asked suspiciously.

They all got quiet.

"It just so happens that on June 19th I'm going to Caesar's Palace in Las Vegas, Nevada where I'll be boxing on the undercard of Evander Holyfield vs. Larry Holmes."

"What the fuck are you talking about?" Luke bellowed. "Why are you making me get outside of myself today? This is a special occasion."

"You're right about that. I got my license today, I'm a professional boxer."

Luke walked over to stand in his face before he said, "The purpose of you going to college was to learn enough to make an educated decision where you won't make an ass out of yourself. Some guys have to take a beating to make a living, that's not you."

Rebecca rushed over to Luke.

"Let it go, Daddy, please," she said, wanting to diffuse the situation.

"Now's not the time, son," Gloria said, pleading with him.

Luke ignored them and kept talking. "You got a fantasy in your head, boy. I have seen what happens to men who have fought in the ring. They lost their intelligence, their minds, and their health. I don't want that for you, son."

"It's not about what you want for me. It's what I want for me.

I don't want a boring life of going to meetings all day, worrying about supply and demand, discussing hair products, and I'm not about to be chained to a desk. That's not my thing."

"It's that thing that kept food on the table and clothes on your back. Where do you think you would be without somebody living that boring life you're talking about?"

"I appreciate that, Dad, but it's my life and my decision."

Luke was furious. "Your momma and I sacrificed…"

"Let him be," John interrupted, "He's young and a young man is like a tiger, he needs to be free to prowl and hunt."

Luke lashed back, "He's not a child, he's grown, and when you're grown you can't do everything you want to do in this life. We have responsibility for other people besides ourselves. If you go through with this, I'm done. I'm not about to finance this foolishness."

Martha walked over to Luke and spoke to him in a low voice.

"Don't burn the bridge between you and your child," Martha urged. "Let him know that if things don't work out he can always come back home. I never felt that and I did a million things I regret. Don't put him in that position."

"I only got one thing to say," Miss Ruby said, going up to Daniel, "Promise me you won't let nobody hurt that pretty face."

"I'm going to do my best, Grandma Ruby."

Luke dropped down on the sofa next to Matthew, resigned to the fact that nothing he said was going to make a difference to Daniel. All of the things he thought were important in this life were in his son. He wanted to turn the company over to him. Then he would be a proud and self-sufficient man. He would never have to grovel, never have to beg from anybody. He could get a good woman and provide for her. The only drawback was that his son didn't want any part of it.

"Hey, brother," Matthew said, patting him on the leg, "It doesn't matter who's right. From where I sit, you both are right.

***

"This is the big time," Wendell said when they walked into the lobby of Caesar's Place in Vegas. "You know you could have saved the cash and stayed at a hotel off the strip. We're only getting a $12 thousand purse from this fight."

"No way, man, this is the way it's going to be from now on," Daniel said, looking around.

They checked in and walked through the casino towards the elevator.

"Somebody over there is trying to get your attention," Wendell said, nodding towards a hostess carrying drinks.

"She's fine but she can forget it."

"It might be good for you to find that special lady," Wendell chuckled.

"I'm going to be on the road, I don't need anybody trying to pin me down."

Inside their hotel room, they sat their bags down and went back out to find something to eat.

"I'm ready to try out the buffet," Daniel said, rubbing his belly.

"You don't need to overeat before this fight tomorrow, man."

"What are you talking about? I don't have no problem making weight."

"You don't need a bunch of shit in your system. You need to eat light. Veggies and protein, fruits and water, that's it."

"You got to be kidding, they have everything in here and I'm hungry. Besides, we're only fighting six rounds."

"You can't look past any man. You can get knocked out and lose a fight in the first round."

Daniel's mind flashed back to several fights he'd seen that went down like that.

"You're right, I got to stay focused."

He filled his plate with chicken and every green vegetable they had in the restaurant. He drank only water and fruit juice. When they were done they went back to the room to where Daniel could take a hot bath and go to bed early.

He got up early the next morning did a short run before weigh-in to relax, and then ate a light breakfast of oatmeal and a banana.

"Don't forget to wear your good drawers, man, you don't want to be on TV looking raggedy."

"You know how I do it," Daniel smirked.

He showered and changed and they walked to the arena

The weigh-in thrilled Daniel. He waited in the back while the other fighters on the undercard went before him. He was just two bouts away from the championship fight. When he heard his name called by the announcer he walked up on the stage with Wendell behind him. Flanked on both sides by women wearing tight blue boxing shorts and midriff tops, he undressed down to his black Calvin Kline boxers. He got on the scale as cameras flashed, threw his head back, and let the applause wash over him. He put his warm-up bottoms back on and then he stood toe-to-toe with his opponent to pose for more photos.

"That's what's up," Daniel said when they were finished.

"Back to the room," Wendell said, "You need to rest your body."

Daniel went back to bed for a nap. He got up around 2:00 and ate a small plate of pasta and a protein bar. He spent the rest of the wait listening to music on this CD player. When it was close to the time for them to head down to the dressing room, he went through the yoga sun salutation to stretch and loosen up.

The dressing room was more like a small locker room. Daniel took off his warm-up suit, put on his protective cup and green satin boxing shorts, and then his black boxing shoes. He did some shadow boxing to warm up before Wendell carefully wrapped his hands and put on his gloves. When he slid on the new matching robe that his Uncle Matthew bought for him he was ready. He started bouncing on his feet and throwing jabs in the air.

"It's time for your coming out party, my man," Wendell said, opening the door for him.

"All right then, my man, let's dance."

***

Luke had refused to watch the fight. Rebecca wasn't about to miss it so she went over to her Grandparents house to watch it with the rest of the family. The TV was already on and they were sitting in the den when she got there. There were several bouts on the undercard so the volume was low while they were talking.

"I'm so nervous I'm shaking," Rebecca said, "I feel like I'm the one getting ready to fight."

"I know, except you won't be the one feeling those punches," Grandpa John chuckled.

"As long as he gives more than he gets," Matthew said.

"I don't know why Luke is tripping so hard," Mark said, "If he was my son I would be out there in Vegas on the front row."

Martha snickered. "I bet you would, now how much money you got on it?"

"You know it's rude to get all up in grown folk's personal business," Mark said in an attempt to sound proper.

"Excuse me, sir," Martha laughed.

"Gloria, get me a beer, I think the boy's coming up next," John said, squinting at the TV.

"Turn it up," Rebecca hollered.

They watched Daniel and his opponent climb in the ring without much fanfare, only half the seats in the outdoor arena were filled. When Michael Buffer began his animated introductions, Daniel began to dance and bounce around the ring like Muhammad Ali. He had imagined this moment so many times.

"Ladies and gentlemen, introducing in the red corner, wearing green trunks and weighing 207 pounds, in his first professional fight, from Philadelphia, Pennsylvania, Daniel Clements.”

Rebecca jumped out of her seat and started cheering.

Michael Buffer continued. “In the blue corner, wearing purple and white trunks and weighing 218 pounds, in his ninth professional fight with a record of seven wins and two loses with four knockouts, from Havana, Cuba, Javier Gonzales.”

Javier ran in place and then raised his gloves high in triumph.

“What’s he got his hands up in the air for, they haven’t even started yet?” Rebecca complained. “He’s about to get a beat down.”

“Daniel’s got his hands full,” Matthew said cautiously.

The referee brought the fighters together and gave them the rules for the fight. Javier, four inches taller, stared down at Daniel with a scowl on his face. Unintimidated by the look, Daniel smiled back. Then they retreated to their respective corners.

“I don’t think I can watch this,” Mary said, “I’ll be in the kitchen.”

“I might be in there with you in a minute,” Gloria said, getting nervous.

The bell rang. Daniel and Javier danced around the ring dodging each other for 30 seconds without throwing a jab. The crowd starts to boo them. Then Daniel threw a right hook that missed but Javier countered with a left jab that landed on his jaw. They trade a few punches before Javier ties him up and tries to work on his body. Daniel pushes him off and throws a right beneath his gloves straight to his body. Javier hits him again with the jab. They mix it up and the bell rings ending the first round.

The whole family watched as Daniel’s trainer squeezed water on his head and in his mouth to refresh and keep him cool in the Las Vegas heat. They see Wendell talking to Daniel, and Rebecca turns the volume way up but they can’t hear what he’s saying.

“This is hard to watch,” Rebecca said. “I might end up in the kitchen too.”

"No worries, he looks good," Mark said with confidence, "He had to feel him out in that round. He's got to pace himself, he's never fought this many rounds before."

The bell rang signaling the second round and Daniel rushes out. From the first round he saw that Javier is an outside fighter. He moves inside throwing double jabs to the body and a right hand over the top. Javier pushes him back and throws a jab and a cross. The fighters circle the ring jabbing and blocking until the end of the round.

"I think it's even," Matthew said, "One round each."

Wendell said something to Daniel in his ear while he was in the corner and when the bell rang he charged across the ring in attack mode. He threw a combination to the head but Javier backed up and threw a jab that landed on his chin. Daniel goes inside and lands an overhand right to the side of the head. Javier starts to run but Daniel pushes him to the ropes leaning in on his chest and working the body. He covers up and throws a flurry of hooks. The crowd roars as the momentum of the fight increases.

"He's got him hurt," Mark said, standing up.

"Finish him off," Rebecca shouted at the TV.

Daniel throws an uppercut that knocks Javier's head back. Javier leans on the ropes trying to clear his head and Daniel throws a right to his belly. Javier's legs crumble beneath him and he drops to the canvas. The referee pushes Daniel aside and counts to ten. He signals to the audience. "He's out."

The house erupts in cheers. They watch as Wendell rushes in and lifts Daniel in the air. "You did it man," they hear him say.

Daniel lifts his glove in victory.

"He won," Rebecca screamed, running across the floor. "I've got to call Daddy."

"I'm glad that's over," Mary said, coming back in the room.

They're talking happily, going over the highlights with each other while Rebecca pushes the numbers in the phone. It rang over and over before Luke finally answered. He was sitting alone on the patio.

"Hello," he said in a subdued voice.

"Daddy, Daniel won the fight," Rebecca said breathlessly.

"Good for him," Luke said without any enthusiasm.

"He didn't get hurt."

"That's good, sweetheart."

Rebecca had believed that her Daddy's reservations were mainly about Daniel getting injured in the ring. Now she realized that he would never accept Daniel's boxing, win or lose.

"I'll be home in a little while," she said.

"Okay, baby," he said dryly.

Luke was hoping Daniel would have got his ass whupped bad enough where he would never want to climb in the ring again. He put down the phone and sank into a funk.

***

A few weeks of feeling the blues was taking a toll on Luke. He was zoning out during important meetings at the company. More than a month ago Rebecca had given him and Matthew a heads-up on a movie called *Poectic Justice* that was being filmed on the West coast with Janet Jackson wearing braids. She had advised him to develop a line of synthetic hair for braiding and the products for maintenance of braid styles but he hadn't even started on it.

Matthew walked into his office at the end of the day on Friday and sat across from him.

"I'd tell you to take a vacation and get your shit together but we don't have time for that, my brother," Matthew said. "If you don't snap out of it there won't be a company here for you to brood over."

"I know that, Matt, and I'm working on it" Luke said, sounding like he was half asleep.

"I don't know why you're going through all these changes for anyway. You're stressing over Daniel for no reason, Becca is the one who should run this thing when you're ready to let it go. She's hardworking, dedicated, she's got fresh ideas, and she wants to do it."

"Working herself to death," Luke griped. "That's not what I want for my baby."

"You can't control either of them or their lives. Why don't you spend some time living your own and stop acting like you died with Ruthie."

"You know where the door is," Luke said angrily.

Matthew shook his head, got up and walked out. Luke sat there for a minute.

"I just need to take the edge off," he said to himself.

He went into his private washroom and freshened up. He was going out to get a drink and relax. He had heard about a new upscale place on Chestnut Street, The Cat Club, where black professionals hang out. There was no way he was going back to Studio West and take a chance on running into Tonya. He had gone out to The Ritz a couple of times and even asked someone out to dinner. He was drawn to women who bore some resemblance to Ruthie but when they opened their mouths the fantasy is gone. Once he even asked one of them not to speak. They didn't have her sweetness or tenderness. They all wanted something from him. His lady love had always wanted to give.

Inside the Cat Club the music was more R&B than rap and the clientele were dressed for success. He went over to the bar and saw that the bartender and hostesses were all female and wearing black cat suits that held onto their curves for dear life. It was more of a laidback atmosphere with upwardly mobile blacks doing more networking than they were dancing.

At the end of the bar Luke saw a petite woman standing with such a regal aura that it was as if she towered above the others next to her. She was pretty and stylishly dressed. Her hair was cut in an asymmetric bob that was parted on the side. She brushed the long front out of her eyes and Luke was mesmerized. He had to meet her. He picked up his drink and eased through the crowd until he was standing behind her.

He cleared his throat, "Excuse me, I would like to buy you a drink."

She turned around and said, "Do I know you?"

Luke winced, her voice was hard and raspy and her two front teeth were outline with gold. The spell was broken.

"Sorry, I thought you were someone I knew."

"No harm done, I would be happy to make your acquaintance," she said, checking him out.

"My name is Luke, I would love to get to know you also but I'm waiting for someone."

"Another time then," she smiled.

"Definitely," he said.

Luke walked away and kept moving until he was out the door and in his car. Trying to meet someone in a club wasn't his scene. The truth of the matter was that he really didn't want a relationship. He decided to do what Matthew suggested.

When he got home he called the escort service on the card Matthew had given him. He told them he wanted a woman who looked like Tammi Terrell.

Chapter Fourteen

It was Monday morning and Rebecca was up bright and early for work. Everything had changed over the weekend. After taking semester overloads and summer classes she had finally graduated from Drexel. The whole family had come to the house to congratulate her and they managed to get through the celebration without any arguments or Luke getting out of himself.

She had waited for this day for a long time. She could have gone over to the house and talked with her Dad there but she wanted to keep it all business. Inside the employee lounge she paced back and forth while her eyes gravitated back to the clock on the wall. At 9:14, one minute before her appointment, she went to make her request.

"Good morning, Daddy," she said, walking into his office.

"Come on in, sit by me," he said, glad to see her. "I saw you were first on my schedule. What's on your mind?"

"Now that I'm out of school I'm ready to talk about an executive position for me. I've been working here for six years. I've worked in all the departments and done management internships during the summers. I want to work directly with you. I think I've earned that opportunity."

"Sweetheart, you just graduated two days ago. Why don't you take some time off, relax, have some fun with your friends."

"The only reason I went to school was because you insisted and said it meant a lot to Mommy. All I ever wanted to do was work here."

"You've worked here so much that you didn't leave anytime for socializing. That's important too, Becca. You should join a club or something to meet new people."

"That stuff doesn't thrill me. I don't need anybody new in my life right now."

Luke was getting more agitated. Why didn't this child of his want to enjoy herself and the life that he and Ruthie had provided for her? His main regret was Ruthie having to work so hard when she was young.

"Didn't you meet an eligible gentleman that peaked your interest while you were at school? You're old enough to get married and have a family of your own."

"I'm not feeling that urge, Daddy, I don't need another person to validate me. I don't mind being alone and I have plenty of family already. I feel like this place was Mommy's baby and now I'm ready to take care of it. I can help it thrive and grow."

"Take it from me, sweetheart, I had someone I loved and now I'm alone, being with someone you love is better."

"People are made up differently. I enjoy my own company very much."

"How can you be so sure, you're not going to meet someone you might want to share your life with if you're in the office working all the time?"

"I don't think you'll be comfortable hearing this but I've been with both males and females while I was in school. I'm not partial to either one. Those relationships didn't give me the satisfaction that I want in my life. Right now I need the mental and intellectual stimulation that I get working more than I need the physical stimulation from a man or woman."

Luke was taken aback. "You're absolutely right," he told her, "I'm not comfortable hearing any of that. As a matter of fact I think I crossed a line and we went too deep. You're my daughter and if you want to work here you have that privilege. I know you have something in mind so throw it out there."

"I don't want a fake title in a fake office. I want to be Chief Operating Officer."

"Whoa, Becca, that's a huge responsibility. I don't think you're ready for that."

"Daddy, I know you've been holding that spot for Daniel since Mommy died. Do you think he's any more ready than I am?"

"That's not the point."

"What is the point, that I'm not a son?"

"Not really, sweetie. I'll admit that I am looking forward to your brother taking over the company when he gets his head on straight but you're my baby girl, I don't want to see you throw your life away working all the time."

"I've told you how I feel and what I want. Daniel is not coming to work here any time soon and I'm here today. You're always telling me what Mommy would want and I'm telling you that she would give me that job."

Luke paused and thought about it.

"You're right. The job is yours."

Rebecca pumped her fist and shouted, "Yes."

"The company is facing some challenges in expanding," he warned, "We had to downsize a few years ago and we haven't made up that ground yet."

"That's a temporary problem, Daddy. Hairstyles are trends, they don't last forever. They all evolve, the conk, the afro, and now the curl. That doesn't mean our business fails. All of them have to be maintained. For as many shapes, sizes, and complexions of black women, there are probably just as many hair styles. The key is to stay current and even create new styles."

"That was what your mother did."

"And that's what I'm going to continue to do, Daddy," Rebecca said, getting up from the table. "The best days of this company are not behind us, you'll see."

***

Daniel drove his fists into the heavy bag over and over trying to tear it apart as if it were the dastardly demon blocking him from his destiny. Wendell had gotten him four more fights and he had knocked two of them out before the end of the fourth round without getting winded. It was obvious they were set-ups, mismatches that he would no doubt win.

"It's what you got to do to build up your record," Wendell kept telling him. "That way we can get better fights and bigger paydays."

Logically he understood what Wendell's strategy was but his gut told him that he needed bouts with skilled fighters to keep his edge sharp. He stepped back and hit the bag once more as hard as he could and the sweat from his forehead spilled down into his eyes. He squeezed them tight and opened them to the sunrays brightening the room from the door opening. A hush spread across the room. Daniel recognized the man who walked into the gym with one body guard beside him and another close behind him. It was Earl Knight. He was notorious and respected as a manager and a promoter in the boxing game. He was responsible for more than a few boxers earning championship belts but he was known to pick their pockets every chance he got.

"I'm looking for Daniel Clements," Earl bellowed out across the gym.

"Why?" Daniel asked, pulling off his gloves.

Earl recognized him too. He and his boys walked towards him.

"Some dinner and some conversation is all," Earl said with a friendly manner.

"I don't have a problem with either," Daniel told him.

"Good, we'll be waiting outside."

"I'll change and be there in a few minutes."

"No rush, take your time," Earl smiled.

Daniel showered and changed into the brown slacks and mock turtleneck he had in his locker. He grabbed his coat off a chair in the front on the way out.

"Don't turn your back on that one," somebody working out in the gym shouted at him.

"I got this," Daniel shouted back.

He stopped and stood outside the limo holding his duffle bag and the window rolled down.

"I've got my own car, where do you want to talk."

"Ride with me," Earl offered, "I'll bring you back to your car."

Daniel got in.

"Can I offer you something to drink?" Earl asked, holding one in his hand.

"No thanks, I'm cool."

Earl had heard Daniel was squeaky clean. When he turned down the drink, Earl wondered if he was a health nut as well.

"You don't have any objections to red meat do you?" he asked cautiously.

"No, none at all," Daniel chuckled.

"Great. Delmonico's," he called out to the limo driver.

Daniel turned off his pager and leaned back to gaze out of the window. He was sure that word about him leaving with Earl Knight had already gotten to Wendell and he would be blowing up his pager at any minute. He didn't mean any disrespect to Wendell but he was his own man and he would make his own decisions.

Inside the restaurant the host greeted them, "Your table is ready, Mr. Knight."

"Thank you, Carl," Earl said, as he followed him to the booth on the left.

"The usual, sir?" the host asked when they were seated.

Earl nodded. "Yes, thanks."

It wasn't long before the table was set with prime rib, lobster, an assortment of side items, served with a carafe of cabernet sauvignon and a bottle of Grey Goose vodka.

"After you," Earl said to Daniel, "You're my guest."

"What else are you offering?" Daniel asked, filling his plate with food. He didn't want to waste time with Earl buttering him up.

Earl leaned on the table and crossed his hands.

"I know Wendell Williams is your trainer, he's a good man and he's got experience, but he's taken you as far as he can. I've got connections he'll never have. I can build your reputation with the right fights. I can make the matches that will help you get a shot at the belt."

"It sounds good but your reputation precedes you."

"Which one?" Earl laughed. "The one based on rumors or the one based on facts."

"Truthfully, I'm not concerned with either," Daniel said, cutting his steak. "I've got a business degree that says I can read a contract and count my own money."

"There's only one thing missing," Earl added. "You got to have a manager. I'm the one you need. If you want Wendell as your trainer that's fine with me. I'll get you the big dollars. Make you richer than Iron Mike."

"It sounds good. Why don't you let me see how it looks in black and white?"

Earl laughed again, "Cheers." He held up his vodka glass, and poured it down his throat.

***

The next day, Wendell was waiting for Daniel at the door when he got to the gym after his four mile morning run.

"So what's up with you?" Wendell asked brusquely.

"We need to have a conversation," Daniel said, walking past him to the locker room.

"I heard you had one already with Earl Knight."

"I did, and now I need to have one with you. Bottom line, I need a manger."

"We've gotten this far without another mouth to feed. I can manage you and train you."

"Yeah, you've done okay but now we've hit the wall. I'm ready for a real shot."

"I'm the one who got you the undercard in Vegas. That was pay-per-view."

"What if that was just a flash in the pan. I got bigger fish to fry. I'm not trying to be another undercard. I want to be the main event."

"It'll happen, Daniel, you need to be patient."

"That's all I've been, patient. Earl Knight says he can get me a shot at the championship within eighteen months. I signed a contract with him for that long. If he doesn't make it happen our deal is done."

"He's a muthafuckin' shyster looking for somebody else to rip off."

"Everybody's a shyster in this game. I can handle him."

"We should have discussed this before you hired him."

"Probably, but in the end it's my decision. I'm the one who has to get out there and fight."

"You're right, man," Wendell said with a salty attitude, "Do whatever you want."

"Don't take it personal, man. I still want you in my corner, that hasn't changed. When I get that belt and the big purse to match, it'll be party time for you too."

"I hope it works out like that. I'm getting to old to be hungry and out in the cold."

"Trust me, man, that's not gonna happen."

***

Earl Knight didn't play when it came to making money. He set up a string of bouts like dominoes for Daniel to knock down one by one. Each one was a step higher in the ranks toward his goal of becoming a major contender. Wendell watched him like an eagle waiting to strike a rat when it shows itself.

Earl had gotten ringside tickets for Daniel and Wendell to accompany him to Heavyweight Champion Lewis Whitfield's second title defense. The Champ's camp had gone all the way to Russia to find this white boy. He stood tall in his corner with his body looking like a monument meticulously chiseled out of stone.

"That white guy don't look like somebody you want to play with," Daniel said, eyeing him.

Earl nodded. "We'll find out shortly."

Earl was an old player in the boxing game and had no doubt this bout was either a fix or a mismatch designed for a payday. The bell rang summoning the fighters from their corners. For more than a minute they danced around each other throwing punches from a distance too far apart for them to make real contact. Boos and groans of displeasure swelled throughout the arena like rising waters of a flood urging them to act.

The first round ended without either fighter answering the crowd's continued demands for a dogfight or at the very least a few clashes. The second was somewhat different than the first with Lewis as an elusive target bouncing around the ring, while the Russian stood stationary without any head movement. More boos and taunts filled the expansive room.

The crowd soon discovered what Lewis's camp already knew; the Russian had a glass jaw. Lewis shattered it with a straight right hand and he fell to the canvas like a toppled statue one minute and forty-seven seconds into the third round. The whole arena was stunned into silence. They didn't know how to react as the referee did his count. An air of conspiracy blew over them. The jam-packed room sensed they had been deceived and robbed. Lewis raised his glove in triumph but they turned on the Champ with jeers and catcalls. Idle cameras and dazed reporters lined the perimeter of the ring.

Perfection, Earl couldn't have scripted it better. It was all a part of the unique love-hate relationship that fans have for champion athletes. They love the build-up, the hype, the glory of a magnificent performance, but they are quick to denounce, humiliate, and ridicule them for any fall from grace. Earl seized the moment. It was like a movie director shouted, "Action." He glided to the nearest camera and went through his rehearsed lines.

"This evening's bout is a travesty for boxing," he said, holding the microphone and staring intently into the lens of the camera. "The fans have come out and bought tickets in good faith to see a prize fight. What they got was a joke, a staged comedy. Boxing fans deserve better and the Champ should want to give them better. He can do that by defending his title against a real challenger."

"Who do you want to see him fight?" the reporter asked, taking the bait.

More microphones reached in closer to capture Earl Knight's voice. He took a deep breath for emphasis before he spoke.

"The premiere match-up for the next heavyweight title defense would be between Lewis Whitfield and Daniel Clements." Earl motioned for Daniel to stand beside him. "This man here, Daniel Clements, is ready to fight Lewis Whitfield whenever he wants to give the fans a real fight for their money."

"I've seen him before, what is his ranking?" another sports reporter asked.

"He's undefeated with twelve profession bouts, seven by knockout. He's ranked #9 by the WBC. The Champ shouldn't have anything to fear about getting in the ring with him, Daniel just wants a shot."

More cameras flashed. More questions were asked but Earl didn't bother answering them. He had accomplished his goal. For the price of four tickets to the fight he had gotten more publicity than he could put a price on.

***

Daniel was hot. Earl Knight's impromptu press conference had made him the flavor of the month. The media couldn't get enough of him. There hadn't been a boxer as pretty and camera-ready as Daniel since Muhammad Ali. The Lewis Whitfield management team was under a ton of pressure to make a deal. During pre-negotiations, Earl called Daniel and Wendell to a formal meeting at his office.

"This ain't good, man," Wendell warned as the elevator climbed to the 22nd floor of Penn Center. "He can't be manager and promoter, it's a conflict of interest."

"I'm not worried about that. What I wanted from Earl Knight I've gotten, that's a shot at the heavyweight championship. I'm not married to him and he doesn't have any papers on me. We're making a business deal that should make us both very happy."

"I trust him about as far as I can throw him," Wendell grumbled.

They exited the elevator and entered the offices of Knight Productions. An attractive woman dressed in a maroon cocktail dress escorted them to a conference room where Earl was waiting.

"Can I get anything for you, food or drink?" Earl asked courteously.

"No, thanks," Daniel replied, taking a seat. "I'm in training."

"Great, we can get right to it. This is sure to be a lucrative fight that can generate upwards of $38 million. I have a figure in mind for your purse that I think I can get for you very easily. What I need to know is what figure do you have in mind?"

"I want $3 million," Daniel said.

"That's very conservative," Earl said, surprised. "We can get you much more than that."

"That amount, my share, will be untouched, free and clear."

Earl lit his cigar and took a drag. Then he leaned back in his chair. "As promoter, there are bills that I have to guarantee will be paid, from promotion to security, hotel accommodations, travel, doctors, an assistant trainer, a cut man, the girls in the ring, even the chair in your corner. They don't come cheap but I have a team in place to handle those particulars."

Daniel fanned the smoke from the cigar.

"My purse will remain untouched for any other expenses related to the event. That's your business. Mine is to come trained and ready to fight. You will have my full cooperation but whatever amount you need to cover my purse, the expenses that will be generated, in addition to the profit you have in mind, is what you need to negotiate."

Earl looked at Daniel with a straight face that gradually turned to a smile and then it broke into guttural laughter. Daniel smiled back at him. Then Earl stood up and reached out his hand.

"I love it, we have a deal. I'll have my attorney draw up a contract."

Daniel shook his hand. "I'm glad."

Earl nodded. "Now all you have to do is win and the world is yours."

Chapter Fifteen

arl did what he got paid the big dollars to do. He offered, countered, and negotiated a deal with Top Rank's Bill Arum and Whitfield's Management Company. It didn't make any difference to Daniel how much Earl got for himself as long as his paycheck was signed, sealed, and delivered with what he asked for.

Knight Productions had arranged for Daniel to be fitted for tailor-made suits. There were several press conferences scheduled in a tour across the country to build up the hype and Earl wanted him to look like a model who just jumped off the pages of GQ magazine. Home Box Office (HBO) arranged to kickoff the publicity junket in New York City.

Daniel stood backstage while the announcer introduced him.

"Ladies and gentlemen, representing the world-renown Joe Frazier Gym out of Philadelphia, please welcome Daniel Clements in the biggest challenge of his career. He is undefeated with a record of 12 professional fights with seven by knockout."

Daniel walked out on the empty stage against a backdrop of huge photos of him and Lewis. Cameras from every angle in the room flashed and he felt like a Hollywood movie star.

Then the announcer introduced the champ. "Ladies and gentleman, here he is defending his title for the fifth time, undefeated with a record of 32 wins and 11 knockouts, WBA and IBF Heavyweight Champion of the World, Lewis "The Lion" Whitfield."

The champ walked out on the stage and the room applauded.

They walked over to meet at the center of the stage and stared each other down. Lewis grinned when he thought about the way he planned to demolish the young wannabe. Daniel gave him a blank look. He would save all of his emotions and tactics for the ring.

Next they posed for the photo shoot. The two men were a contrast in looks, background, and style of boxing. Daniel was handsome, clean cut, tall and athletic, a college grad, and a boxer. Lewis was rough-looking, bulky, scarred from battles in and out of the ring, an alumni of the penitentiary, and a brawler. It was just the start of the promotion that had Daniel traveling from Club Nokia in Los Angeles to ESPN in Atlanta for interviews and exhibitions.

Wendell complained the whole time. "This is a waste of time, man. We need to get back to the gym. None of this bullshit is going to help you when you get in that ring."

"Chill out, man. We're making easy money. I haven't had to take one punch. These appearances are paying big-time," Daniel told him. "We'll be back in Philly by the weekend."

They brought the enthusiasm home with them. The gym was full everyday with spectators wanting to see Daniel train. It got on Wendell's last nerve but Daniel loved it. It had taken him three years to get to this moment. He trained for eight hours every day. He was feasting on the spotlight and exhilaration he had craved from watching his hero, Mike Tyson, nine years ago.

The fight was scheduled at the MGM Grand in Las Vegas on November 19, 1994. Earl Knight assigned a team to travel with Daniel and Wendell to Vegas a month prior to the fight to live at an estate he'd rented. The team included security, someone to take care of his wardrobe, another for his meals, an assistant trainer, sparring partners, and a driver to get them around.

Earl even threw him a party for his 25th birthday on Halloween but Daniel wasn't in the mood. He missed the people who really cared about him. He missed his family. He went to his room and called home. Rebecca answered the phone.

"What's going on, girl?"

"It's all about you, Daniel," she answered cheerfully, "Happy Birthday."

"Thanks."

"Where are you?" Rebecca asked, sensing his mood.

"I'm in Vegas already. Are you and dad coming out for the fight? I sent tickets."

"I don't know but I doubt it. The fight is around his birthday and the time Momma died and you know how he gets around that time. Plus, you know he wants you to quit and come home."

Daniel sighed. "He needs to get over all of that."

"Yeah right. Hold on, I'll get him on the phone."

A minute later Luke said, "Happy birthday, son. How are you doing?"

"I'm great, Dad. My training is going well and I'm feeling good. I wish you and Becca would come and be here. I could use some family support."

"Becca can come if she wants but I've got a family business to run."

"It's one night, the biggest night of my life."

"I want to support you, son, but I can't be there and watch you get hurt unnecessarily."

"It's a sport not the Gulf War, Dad."

"It's your well-being, you're too smart for this."

"Rebecca's the brain of the family."

"You got your share too. Why you would rather let somebody beat them out of you I'll never know."

"I got to go, Dad. I love you."

"I love you too, son."

Daniel hung up the phone. He swore he wouldn't call him again until he was the champion.

***

Daniel takes the long walk down the aisle of the darkened arena of the MGM Grand with the lights shining on him. He can feel the energy of the crowd cheering in the thickness of the air but he can't hear them or the loud music playing. He is completely in his zone, focused on one thing, the job he has to do. He climbs into the ring and watches as the lights shift to Lewis dancing down the aisle trailed by his entourage. He sees the ring announcer go through his introductions, and his eyes follow the lips of the referee giving them the rules of the fight. Back in his corner he feels Wendell's breath against the side of his face. Then the only thing he hears is the sound of the bell.

Daniel raises his gloves and moves to the center of the ring to meet his opponent. For the first few rounds the boxing match is even with the fighters trading jabs. Lewis's strategy is to carry his challenger for a few rounds to satisfy the crowd before he knocks him out. The lack of intensity makes it feel like a sparring match to Daniel. In the fourth round Lewis hears boos, whistles, and rumbling beginning to resonate in the stadium. This is his signal that it's time to up the action. He fires a flurry of punches that back Daniel into the ropes. He follows with an overhand right to his head, a left hook to the body, and smothers him with short jabs. The bell rings, giving Daniel a chance to breath.

"You need to come alive," Wendell said with urgency as he massaged his neck, "You can't let a round go."

"I got it," Daniel said before Wendell swabbed his face with Vaseline and put in his mouthpiece. He nodded and rose to his feet.

The bell dings for the fifth round. Lewis sprung at Daniel like a hulking mass of muscle throwing quick jabs with his right hand. Daniel kept his arms raised to protect his head from the blows. He felt a punch to the left side of his torso from a right hook. He counter-punched leading with his left jab and following with an upper cut with his right hand. Lewis wrapped his arms around Daniel's tying him up and wiping his sweat covered head near his eye. Daniel pushed him off and before Lewis could find his balance Daniel hit him with a left to the body. The pain from the blow shocked Lewis back into action. He began bouncing, first to the right and then to the left before he attacked with another flurry of jabs to the body. Daniel threw a straight left to the middle and a right hook. He sprung back using his footwork, moving in to land his punches and then moving back out. The crowd roared loving the action.

Lewis started out the sixth round throwing a lot of punches but the snap was gone. By the seventh round there wasn't much power behind them. His punches tired him out more than they hurt Daniel. He covered up and leaned in on his challenger's shoulder. Daniel loaded his right fist with all the power of his inner core and brought it up from his knees to Lewis's chin and followed with a left that hit him straight in the eye. Things went into slow motion as the punch connected. Daniel watched as the split above Lewis's eye opened like it had been sliced and blood ran down mixed with his sweat. Lewis tasted his own blood and growled as he lunged towards Daniel. He was met with a right cross to his temple that knocked him off his feet. He jumped up but his balance was off as he staggered around the ring. The referee grabbed his wrists looked him in the eyes and waved to the audience that it was over.

Pandemonium breaks out in the arena. "Daniel, Daniel, Daniel!" the crowd chanted, on their feet while he jumped up and down elated with the win. Almost instantly the boxing ring is filled with security, cameramen, trainers, promoters, Lewis's entourage and even his wife. Wendell grabbed Daniel from behind and hoisted him up into the air.

The ring announcer moved to the center of the ring and raised his microphone. "Ladies and gentlemen, the winner and new Heavyweight Champion of the World, Daniel Clements."

The crowd roared and then continued to chant.

Larry Murchent sidled up to the winner for an interview.

"Daniel, as the underdog coming into this fight how do you feel?"

Still out of breath, Daniel said, "I feel great. I dreamed about this moment for a long time."

"What was your game plan preparing for this bout?" Murchent asked.

"To win, that's all, I had to win."

"Well you did that, congratulations."

"Thank you, and I want to dedicate this championship to my mother. She always believed I would do something great. "I love you, Momma."

Daniel feeling his deep emotions rising to the surface turned away from the camera. Larry Murchent then moved through the throng in the ring over to Lewis. Lewis ignored him and showed him his back; he wasn't in the mood for an interview.

"Lewis," Larry called out behind him, "Would you like a rematch?"

Lewis ignored his question and left the ring.

Earl Knight grabbed the bottom of Larry's microphone and pulled it up to his mouth to speak.   "There were doubts about this being a legitimate match-up but I have proved the naysayers wrong again. They said Lewis was heavier and a more seasoned fighter, they forgot Daniel was younger with more skills and patience. They said Daniel didn't have a chance in the ring with "The Lion" but today Daniel was "The Lion Killer." I also want to let the Whitfield camp know that we'll gladly grant them a rematch whenever they're ready."

"There you have it," Larry Murchent said, "In a spectacular demonstration we crown a new Heavyweight Champion of the World tonight."

***

Most of the Clements family were yelling their heads off in the great room at Luke's house. They were ecstatic over Daniel's win.

Luke sat by himself in his study. He should have been on top of the world when his son won the championship but to him it felt like another tragic death, as if he had lost his son forever. He reached for the cordless phone and pushed in the number.

"Hello," a soft voice answered.

"Can you meet me at the hotel?" Luke asked.

'I'll be there within the hour."

Luke hung up, put on his coat, and grabbed the keys to his car. He left without anyone in the family noticing. He drove downtown to the Latham Hotel on 17th Street where he kept a room for them to meet. He gave the valet his keys and went up to the eighth floor. He poured himself a drink and stood at the window to wait. He watched the pedestrians along the sidewalks and the cars that navigated the streets below. All of them were unaware of the contemplations that filled the hearts and minds of another. Each caught up in the turmoil of their own lives.

The door opened behind him and she asked, "Have you been waiting long?"

He turned around and said, "No, not long. It's good to see you."

"You look like you're down, let me massage your back for you."

"That sounds good," he said taking a seat on the bed.

Joyce knew how to make him feel good. After numerous appointments over the past three months she considered him a regular. She learned that he wanted the closeness, the sensitivity, and the sex, but his emotions were never involved. She was merely a substitute for the one he loved. Sometimes he didn't talk. It was all business.

She felt his muscles relax under her fingers. Then he pulled her down beside him and kissed her. He preferred to be the aggressor although he was a gentle lover. When it was over he held her tightly which was unusual for him.

"Is everything okay?" Joyce asked softly. "Do you want something?"

All he said was, "I've got to find a way to bring him back home where he belongs, Ruthie."

***

The after-fight party at the Tabu Ultra Lounge of the MGM Grand was like nothing Daniel had ever seen before. The reason Vegas was called 'Sin City' didn't need any further explanation. There was food, drinks, drugs, and more women, all for the taking in one place. He was the man of the hour and there was nothing he wanted that he couldn't have.

The club was wall-to-wall with celebrities and stars but it was his time to shine. Being crowned the Champ was like a rebirth. Instantly he became 'somebody.' They all wanted to meet and talk with the Heavyweight Champion of the World. They passed him around like a new-born baby taking pictures with oohs and ahhs, pulling him from person to person before he could finish a conversation.

After a few hours into the celebration Daniel felt like he had been caught in a tornado that had spun him around and around taking him higher and higher. He was worn out and light-headed. It had been an epic day.

"I'm beat," Daniel said, smiling. "I've got to call it a night."

"You've earned your rest, my man," Earl said. "I got you a penthouse suite to celebrate."

Daniel glanced across the room at Wendell who was huddled in a corner with an attractive young lady.

Earl whispered to him. "It'll give Wendell some time to have the room to himself."

Earl escorted Daniel to the room with one of his security guards. He opened the door and handed Daniel the room key. Inside there were two women waiting.

"My gift to you," Earl said, shaking his hand.

"I can get my own women," Daniel responded, slightly agitated.

"Hey, I'm sorry if I overstepped. I didn't mean any harm. Do you want them to leave?"

"Good night, Earl. I can handle it from here."

Once the door was closed behind Earl and his man, Daniel sat down on the gigantic sofa in the middle of the luxurious room. If either of his guests told him their names he didn't remember them. He tried to get to know them but they were smothering him with kisses while they took off his clothes. Then they pulled and tugged on him like vultures wrestling over a piece of meat.   Daniel stopped trying to love on them and laid back and let them play. It wasn't real, it was all fantasy. They both wanted to have sex with the Heavyweight Champion of the World, and he was sure they were getting paid. He couldn't judge them, he had just knocked another man out for money.

He woke up in the morning a few hours later and one of the women was gone. He told the other to get out. He thought about ordering up some food but the fridge was completely stocked. He was making himself some eggs in the spacious kitchen when there was a knock on the door. He opened it and Earl was standing there wearing a wide grin.

"How was your night?" he asked Daniel with a grin.

"It wasn't bad, a little crazy though. It'll be good to get back home and get back on my routine. I've been out here for a whole month."

"No time, Champ," Earl said, sitting down. "You're booked for the next two months. It's going to be a whirlwind of interviews and guest appearances."

"That's all good but if I want to stay the champ, I can't forget what I had to do to get here. I need to train to stay in shape."

"No problem, I'll make the arrangements and make sure you have time for that. If you don't mind, I can get you the best trainers in the game, state of the art. Wendell did a great job but now you're in the big leagues."

"Not right now, I'm comfortable with my trainer."

"It's your call. Take some time to eat and do what you do. I'll pick you up this afternoon. We're flying into Los Angeles for "The Tonight Show" with Jay Leno tomorrow."

"No way," Daniel said, excited.

"Oh yeah, man, and the next morning we're flying back east for an interview with Bryant Gumble on "The Today Show.""

"Wow, it doesn't even seem real yet."

"This is living the dream, baby."

Daniel took a long shower after Earl left before he went back to his room to catch up with Wendell. The room was quiet when he walked in. Wendell was still asleep, curled up next to the woman he had pinned in the corner last night. Daniel shut his bedroom door and started to pack up his things.

Chapter Sixteen

"**S**herry, get Rebecca and Matthew in my office ASAP," Luke said, full of excitement.

"Yes, sir, do you need anything else, coffee?"

"No, we'll be fine."

A brainstorm had come to Luke as he stood under the shower that morning, he felt like it would make all the difference in the company and his relationship with Daniel.

"Where's the fire?" Matthew asked, coming through the door.

"No fire yet but I'm about to light one," Luke said with his face beaming.

"I'm not sure if I should be happy or run for cover," Matthew said curiously as he sat down.

"You'll know soon enough," Luke told him.

They sat in silence except for Luke drumming his fingers along the table. He was eager to put his plan in motion. Then Rebecca walked in.

Luke smiled. "Come on in, sweetie, join us."

When Matthew and Rebecca were seated on his right and left at the table Luke clasped his hands together, sat up tall in his chair, and started the meeting.

"I have a fantastic idea for next year's promotion," he said enthusiastically.

Rebecca was puzzled and confused.

"Daddy, we already decided on that a month ago and the budget has already been assigned to developing a hair line for extensions

"

and weaves," she reminded him.

Luke shrugged his shoulders and said, "That can wait. This is the prime time for us to capitalize on Daniels boxing success. He's a major celebrity now and that will be a great boon for the company. My idea is to launch a cologne line using his name."

"Come on, brother," Matthew lamented, "I know what you're trying to do but we don't know the first thing about creating fragrances and financially this is not the time to make any large investments that won't guarantee us a return."

"If Ruthie and I hadn't taken risks we wouldn't be sitting here today, there wouldn't be a company," Luke argued.

"That market is saturated and very competitive," Rebecca added, "I don't see how that can pay off for us."

"More important than profit it will get Daniel involved with the business and that will pay off for us in the long run," Luke explained.

"We've made plans for other products that will pay off immediately," Rebecca said, "We can parlay the success from those deals into a venture for your fragrance line in the following year."

Luke pounded the table with his fist and said, "I don't mean to be abrupt but I don't know why we're still discussing this, my mind is made up."

"If that's the case, I don't know why I'm still sitting here," Rebecca said, getting up and stomping out of the room. She couldn't stand to hear this same tired song again.

"You haven't been listening and you're being stubborn, Luke," Matthew said, trying to talk some sense into him. "Daniel isn't thinking about this company. You've got to let the kid live his own life. I can't believe you would sacrifice everything that you and Ruthie built. This cologne idea could jeopardize it all. Does it really mean that much to you?"

"Damn right it means that much to me. What father wouldn't

want to pass on the life they've built to their son? It's the legacy for our family. He's the only one who can keep it going."

"You're blind, my brother. Rebecca is the one who can carry Clements Cosmetic into the new millennium. If the truth be told, it's her ideas that have helped us transition our product line from dependence on the Kush Kurl. Without that I don't know where we would be. Why don't you give her some credit?"

"She's my baby girl. I don't want her to have to work as hard as her momma did. It would break my heart if something happened to her."

"You're breaking her heart. Here she is trying to be here for you and the company and the only person you're concerned about is Daniel."

"You know how it was when we grew up. I don't want to be like Pops. I want to give them something in this world so they won't have to struggle."

"That's a done deal. They haven't struggled a day in their lives. Now let them live and do what makes them happy. Give Rebecca a free reign in the business and the next time Daniel fights get a ringside seat. Get back to living your own life, you're not dead."

"I might as well be, they're the only thing I have in this world to live for."

"Fortunately for you, that's plenty enough reason," Matthew said on his way out.

***

Luke was gung-ho about his plans to develop a cologne line for Daniel and wanted the company focus to be on the fragrance. The problem was that much of the budget for new products had already been spent on the hair line. Luke needed more capital to move forward even after he had halted the projects that Rebecca had been working on. For expediency he proposed his new venture to an investment banker.

He was a few minutes early for his appointment but the executive assistant, a petite middle-aged woman with curly brown hair, who introduced herself as Alice, greeted him and escorted him back to one of the offices behind the thick heavy glass door. A short man, red and peeling from what appeared to Luke as sunburn, invited him in.

"Hello, Mr. Clements, come on in. I've been expecting you. I'm Christopher Crowley, one of the managing directors here at HLS Capital."

"Thank you, Mr. Crowley, it's a pleasure to meet you."

Luke shook his extended hand and sat down in one of the four large wingtip chairs that had been placed at 90 degree angles around a coffee table.

"Call me Chris, hopefully we're about to get in bed together so to speak."

Luke laughed, "Then by all means call me, Luke."

"Certainly," Chris said, smiling. "Nonetheless, Luke, in all seriousness HLS is delighted to be able to assist you on this new project for your company. I can only imagine how proud you are of your son and what he has accomplished."

"This is a great opportunity for me to build a bridge between my son and his public image to the Clements Cosmetic Company."

"This expansion into the fragrance market is a promising perspective for Clements Cosmetic, the perfume and fragrance business has a multi-billion market. Have you ever considered taking the company public? It would create a shitload of capital for your company."

"I don't doubt that but Clements began as a family business and that's the way it will stay."

"I can respect that," Chris said. "According to your evaluations, the amount of financing that you need for this segment of your business plan for development, bottle design, packaging, and marketing is $5 million conservatively."

"That's correct."

"The firm has agreed to provide you with the financing if you have no objections to the terms of the agreement that we negotiated."

"I had some issue with the time limits stated but we intend to expedite this project. I don't have any reservations or objections about the deal."

"Fantastic," Chris exclaimed, pouring them a drink from the carafe on the table. "Let's toast to the future success of this collaboration."

Luke took the glass and raised it. "I'll definitely drink to that."

***

Six months later Daniel was still on fire. He had gone through countless interviews and special appearances and was back to training at Frazier's Gym, but he was always having to go to a photo or commercial shoot for a magazine. Sponsors loved him. He was beyond reproach, a college grad, no drug history, no baby-mamas, no criminal record, and no sob story. He was getting endorsements for energy drinks, exercise attire, breakfast cereals, and even detergents.

Daniel's mind drifted while he beat on the speed bag. It was a firm hand on his shoulder that brought him back.

"It's time, champ," Earl Knight said.

"What time is that?" Daniel asked, wondering what other place he wanted him to show his face and put up his fist.

"We're going back to Vegas. It's time to defend your title," he said dramatically.

Daniel stopped punching the bag. This was exactly what he wanted to hear.

Earl continued. "We don't want to lose the momentum you have behind you. The excitement from the last fight is still there and the fans want to see you back in the ring."

"So Whitaker wants a rematch?"

"I have no idea, he probably does but I haven't heard from his camp. The big money wants to see you fight Michael Moore. He's been doing a lot of talking and it seems like promoters have an appetite for what he's been saying."

"Any place and anytime, I'm ready."

"I'll let you know the details after we iron out the financial piece. My guess is that we'll be inside of three months."

"Good looking out," Daniel said as Earl walked away.

Daniel's thoughts went back to the subject he had been thinking about before Earl had come by. It was Wendell. As long as he was broke, there wasn't a better trainer in Philly. Now that he had gotten a few paydays he was out of pocket. It started in Vegas. He was Daniel Clements' trainer so he got women by proxy, except these women didn't want to be wined and dined. They wanted Patron and cocaine. Wendell kept some on hand to make them happy and then one of them encouraged him to partake for his own pleasure. It only took one time and he was hooked on the feeling it gave him.

*****

Wendell strolled into the gym an hour after Daniel had finished his morning run. Daniel was drinking a bottle of orange juice.

"We need to talk," Daniel said, tossing the empty bottle in the trash.

"You need to get up off your ass and train," Wendell said.

A hush came over the room as those in earshot prepared for the fireworks.

"Let's take a walk," Daniel said, not wanting an audience.

They were a block away and Daniel still hadn't said anything.

"Look here, man," Wendell said impatiently. "What are you tripping over? We're wasting time out here in the street?

"You're high, man," Daniel said, finally. "You need to check yourself."

"What are you talking about? I can handle myself."

"You can do whatever you like but I need somebody I can count on in my corner. Earl has scheduled a title defense for me in less than 90 days, I don't have time for the nonsense."

"Come on, Daniel, we got here together."

"I know, that's why I want to keep you on my team, but you're slipping. I can't go down with you. It took too much for me to get here."

"It's not that serious, man."

"It is for me, go home and think about it. You've got some decisions to make."

***

A week later when Daniel arrived at the gym after his run, Wendell was waiting.

"I'm ready to do this, man," Wendell told him.

"I need somebody I can rely on, this ain't no joke," Daniel said, having some doubts.

"You know me, man."

"I don't know anybody. You kept telling me Earl Knight was going to be the one to screw me over and kick me to the curb but you were the one who got out of order."

"Come on, man, you know that's not true," Wendell said in his own defense. "I got caught up. I ain't never seen that many open bottles and open legs in my life. All of sudden it was like I was somebody else. I didn't have a worry in the world except how to spend my money."

"Yeah, I know what you're talking about, but this is business and you forgot about that."

"Hold up for a minute, man. When I first saw you in here you were just a spoiled kid with your mama's milk still on your breath."

Daniel grabbed him in the chest. "Don't go there or I'll kick your sorry black ass, one eye or not. You didn't make me."

"Cut me some slack, man, I'm sorry. I got my head on straight now. I'm ready to go to work."

"Is that right? Why should I believe you?"

"Look here, I started partying and I couldn't stop. I spent half the money and I don't know what happened to the rest. This chance is all I got, man."

Daniel thought about it for a second, he didn't have time to find another trainer he could trust. He and Wendell had worked well together. After all, he had got him this far.

"You got one more time to fuck up and you're gone."

"That's what I'm talking about, Dan my man, we gonna do this."

Daniel trained hard but not like he did for his bout against Lewis Whitaker. How could he, there was always some guest appearance that Earl needed him to do to promote the fight that distracted him. Wendell kept a straight face on the job but when he and Daniel parted ways at the end of the day he wasn't ready to go back to his old life of watching TV alone with only a Schlitz Bull for company. He was his own man and he wouldn't take anything for the thrills he got from the women and the coke.

***

The press conference about Daniel defending his championship title caught Luke by surprise. He had hoped to have a product to present to his son before he fought again but the progress in selecting the fragrance blend had been delayed. He called Rebecca and Matthew to schedule a meeting to escalate the campaign.

Matthew was in the conference room pacing across the floor when Luke got there. His facial expression was a mixture of concern and betrayal.

"Sit down, brother man," Luke said, "Wearing down the carpets won't solve anything."

Matthew took a deep breath and responded. "Clements Cosmetic Company is your baby and I respect that. I also appreciate the confidence that you had in offering me the position of CFO. What I don't understand is how you could make a deal with HLS without consulting with me or at least letting me know about it."

"It was an executive decision and I didn't want to argue about it with you," Luke told him. "It's done, all we need to do now is put a rush on the Daniel campaign."

Rebecca walked in the room with the scents of sample blends wafting around her. Luke breathed it in and thought about Ruthie smelling like cake and cookies.

"Sorry I'm late," she said, taking a seat.

"Are you for real?" Matthew asked Luke, exasperated. "You were so pumped on making this deal that you didn't bother to read it or either you didn't care about the rights you gave to those rip-off artists. Don't you know what's going to happen if we don't have the balloon payment after eighteen months?"

Rebecca still dizzy from sniffing cologne scents listened as they argued back and forth. When she got the gist of the dispute, the risk her Daddy had taken, she wanted to pass out. The only reason she didn't was because it wasn't in her will to lose consciousness. She slammed both hands on the table and they stopped mid-sentence.

"How much, Daddy?" she asked staring at her hands.

Luke spoke matter-of-factly. "Five million dollars, $5.5 million balloon payment 18 months from the date of the loan or they can buy us out or take us public to regain their investment."

"Uncle Matt, how much liquid cash do we have?" Rebecca asked.

"The Kush Kurl revenues are continuing to slip and we haven't done any additional cost cutting measures. Aside from running expenses and payroll for that time frame, we have half of it. The fragrance has already gone over budget and is sucking us dry."

"I don't see any way out of it," Rebecca said, "We have to follow through. It will mean that we have to work around the clock until we get the right scent."

"As I was telling you, Matt, there's no need to go ballistic," Luke interrupted. "The bottle design has been selected. I have a prototype for both of you to see."

Luke opened a box sitting on the table. Inside was an emerald green bottle shaped like the torso of a muscular boxer wearing shorts with his boxing gloves pressed together. Daniel was written across the shorts.

"I don't think we should use Daniel's name on the product," Rebecca commented, thinking about the implications it could bring.

Luke looked at her as if she had lost her mind. "If we don't that defeats the whole purpose."

"Being the spokesperson and face of the cologne will be enough," she clarified. "We could call it "Champ.""

"Absolutely not," Luke protested, "It's going to be called Daniel."

"It's about image, Daddy. If Daniel gets a parking ticket it's going to reflect on the company."

"I'm not worried about that," he said impatiently.

"You don't seem to be worried about anything," Matthew interjected.

"Are we here for any other reason because I've got things to do," Rebecca said, standing up. She knew full well that trying to change her daddy's mind was like talking to a wall.

Luke stood up too and walked her to the door. "Look, sweetheart, I know you're a little sour on this project because it pushed back your hair line but I need you to get this done as quickly as possible."

"No problem, Daddy," she said leaving.

***

Standing outside the entrance to the Caesar's Palace arena on the night of September 14th 1995, Daniel's skin tingled. All the nerve endings in his body were excited. He jumped up and down to release the energy building up inside him. He lived for this moment, the allure, the anticipation, the nerves before the fight, and walking into the stadium as the Heavyweight Champion of the World.

The music of Dr. Dre rapping, *Keep Their Heads Ringin,* started booming and the huge doors at the entrance glided open and security parted the way. Daniel began his trek to his stage, the ring in the center. Lights flashed all around him as if they were all bursting in a pyrotechnic display. The room had a life of its own, like an alien being with stretched hands moving and clawing at him as he made his way through. The sounds of screams, cheers, and loud voices yelling his name blended together like a ferocious growl. Security guards surrounded him and his entourage moved forward. He stepped up to the ring where his challenger Michael Moore was waiting, pulled the ropes wide, and climbed in.

Timmy Lennon welcomed the audience, introduced the judges, and presented both fighters with much fanfare. The referee brought them together to deliver the rules for the match. Moore stared at Daniel with eyes that threatened to demolish him. Daniel stared back and smiled before retreating to his neutral corner.

"Think about how bad you wanted this, Champ," Wendell said, putting in his mouthpiece, "Don't let him take it from you."

"Not tonight," Daniel said, jabbing in to the air.

The bell rang and the fighters rushed to meet. Moore comes out quick and pushes Daniel aggressively with his forearms and lands a combination to his chin. Daniel is stunned and can't get his jab going. Moore nailed him with a left jab. Daniel is confused by the speed of the punches thrown at him. He holds his gloves firmly in place to block a left hook. Moore continues his attack with a flurry of jabs to the body and combinations to his head. Daniel can't find his rhythm. The crowd is shocked and on its feet feeling a knockout is imminent, then the bell signals the end of the round.

"What's your problem, man?" Wendell asked frantically, "You look sleep out there. You're not using your footwork. Where's your head movement? He's using you for target practice."

"He's a southpaw, it threw me," Daniel said between breaths.

"You can't stand there and take his shots, it only takes one."

"I hear you."

"Eye on the prize, baby," Wendell said as the bell summoned the fighters back.

The exchange between the fighters in the second round was even and busy as the action slowed down and Daniel adjusted to the power punches from the left hand. On the offense the champ lands a straight right between Moore's gloves. The challenger clinches him and the referee steps in to separate them. Daniel comes back in with a combination of shots to the body. Moore lands a left hook and Daniel counters with an uppercut through the middle of his gloves. Daniel moves in banging with his right hand. Moore's nose is dripping red and a welt is growing over his left eye. He tastes his blood and wraps Daniel up until the bell rings.

"That's right, Champ," Wendell said, pouring water into his mouth while he sat on his stool, "Weave in, land the shot and weave out."

Daniel stood up, "I got him."

Moore lurches forward with a left cross wanting to hurt Daniel but it was short and grazes him. Daniel hits him with a double jab to the head. On the defensive, Moore tries to land a left hook that is blocked. Daniel moves to the inside working the challenger's body. When Daniel feels Moore's belly go soft behind his punches he backs up and throws a spectacular overhand right. Moore stumbles and then falls to one knee before his back hits the canvas.

The crowd roars and counts with the referee even though no one believes Michael Moore is going to get up. Daniel goes to his corner and Wendell pulls off his gloves. Doctors come into the ring to attend to the challenger while Daniel smiles and waves to his fans. The ring announcer re-enters the ring.

"Ladies and gentleman, we have at the time of two minutes and 36 seconds in to the third round a knock-out victory by and still Heavyweight Champion of the World, Daniel Clements."

The referee lifts Daniels arm high as the winner and the room erupts in applause. Larry Murchant trailed by a camera edges in for a short interview.

"Daniel, you have successfully defended you title tonight, to what do you attribute the win?"

"Sheer determination, I had to win."

"What is your motivation to go through the pain of boxing and prize-fighting? You come from an affluent family."

"I'm a champion. I fight for the glory."

The crowd answered that with chants of his name, "Daniel, Daniel, Daniel.

***

Luke had watched the fight alone in silence counting the number of blows to the head that the challenger had landed. He was comforted by the fact that limited damage had been done. Most of the family, including Rebecca, had flown out to Las Vegas to be there for Daniel in person.

"Once I launch the cologne line, the whole world will be calling for Daniel," Luke murmured to himself, "He'll see what I've done for him and he'll come home."

Chapter Seventeen

"Congratulations again, Clements, you defended your title," Earl Knight said over lunch at Delmonico's a few days after the fight. "Now it's legit, you're a bad dude."

"Thanks, man," Daniel said, giving him a soul brother handshake. "I couldn't have gotten here without you."

Earl reached into his suitcoat pocket and pull out several checks he had for Daniel.

"This is what makes it all worthwhile," Earl said, handing them over with a smile.

Daniel looked at the checks satisfied. "It's been a pleasure doing business with you. With the word on the streets about you I thought I was going to have problems regarding my money."

"Don't believe half of what you hear, young brother, truth be told we'll all crack a nut if we find one."

Daniel laughed, "You're probably right.

"Out next move is to take this show on the road, champ," Earl said, being serious, "It's time to put some icing on the cake, baby."

"I wouldn't mind taking a rest right about now," Daniel said.

"Who's talking about rest? Oh no, you are the Heavyweight Champion of the World and it's time for you to go out into the world and let the people bask in your greatness."

"How much is this going to cost me?" Daniel smirked.

"This is the opportunity to make real money, my man. Appearances and exhibitions. You don't get to this level and not take advantage of it. Folks pay top dollar to see the champ. Heads of State and royalty want to sit at your table."

Daniel nodded his head in agreement. "I'm ready, let's do it."

***

Earl Knight and his entourage of security accompanied Daniel minus Wendell on a tour that spanned the globe. They made stops in Japan, Russia, and even Brazil. Daniel was in a whirlwind and loving every minute of it. He couldn't keep track of all the women of every color, size, and shape, taking turns in his bed as they traveled from hotel to hotel. When they got back to the states Daniel did cameos in two Hollywood movies and some modeling for Hugo Boss menswear before returning back to Philly.

On his first day back in the city while he was on his morning run he was accosted by fans and couldn't make it one mile from his apartment. He called Rebecca as soon as he got home.

"What's up, baby sis," he said cheerfully when she answered.

"It's about time, Dan, I was wondering how long it was going to take for you to call, even E.T. knew to phone home."

"You don't know how crazy my schedule has been, but I'm going to be around for a few months. I'm getting out of shape."

"Living too much of that good life will do that to you."

"You wouldn't believe it. I can't even go out of my own house without people coming up to me for autographs and wanting to take pictures."

"You did know that was going to be a part of it," Rebecca said with a dash of sarcasm.

"I guess you don't realize how much until it happens. I might need to buy me a place further out of the city where I can get some privacy."

"I hope you haven't gone crazy like these other brothers who make some bread and buy a huge mansion out in the middle of nowhere to live in by yourself."

"Not yet, I'm not going out like Evander Holyfield, but we'll see."

"Anyway, I'm glad you finally called because we need to talk, I mean seriously. Dad has invested a ton of money in a cologne line for you and I need you on board for promotion."

"Yeah, no problem, we can do that. Let me take you out on the town tonight."

"Now that's what I want to hear. Get out of those strip joints and drop some of that cold cash on your sister for a change."

"You know you're wrong," he sniggered.

"Uh-uh, I know you."

***

Daniel picked Rebecca up in a brand new black Aston Martin.

"Now this is rich," she said, easing down onto the smooth tan leather seat.

"What's the sense in making it if you can't spend it," Daniel remarked.

"I never thought I would say this but you're sounding like Daddy."

Daniel shook his head. "Now that's scary."

When they walked into the Sky-High Lounge they got the full VIP treatment.

"I guess being famous has its advantages," Rebecca said.

"So what did you want to talk about that is so serious?" Daniel asked after their hostess brought them their drinks.

"You know Daddy is really hyped up on this cologne line for you with your name on it."

"Yeah, Uncle Matt told me about it when you all were in Vegas for the fight."

"Well, he sunk most of the company's capital in it and he's borrowed more than that. He's banking on this campaign being super successful. Bottom line, if we don't break even we lose the company to our lenders."

"What was he thinking about to take this kind of risk?" Daniel asked, getting angry and frustrated at the same time.

"He was thinking about you. He did it for you. He's hoping you'll be impressed enough to come home and be a part of the company."

"I don't care nothing about a cologne with my name on it. It's ridiculous, I don't need that."

"Look, I wouldn't ask if I wasn't up against a wall but I need you to do some print work and some commercial work to promote it. After all, you're Daniel."

"This is bullshit, its blackmail. He's just trying to tie me to the company."

"It is what it is, brother. Nevertheless, I need your help."

"I'm living my dream right now, doing what I want to do. I already spent four years in college paying my dues to the family."

"I know that but I need your help. The company is my dream now."

Daniel paused for a moment and then sighed. "Damn. I'll do it for you, Becca, not for him."

***

Clements Cosmetic Company was surviving on borrowed time but Luke felt better than he had in years. Daniel had been in and out of the building for almost three weeks. He had done two photo shoots for advertising to use in magazines, bus stops and shelters, and billboards, and they were working on a commercial shoot for television. The costs were building up but he was sure that his son was finally making an emotional connection to the company. Luke went by the set when they were finished shooting to have a talk with him.

Daniel was changing back into his street clothes.

"It's been good to have you around here, son," Luke said, "We haven't spent much time together for a while now. I missed you."

"That's your choice, Dad," Daniel said coolly, buttoning up his shirt.

"Not really, I've been preoccupied with the business here."

Daniel put on his shoes. "It's all good, Dad, I've been pretty busy myself."

"You know your momma and I built this company not just for ourselves but to have something to pass down," Luke said, watching him. "We didn't want you to have to start out with nothing like we did."

Daniel stood up. "I appreciate all of that and it has helped me get where I am now."

"This campaign is going to make you a superstar," Luke said.

"I'm already a superstar, Dad," Daniel said, looking him in the eyes.

"Okay, you're a big man for now, but what you have here in this company is something that can last a lifetime. Boxing, even for the best is a temporary thing."

"I'm happy, Dad. I don't have any complaints no matter how long it lasts. Everywhere I go, anywhere on this earth, I get the best table, the best food, the best liquor, and the best ladies. All of it because I am the Heavyweight Champion of the World."

"One thing you need to know, son, is that you don't have to let another man bash your head in to eat, drink, or get some pussy from these money grubbing gold-diggers. For that, you just pull out your wallet."

Daniel couldn't do anything but shake his head and walk away.

***

Now that Daniel had paid some more dues to his father on the cologne campaign he need to get his party on and celebrate that it was over. Back at his house he cleaned up and changed clothes. He chose to wear his green leather suit he had made in the same color as his boxing trunks and robe. He splashed on some of the cologne with his name on it and checked himself out in the mirror. He didn't care what his dad said; there was no doubt about it. He was the man.

He drove by Wendell's place to pick him up to ride with him.

"Where are we headed?" Wendell asked eagerly, closing the car door.

"Bahama Bay, baby."

"Sounds like a plan to me."

Daniel parked his own car, he seldom used the valet. When he was ready to go he was ready to go, he didn't have time to wait for his car.

The music was pumping and bouncing off the walls inside the club. It seemed like everybody there froze for a second when Daniel walked in. Then the DJ put on an old school rap, Whodini's *Five Minutes of Funk*, and the room filled with a current of energy as the bass vibrated from the floor up to the ceiling, the whole vibe changed. A bold and sexy female in a body-hugging yellow dress grabbed Daniel's hand and led him to the center of the dance floor.

Daniel stretched his arms wide and rocked from side to side like he owned the place. The crowd backed up to give him some space. He took off his jacket, handed it to Wendell, and gyrated his hips to the funky beat. All the ladies hollered.

When the song ended a hostess led him to the VIP area where he ordered champagne.

"That's how you enter a room, player," Wendell said, holding up his glass in admiration.

Daniel lifted his glass too before he downed it. "It's one of the perks of the job."

"Here comes another perk," Wendell said as the girl from the dance floor approached them.

She struck a pose beside their booth and said, "May I join you?"

Daniel looked her up and down with approval. Wendell gave her a toothy grin.

"Certainly, be my guest," Daniel said, "Would you like a drink?"

"Yes, that would be nice," she said taking a seat.

"You probably already know this but I'm Daniel and this is my trainer, Wendell."

"Yes I know who you are, it's nice to meet you, and you also Wendell."

"May I ask your name?" Daniel asked seductively.

"It's Desiree."

Daniel took her hand in his. "It's my pleasure, Desiree."

"I was really surprised when you walked in here tonight. I've watched your fights on pay-per-view and I know I'm your number one fan."

"After seeing you move on the floor, I'm becoming a fan of yours," Daniel told her.

Desiree smiled and slid close enough to Daniel for their thighs to touch.

"I know you just got here but I really like the atmosphere at the Zanzibar. It's more laidback and romantic if you're interested."

"Hell yeah, I'm interested," Daniel whispered in her ear."

Right at that moment a burly wrestler looking guy rushed up to their table so swollen up with rage that his chest was heaving. The bouncer from the entrance was standing beside him. Desiree slowly eased away from Daniel.

The big guy with the problem leaned on the table and shouted, "No nigga, you not gonna come in my club and disrespect me. I don't care who you are."

Daniel stared at him totally confused. "What are you talking about?"

"That's my woman you're all hugged up with," he said, raising up a fist.

"Your lady stepped to me, man. Your beef is with her not me. I didn't come here to cause any trouble. I came out to have a few drinks and enjoy myself."

Wendell reached in his jacket pocket for the piece he started carrying after the first fight in Vegas. Desiree got up and took the guy's hand.

"This ain't the place for you, champ," the guy said, calming down.

"Sorry to hear that," Daniel said, standing up and walking out.

Wendell hurried out behind him still holding his hand on the gun in his pocket.

When they were in the car Wendell said, "We can't party with civilians out here, man, they not used to celebs, that's only in Vegas."

"In that case we need to catch a plane out of here," Daniel said, burning rubber on his way out of the parking lot.

"You ain't said nothing but a word," Wendell said, slapping him five from the side.

***

Daniel had a ball flying from coast to coast partying and making it rain, and it wasn't liquid sunshine. Daniel was throwing money around like it was confetti. Since his last fight he had purchased an estate out in Villanova, two cars that included a Bentley, invested heavily in the stock market and opened a club in Center City. He woke up one morning and discovered he was strapped for cash. He needed another payday. He called and set up a meeting with Earl Knight.

"How's it going, my man?" Earl asked when Daniel walked in. "Are you enjoying yourself?"

"It's cool," Daniel answered, taking a seat.

Earl crossed his legs, lit his cigar, and took a drag.

"So to what do I owe the pleasure of this visit?"

"I want another fight, man."

"Whoa, slow down, champ. You have six months before we even have to think about another title defense. Savor this time."

"I need the money. All my funds are tied up."

"I can float you a loan, no problem."

"I'm not going to ruin our business relationship by borrowing money. I need to go to work."

"Your timing is all off. Since Mike Tyson got released, he's on a tear to regain the title. Once he becomes the number one contender you can make enough money, win or lose, where you won't ever have to take another punch. He'll be where we want him to be in six months."

"I can't wait that long, I got bills to pay. I have Wendell, sparring partners, and a staff to pay at my gym."

"If you won't take money from me, why don't you ask your father?"

"It's complicated and I'd rather not," Daniel said, getting irritated. "I'm telling you I just need a fight."

Earl sighed, discontented. "Give me a few days. I'll see what I can do?"

***

A week later, Earl drove by the gym while Daniel and Wendell were training. One of his security guys came in and asked them to come out to the car where they could talk privately. Daniel put on his robe and Wendell followed him out to the long black limo parked on the curb.

"What's the word?" Daniel asked, leaning forward on the seat.

Earl leaned forward towards him to talk. "If you really want to do this, man, I can get you a fight with the Russian that lost to Whitaker. It's not a gigantic draw in the states but if we schedule the fight in Germany where they want it, we can pull a decent payday."

"Let's do it," Daniel said, pleased.

"How soon are we talking about?" Wendell asked with some misgivings.

"Inside three months," Earl replied.

"Get the contracts together and call me," Daniel said, getting out of the car.

"What's going on, man?" Wendell asked, feeling uneasy. "You know how we been living, I don't know about taking a match this soon, we need more time than that to get you ready to fight."

"I need to make some money, I'm tapped out. We can do this, man, no problem. Don't start freaking out on me. We did it before, we'll do it again."

"Where we started is different now. You've gained some pounds and it ain't muscle. You barely have enough time to get the liquor and that extra stuff out of your system."

"Starting today, I'm back to the drill and a healthy diet. No drinking, no women, and no extra stuff until after the fight."

Wendell wanted to argue but his pockets were getting thin too.

"All right, whatever you say, you're the boss."

***

Luke, Matthew, and Rebecca were tense after Chris Crowley summoned Luke to HLS for a management conference.

"I don't know why you both have insisted on coming to this meeting, I can handle any issues with HLS without needing a babysitter," Luke said grumpily on the elevator.

"As the CFO of the company I should have been in attendance on all the meetings here," Matthew reminded him, "I don't trust Chris Crowley any more than a rattlesnake. If we get caught with our pants down he's going to bite us in the ass."

"We all need to be here, Daddy," Rebecca added, "As far as the fragrance line is concerned you have lost your objectivity. It wasn't the beginning of the company and I hope that it won't be the end of it."

When they reached the floor they could see Chris's executive assistant, Alice, waiting to greet them. She led them to their company conference room where Chris and two other directors were already seated. The table was full of refreshments and fresh coffee.

"Good morning, welcome," Chris said graciously, nodding to Rebecca and Matthew. "Help yourselves to the spread we have here."

Luke sat down and made introductions. "This is Matthew Clements, my CFO, and Rebecca Clements, my COO."

"It's a pleasure to meet you both," Chris said, "I'm Chris Crowley and these are my associates Jeff Scales and Roger Mayfield. We wanted to get together and make sure we're all on the same page."

"I think that's an excellent idea," Matthew said, looking at them suspiciously. He thought they looked like the Three Stooges wearing thousand dollar suits.

"The project has taken more time to get to market than we anticipated," Luke offered, "However, I'm sure we'll have a very profitable debut."

"There are some important new developments on this venture that we need to evaluate," Chris informed them with a glance towards his associates.

Luke frowned. "I'm a little puzzled as to what you feel we need to discuss."

"Well, Earl Knight Promotions has announced another title defense for Daniel that will take place in Germany around the projected date of the fragrance line hitting the shelves."

'I don't see any disadvantage with that," Luke said, "The extra publicity should be a bonus for marketing."

Chris cleared his throat. "We've kicked the issue around among ourselves here and we have some hesitations about releasing the product with him not being present at the launch party. We don't want to lose our thunder in the promotion for the fight."

"I think it would help drive sales," Rebecca interjected.

"Possibly, but as the major investor in this project we think the timing is significant. The focus should be on the cologne and for the next two months, more or less, it will be on the boxing match."

"That's something we'll take under consideration," Luke said, wanting to end the meeting.

Jeff Scales shifted in his chair and spoke, "I don't think we need to remind you that HLS has executive approval on the fragrance line until the loan is completely satisfied."

The room filled up with tension, it was like a lethal gas and they were all holding their breath lest they be consumed. If Luke and Matthew could have flashed back to their days on Franklin Street it would have been time for the brothers to kick some ass.

"That won't be necessary," Rebecca said, rising out of her chair. "We'll confer on the release date and get back with you."

Luke and Matthew followed her out and they didn't utter a word until they were outside the building waiting for their driver.

"You know what this is about don't you," Matthew said to Luke.

Luke was still too outdone to speak.

Rebecca answered for him, "If they postpone the release we'll be closing in on the due date of the balloon payment. If we miss it, they have control."

"This was nothing but a tactic to get the company away from you, brother."

"Why don't you both shut the fuck up," Luke yelled, "All this second guessing is getting me out of myself."

***

Luke was more angry and disappointed with himself than he was with anybody else. He had let his emotions get the better of him and it caused him to make a terrible business decision. When they got back to the company he stormed into his office and slammed the door to think.

"Come with me," Matthew said to Rebecca in the corridor.

"So how do you think we ought to handle this?" Rebecca asked him once they reached the privacy of his office.

"Your daddy made a deal with some devils and he had all the power to do so. The only way out of it is to pay back the loan."

"We only have two options at this point," Rebecca said, discouraged. "We can raise the money or we can borrow from Peter to pay Paul."

Matthew shook his head. "There's no way in hell we can get another loan right now, we're leveraged up to our eyeballs between this campaign and the hair line you were working on. The revenues are barely covering payroll and keeping the electricity on."

"Then our only choice is to raise the money."

"We're talking millions of dollars, baby girl. You might have better luck playing the lottery."

The company had taken some hard hits and they were in trouble but Rebecca wasn't about to throw in the towel at this point.

"I know you haven't forgotten the teaching of your dear departed religious leader," she told her uncle.

Matthew lifted his eyebrows in a questioning look.

"By any means necessary, Uncle Matt," she said, leaving his office.

Rebecca never made it to her office. There wasn't any money lying around in there. The only person she knew that could help them was Daniel. She knew her daddy would never ask him so she would have to do it herself. She got in her car and drove out to his estate where he was training in his private gym.

Daniel was in the boxing ring working out with his sparring partner when she walked in. She sat down on a bench near the wall to watch until they were finished. Daniel took out his mouthpiece and smiled when he saw her. He climbed out of the ring and put on a terry cloth robe to soak up his sweat.

"Hey, girl, what's going on?" he said, giving her a loose hug.

"Why is it I have to drive damn near an hour out here just to see my big brother?" she said, half-teasing.

"Give me a break, all you have to do is call and I'll be there."

"Well I'm calling you in person. Can we step outside and talk?"

"You here in the middle of the day, it must be serious," he said leading her outside.

"I guess I don't have to pull any punches with you."

"No, go ahead and lay it on me."

"Daddy went way overboard on this fragrance collection for you. He borrowed a ton of money and we have to pay it back in less than six months or we could lose the company."

Daniel closed his eyes and kicked an imaginary can before he asked. "Why in the hell would he do something that out of order?"

"You know why, but I don't have time to deal with that. I need to make sure that we can make that payment on the first of the year. That's why I'm here. I need to borrow money."

"How much did he borrow?"

"Five million, the payment is $5.5 million."

"I don't know what to tell you, baby sis. I don't have it."

"Excuse me, I know I'm out of line, but didn't you make $25 million on the last fight."

"Uncle Sam took half of it, then I had expenses to cover. I got the house, built this gym, a couple of cars, and then made some investments. The next thing I knew I was tapped out. That's the only reason I'm flying overseas for a fight."

Rebecca was totally flustered. "That doesn't make any sense to me, Daniel. Nothing around me is making sense right now."

"I'm really sorry. I would help you if I could."

"Let me ask you this," Rebecca said, mulling it over for a second, "Will the amount of your purse just bring your head above the water or will you be flush again?"

"I hope to be good but I may not be able to swing $5 million, one or two maybe."

"Don't stress it, you got enough to think about. I'll work it out."

"So, how is Dad taking it?"

"I don't know. His reality and the rest of ours are in two different worlds."

They walked back to the gym and Rebecca stopped outside of the door.

"Why don't you hang around," Daniel asked, feeling powerless, "We could get something to eat?"

"Another time," Rebecca said, "I've got another stop to make.

Chapter Eighteen

Earl Knight had called Daniel and asked him to meet him at Delmonico's, he needed to talk with him about the scheduled match. When Daniel got to the restaurant, Carl, the maître d, led him to Earl's table. He passed the ever-ready security guys drinking at the bar on the way.

"You're looking good, Champ," Earl said without his usual grin. "Sit down, make yourself comfortable, there's plenty to eat."

"Thanks, man," Daniel said, sitting across from him. "I hope there isn't a problem with the match."

"Yes and no. Some significant circumstances have changed in the last few weeks and we need to decide if we want to change with them."

"Okay, so what are we talking about?"

"First let me explain a few things. This fight game is about money, but even more than that it's about timing. Who you fight and when you fight determines the prize. The fighter is in this game to get the biggest purse possible whenever he gets into the ring."

"I know all that. What's the point?" Daniel asked, wanting to skip the lecture.

"The point is Mike Tyson just got stripped of his WBC title. His camp is ripe for making a mega deal where we can all make a killing, except we have a problem."

Daniel raised his hands, baffled. "What's the problem?"

"This match we made in Germany is the problem. If we can get out of the deal we might be able to schedule a match between you and Tyson early in the year."

"That won't work for me, man. I got obligations that won't hold."

"That's too bad," Earl groaned, "Even if you knock this Russian out 30 seconds into the first round we're going to be taking a huge loss."

"What can I say?" Daniel said regretfully.

"Nothing, man, that's life," Earl said, tossing his napkin in his plate. "Have some food. We'll get our shot with Tyson later."

Daniel ate just enough to be polite and then he left. He drove by Wendell's house and picked him up to go out for a drink in a bar down on South Street.

"Man, I thought it was no more alcohol for us until after the fight," Wendell said, cradling his second gin and juice.

"This is just a moment of release, man, since I can't kick my own ass."

"What are you talking about?"

"I just blew off a chance to fight Mike Tyson."

"Cut the crap, you're not that stupid."

"Evidently I am," Daniel said, staring into the brown liquor.

"I knew that Earl was gonna screw you when he got the chance."

"It's not his fault. It's all mine. I blew my finances to bits and it's rushing me back too soon. If I could wait, I would make three times the payday."

"Well, I'll be damned," Wendell said, "You just hit me below the belt."

"I don't even want to think about it. I got to let it go."

"Man, if I wasn't on my second round of gin I would kick your ass myself."

"I hear you talking that shit," Daniel chuckled. "You couldn't half see before the first round."

"I guess it's like they say, you win some and you lose some."

Daniel raised his glass. "I'll drink to that."

***

Rebecca hadn't been back at the family house in some months but it looked the same. She pulled her car up into the driveway so she could dodge the sprinklers that were watering the fresh cut grass in the lawn. She wondered if her Daddy had company because there was a car she didn't recognize parked on the curb. "I hope it's not the secret woman he thinks he's hiding from everybody," she said as she opened the door and when in. She heard voices and followed them into his home office.

The voices were her Daddy talking to someone on speaker phone. He cut the call short when he saw her come in.

"Hey sweetheart, I didn't expect to see you again today."

"Me either but I really need to talk to you."

"Sure, let's go in the kitchen and I'll make you something to eat. We might as well be comfortable while you chew me out."

"I didn't come here to give you a hard time. I came to try to figure out a solution."

"Okay, what's on your mind?" Luke asked, making her a sandwich.

"I think we should do some liquidating and some refinancing."

"There's nothing I can do with a lean on the company assets, sweetie."

"I'm not talking about the company. I'm talking about this house, my condo, the old house, and the expensive cars. If we can raise half the payment I think Daniel can come through with the rest after his fight."

Luke took a breath to calm himself before he spoke. "Rebecca, I'm sure you mean well but there is no way I'm going to sell your mother's house or the first house we bought together. Besides, what am I supposed to do, throw you grandparents out in the street."

"Right now we have to regroup, Daddy. It's only for a few months and we should be able to get things back on track."

"I don't want you to be worrying yourself about all this business stuff. I'll handle it. I promise. I'll get the money. What I want you to do is take some time off and enjoy yourself. It's summertime. Go up to Wildwood for a few days."

Rebecca refused to dignify any of that foolishness with a response. There was no way she could go off to the beach and pretend she didn't have a care in the world.

"I'm exhausted, it's been a long day," she said, slouching down in her chair.

"You're welcome to stay here tonight. Your room is just like you left it."

"That's all right, I've got to feed my cat."

"Okay, baby, I'll wrap up your sandwich and you can take it with you."

Driving back to the city, Rebecca drifted back over the last nine years and began to seriously wonder if her father had gone through a breakdown after her momma died. He hadn't been the same since. She loved and respected him and she knew he was a shrewd man in business, yet for the last year or more he had been out to lunch. An hour later she turned the key in the door of her condo. She didn't have a solution but she wasn't about to give up.

***

The next month raced by with no further discussions between Luke, Matthew, or Rebecca about what they were going to do about the balloon payment. HLS was blocking them from releasing the fragrance unless Daniel would be present for the debut promotion party. So with his upcoming bout in Germany the "Daniel" launch would have to wait. At any rate, it wouldn't make much difference for the company. Even if Daniel cancelled the fight and put on the show they wanted for the media, they didn't have enough inventory to make the money they owed HLS if every bottle of cologne was sold.

Matthew, tired of playing the game of denial, trudged down the hall to Luke's office to see if he was still playing crazy. When he got there Mark was kicked back in a chair smoking a cigarette. It didn't take a brain surgeon to figure out what was up.

Matthew was about to hit the ceiling. "What is he doing here?" he asked Luke.

"Chill out, Matt," Mark said, blowing out a stream of smoke, "I'm here to help our little brother with a cash flow problem."

"Naw, man," Matthew argued, looking at Luke. "Things aren't that desperate yet?"

"So you think you too good to accept help from your brother," Mark asked, offended.

"Come on, Mark," Matthew said, "I know where you coming from and we're not going there with you."

Mark stood up and yelled at him, "We come from the same place, my brother, the same seed and the same womb, you not no different from me. Luke ain't either."

"This is a place of business, lower your volume, you're not out in the streets," Luke said, getting between them.

The uproar had traveled down the hall and Rebecca was the only one in the office who had the nerve to go in and see what was going on.

"Daddy, Uncle Mark, Uncle Matt, you all need to hold it down. Sherry was about to call the police. What's going on?"

"It's nothing for you to worry about, baby girl," Luke insisted, "I called your Uncle Mark here to talk some business. He and your Uncle Matt had a misunderstanding."

"No, Becca," Matthew said, staring Luke down. "Your Daddy must have truly lost it if he's willing to go in the gutter. We don't need dirty money."

"Is there such a thing as clean money?" Mark asked with sarcasm.

"No disrespect, Uncle Mark," Rebecca said calmly, "We already have white collar crooks trying to roll over us. The last thing we need is some hardcore hoodlums trying to take us out."

Mark moved towards the door. "It's cool, niecy, but don't forget I'm part of this family too."

When he left, Luke and Matthew resumed their argument yelling at each other in hushed tones. Rebecca didn't make any effort to stop them. A light had come on in her head and her thoughts were racing toward it. If things worked out like she had a feeling they would she would at least make enough money to buy Clements Cosmetic Company some time.

***

Daniel, Wendell, their crew of sparring partners, his massage therapist, and nutritionist had just landed in Germany on September 7th; the fight was scheduled for September 21st at the Olympiahalle in Munich. They were met by a guide at the airport and driven by a custom van to a rented villa where they would stay for the next two weeks.

"This place is really nice," his nutritionist said after checking out the place. "The kitchen is fully equipped."

Her name was Faith Brooks and she was the only female in the crew. She worked with a number of high-profile athletes but she also owned a popular café down on South Street. She was young and pretty, medium brown-skinned, brown eyed, with long hair she always twisted up in a bun. None of the guys bothered her because they thought she was Daniel's lady but their relationship was purely professional. She had been highly recommended to him by Bernard Hopkins for controlling his weight while training.

"It's got everything, man," Wendell added happily, "An indoor heated pool, a sauna, a gym, and a high fence and shrubs for privacy."

"It should be all of that, Daniel said, unenthused, "It's costing me a grip."

"You don't need to be worried about anything but this fight from now on," Wendell said, "It's good we came here early to clear your head. You've been too distracted lately."

"You're right, man," Daniel said, slapping him a low five, "This is boot camp time. I'm about to battle it out with that overgrown Russian in two weeks."

It didn't take long before Daniel's camp had established a routine and he was looking sharper than he had since his last fight. He had to do a number of scheduled public appearances with his challenger to hype the fight when Earl's plane arrived, but when they were completed he went right back to his training routine afterwards.

Faith made all of his meals but she let the other guys know that she wasn't the house cook and they had to fend for themselves. On the night before the fight she sat down to chat with Daniel while he ate. Cooking for him and designing his meals, they had spent quite a lot of time together over the last two months. She liked that his ego wasn't too big for them to fit in a room together. He was easygoing and he listened. They had talked casually but she really didn't know that much about him, they hadn't had a real conversation.

Faith noticed that he took his time eating his food instead of wolfing it down like somebody was about to snatch his plate.

"So, how did you start boxing?" she asked curiously, "You don't seem like the typical kind of boxer I've worked with?"

"Is that right?" he said with a small grin. "What do I seem like to you?"

"Granted, you're strong and built like an athlete, but you don't have the disposition of a fighter. You're not mean enough."

Daniel put down his fork to explain. "It's not about being a killer. It's about out-training and outsmarting your opponent. Have you ever played chess?"

"I have but it's not my board game of choice."

"Well, it's not much different than that. The object is to be the best, have the best skills and the best strategy. Boxing is a sport you know."

"It's also the most brutal, it's not a game of chess."

"I can't argue with that," he said, giving in. "So in your opinion, what should I have done?"

"Let's see," she said, looking him over with a discerning eye, "You're not quite tall enough for basketball and too muscular for track and field. I would say maybe a wide receiver."

"Football," he laughed, "Are you saying that doesn't require the disposition of a fighter?"

"Touché," she giggled, "You got me on that one."

"Anyway, I'm not a team player. I go more for the individual sport."

"Okay," she said, still smiling. "Then why don't you take all that power in your right hand and swing a tennis racket or throw a bowling ball?"

"My dad would love you. He's been asking me the same questions for years."

"When we get back home why don't you let me meet him?" Faith asked, dropping Daniel another hint that she was interested in getting to know him on a more personal level. "It seems like he and I might have something in common."

He looked back at her and considered it for only a second. She was different from the dolled up women in short skirts and high heels that he always went for, most of the time she wore warm-up suits and sneakers. Yet she had everything any man could want, she was attractive, even-tempered, independent, and she could cook her ass off. Except Faith was the kind of lady you marry and settle down with. He stayed away from her type. With them came the obligations that would get in the way of his boxing career. Even more than that, he was almost sure he never wanted to love anyone that deeply. The hurt his dad carried after his momma died looked like it was too much to bear. He'd rather not go through it.

"We haven't been that close lately," he told her, thinking about the wall between them that stretched higher and wider every day.

Faith let it go. She wasn't going to push the idea if he wasn't interested.

"Sorry to hear that," she said, sliding her chair back from the table. "Don't stay up too late. Your body will need all the rest it can get."

"I'll probably get a massage first. I'm feeling too wound-up to sleep."

"That should help," she said, leaving the room.

Daniel watched her walk away and then shook his head. He wasn't crazy enough to think he could have it all. He had made his choice.

Chapter Nineteen

Rebecca went back into the bathroom and threw up. That was the second time today. Her insides were twisted so tight she couldn't keep anything down. She rinsed her mouth and went back out to the den where the family was waiting for the fight to begin.

"You all right, baby?" Grandma Gloria asked, sounding concerned.

Rebecca flashed her a fake smile and said, "Yeah, I'm fine. I must have eaten something that isn't agreeing with me."

"My belly is giving me the willies too," Grandpa John said. "Every time I watch Daniel fight my nerves get bad."

Gloria chuckled. "It's nothing but that beer you drank on an empty stomach, old man. You can't carry on like you used to."

"Where's Luke?" Matthew asked coming in the door.

"He's not coming," Mary said, "Martha went over there to spend some time with him."

"Come over here, niecey, and sit by your uncle," Mark said to Rebecca, patting the spot on the sofa next to him. "I hate to see you feeling bad."

Rebecca sat beside him and grabbed his hand and squeezed it to stop hers from shaking.

"That was a bold move," he whispered so only she could hear. "If I was in your shoes I'd be sick as a dog too."

"Nothing I can do about it now but wait," she whispered back.

***

Wendell wrapped and taped Daniel's hands without talking in the dressing room. It was only a few minutes away from show time. The first undercard bout was already done and the next one was only going six rounds.

All of sudden Wendell blurted, "Call it off, man."

"Are you high?" Daniel asked, confused.

"I don't think we're ready," he said in a panic.

"I thought I was the one who was supposed to get nervous."

"I don't have a good vibe, man."

"This ain't the time, man," Daniel said, shaking his head.

"We can say you're sick or you pulled a muscle, anything."

"Why are you tripping out on me?"

"Man, I been slipping," Wendell said, wishing he could get a hit. "We haven't even watched the tapes of this guy."

"What you need to do is pull yourself together, get in my corner, and do your job."

"You're right, Dan. I guess I got more jitters than you."

Wendell's attitude was ruining Daniel's concentration. A lack of confidence wasn't the mindset he expected from his own trainer.

"I don't need weakness around me," he told Wendell. "If you can't handle it, man, let me know. Glenn is here as a back up."

Wendell hated to hear it but he had been weak. That lighter than air powder he sniffed up his nose was stronger and more relentless than any fighter he had ever faced. It had him wrapped up for right now but he would beat it. He wasn't about to lose his meal ticket.

Wendell picked up the championship belt and put it over his shoulder and said, "We got to the top together and we gonna stay on top together."

A knock on the door brought them back to the business at hand. Wendell opened it and there was an attendant with security behind him. He was speaking in German but they knew what he was saying. It was time to take that long walk into the stadium. Daniel's small entourage was outside behind them to escort him into the ring. He could feel the pulsation of the music under his feet as he walked to the entrance.

The crew stepped inside the stadium. All the lights were cut off. The colossal arena was almost black except for the bright lights of the boxing ring that seemed like a half mile away. Then a display of lights began flashing in long beams shooting to the ceiling making it feel more like the Super Bowl half-time show than a boxing match. The blaring music could barely be heard over the cheers and roars from the crowd as Daniel led his group towards the center. Whistles from the spectators rang in his ears as he entered the ring.

Daniel looked around at the monochromatic mass of people that was so different from the mixed crowds that he saw in the states. The ring announcer spoke first in German stating the rules of the bout and it was repeated in English by a familiar voice, Michael Buffer. The three judges were from the United States, South Africa, and Hungary. The referee was Carl Edwards from the United States.

"Keep your distance," was the last thing Wendell whispered in Daniels ear before the bell rang signaling the first round.

***

"It's starting," Rebecca heard Grandma Gloria yell out to her. She was back in the bathroom dry heaving into the toilet with nothing left in her system to come up. Feeling like she was sick with fever, she rinsed her face in cold water to quell the heat that seemed to rise from the floor around her. Rebecca stared in the mirror searching for the courage to go out there and watch the fight but it wasn't there. There was just too much riding on it.

"Uh-oh, that Russian almost got him with that right over his head," Grandpa John said, scooting to the edge of his easy-chair.

Gloria grabbed her chest. "Good thing he ducked.

Daniel countered back and loaded so much power in his right hook that he lost his balance.

"That wasn't a knockdown," Matthew said nervously.

"That's right the referee said no too," Mark added.

Daniel starts to move inside to attack but he can't find his target. Every time he goes in the Russian hits him with a right jab, then a combination, and he's back on the defensive. The two fighters trade shots and neither is hurt for the first three rounds. When Daniel gets back in his corner the family can hear Wendell talking to Daniel through the cameraman's microphone.

"You're fighting flat-footed, man. Where are your legs?"

"I'm good," they heard Daniel answer.

"You're taking too many shots, reach in with your right. I want to see fast feet and hands."

Daniel stands up just as the bell rang.

The next four rounds thrill the crowd as Daniel dominated two and then the Russian came back dominating the next two.

"I don't see why Daniel can't put this big muthafucka down," John fussed, squirming in his seat. "He should have finished him in the fifth round.

"Watch your mouth," Gloria said anxiously.

They could hear his trainer saying, "Don't let him get you on the ropes. Your jab is missing."

Still in the bathroom, Rebecca lowered the top of the toilet seat and sat down. Her stomach felt like it was tied in knots being pulled in opposite directions.

"Daniel ain't never gone past the eighth round," Mark said as the ninth round started.

"It's still his fight," Matthew reminded him.

"Yeah but he's not landing any big shots," John chimed in.

"Neither is the other guy," Matthew added, "He doesn't have any snap in his punches."

The crowd grew frustrated with the lack of action in the next two rounds but in the eleventh they began to groan and boo both of them. In the last round with Daniel displaying some fatigue, the Russian became the aggressor, roughing him up on the inside. Daniel clinched him hoping to catch a second wind. The referee only granted him a few seconds before he broke them apart. Daniel took a step back and threw a left jab. The Russian moved closer and stood toe-to-toe in front of him. Daniel could see his chin jutted out without any head movement and loaded his right for an uppercut just as the final bell rang and the referee dived between them.

"It's over, niecey," Mark called out loudly.

"Thank God," Rebecca whispered to herself. She wiped the sweat from her head and temples and came out to face the verdict.

"It went the distance," Matthew said when she walked into the den.

"The whole thing didn't make no sense to me," John said, sliding back in his chair. "The boy was tight, he couldn't get most of his punches off."

"One of us should have gone over there with him," Mary said, worried.

"He's the champion," Gloria responded, "That other guy didn't do enough to take it from him. It looked even to me."

"You'll know in a minute," Mark said, draining the last inch of liquor in his glass.

Rebecca stood there like a statue in the middle of floor while the ring announcer prepared to read the decision of the judges. Then the bell rang again signaling that the decision was in.

"Ladies and gentlemen, going to the score cards we have a split decision. Judge at ringside from South Africa scores the bout 115-112, the judge from Hungary scores the bout 111-116, and the judge from the United States scores the bout 113-114 in favor of the winner and new Heavyweight Champion of the World, Boris Kabinov."

Cheers went through the enormous stadium and grew to a thunderous roar. It was a huge upset. In the den of the Clements family home, they were stunned into silence.

Rebecca fell to the floor on her knees screaming, "Hallelujah, to God be the glory."

"Have you lost your mind?" Grandpa John asked, looking at her like she had gone insane.

Rebecca had dropped down to her hip and was pounding the floor. Matthew still hadn't found the words to speak. Gloria's eye bounced between the TV screen and Rebecca and she didn't know what to say.

"No, she ain't crazy," Mark said, grinning. "She just made a mint on the fight."

"What are you talking about, fool?" Matthew asked, confounded.

Mark pumped his fist with satisfaction. "I told you. Niecey, just got paid big time."

John struggled out of his chair and onto his feet. "You mean to tell me you bet against your own brother. What kind of shit is that?"

"The odds against him were better," Mark laughed.

Rebecca inhaled deeply to compose herself before she answered. "It wasn't anything against Daniel, Grandpa. I could tell his mind wasn't on it when I last talked to him. He was stressing over money and he didn't look ready, he was a little soft around the middle."

"How much did you bet?" Mary asked curiously.

"I mortgaged my condo, sold my car, emptied out my bank account, and bet it all," Rebecca said, still overwhelmed by the decision.

"Stop, no you didn't," Mary said in unbelief. "What if you would have lost, child?"

"I didn't have a choice, Daddy borrowed a ton of money and we have to pay it back or they'll take control of the company. If Daniel won I would have needed Plan C for real."

"Well, I'll be damned," John said, sitting back down. "Somebody get me another beer."

Mary went into the kitchen to get one for him and one for herself.

"That was a big gamble, Becca," Matthew said, shaking his head.

"Uh-huh, and it paid off," Mark said, reaching out for a high-five.

"Somebody oughta call my other knuckleheaded son and let him know what happened," John said after Mary handed him the beer.

"I better go over there," Matthew said, checking for his key, "There's no telling how he's going to react. This was the only time he probably wanted him to win."

*****

"It was his night," was all Daniel said in the after-fight interview. Wendell put a white towel over his shoulders and they left the ring. Some of the onlookers shouted jeers and taunted him but their words were lost, he didn't understand the language. Back in his dressing room he couldn't believe he lost the decision.

"This is a fucking nightmare," he said to Wendell. "He didn't beat me."

"They say he out-pointed you, man."

"To take a man's title you should beat his ass down to the ground."

"That's how it is supposed to be, man, but we're over here in Germany."

"It's my bad, I was playing out there. I should have taken him out."

"It's my fault, Daniel, I wasn't on my game," Wendell said, feeling bad. "I know I said I was going to stop drinking and all that stuff but I didn't. I couldn't help it. I didn't have enough time to clean up."

While he was doing his confession, Earl came into their dressing room with his usual sidekicks talking and smiling as if Daniel hadn't lost the decision.

"I guess that Russian learned how to protect his jaw," Earl joked. "Good show, champ."

"Are you drunk?" Daniel asked, totally outdone. "I lost my belt out there."

"It's not the end of the world," Earl said light-heartedly.

"For you or me," Daniel snapped.

"Win or lose, you made your money."

"It's not only about the money for me, an hour ago I was the champ."

Seeing Daniel wasn't in the mood for humor, Earl put on a serious face. "I know it's tough on you tonight, my man. But it's only a small setback, which is nothing but a setup for a comeback. This is the prize fighting game, it's all about the money, baby. A loss makes you even more attractive for matchups. Nobody signs these contracts to get beat."

"I surely didn't."

"Rest up, get your head together, then call me, and we'll talk about your next move."

"Yeah right," Daniel said.

Earl slapped him on the back and walked out between his two body guards.

"What do you want to do?" Wendell asked timidly, cutting the tape off his hands.

"I want to get on the next plane out of here," Daniel answered.

***

Something clicked in Daniel's head after he lost the fight in Germany. For him it was devastating. Not so much for his boxing career but for his life in general. Not winning was hard to take for someone who didn't know anything about losing. Everything had changed and he didn't know who he was anymore.

In all of his twenty-six years, the only day that didn't go his way before the fight was the day his momma died. He didn't even sleep until he was back home in Philly and when he did his dreams were nightmares, alternating between the loss of his momma and the loss of the fight. He dealt with it by living like a vampire, a werewolf, or other creatures that come out in the dark of night to feed their sense of self. He dulled his senses with alcohol and dope, partied, gambled, and ran around with nameless women.

He was about to leave for another night on the prowl when he heard the doorbell ringing. He could see through the glass on the door that it was Faith shivering in the wind with her arms full of groceries.

"I don't need your services anymore," he said, opening the door. "As you probably know I'm not training right now."

"You might not have a fight scheduled but that doesn't mean you shouldn't continue with your regimen," Faith said with a smile.

"Right now I prefer to forget about all of it," he replied bluntly.

"I don't blame you for that, I just want to cook you a nice dinner."

He opened the door wide for her to come in. Struggling with the bags she made her way inside and took a step towards the kitchen. She stopped when she realized Daniel was still holding the door open. She gave him a questioning look.

Daniel turned away, he didn't want to see her face when he said, "Do what you want, I'm going out, and you really shouldn't be here when I get back."

"All right," Faith said, unfazed, "Have a great time."

She had seen this behavior before as a nutritionist for top athletes in Philly and she was sorry to see it happen to Daniel. The rocket that had blasted him to fame and fortune was off course and spinning out of control in freefall. Something had to give or he was going to crash and burn. She went in the kitchen, turned on some smooth jazz, made him a three course gourmet meal, and locked the door behind her when she left.

Chapter Twenty

It took more of an effort each day for Luke to pull himself out of bed and not just because of the cold winter weather. Despite it being the holiday season, he was heartsick, body worn, and his mind was troubled. When Daniel was defeated he couldn't keep pretending that everything was going to be all right. The protective bubble around him that he floated in above reality had burst and he had to face the truth. His irrational behavior had practically ruined his company, disappointed his daughter, and alienated his son.

Today he was going to have to face the consequences of his actions in the meeting with HLS. It was thirty days before the balloon payment was due. Matthew picked him up so they could ride in together.

"Where's Rebecca?" Luke asked when he got in the car.

"She's going to meet us there," Matthew answered as he pulled away.

Matthew hummed to the radio while Luke drummed his fingers on his leg to the beat of the blood vessel thumping on the left side his head. Traffic was unusually light with it being a few days before Christmas. They made good time getting to the HLS Capital office. They parked in a visitor spot and sedately walked into the building.

Fuming, Luke wondered if his executive assistant, Alice, always stood at the door when Crowley's clients were coming in or was it special treatment for those they were leading to the slaughter house.

"Follow me, Mr. Clements," Alice said politely, but she needn't have bothered, he knew the way to the conference room. The irony of it all was that he wished he didn't.

"Join us," Chris Crowley said, sounding upbeat when they got to the doorway.

Rebecca was already sitting on one side of the table waiting patiently. She nodded and smiled when they came in. The executive assistant took a seat to the left of Chris and they paused while Luke and Matthew sat in the first and second chairs to the right of Chris.

Then Chris began speaking. "I've called you all here for this meeting because there have been some major developments that will most likely have an adverse effect on the environment of the market for the fragrance line."

Luke replied firmly, "If you're referring to Daniel losing the championship and how that will affect sales of the cologne, that development would be an internal issue for our company."

"I'm sure you understand that at this point, thirty days from full payment, that we are closer to being partners on the venture than financiers."

"That would be premature, at this point and time you are lenders," Matthew reminded him. "You reserved some judgement on when the fragrance line would be released and you have exercised that right possibly to the detriment of our company."

Chris took a big gulp of water before he responded. "That would be unfair to say. My utmost concern is the continued success and profitability of Clements Cosmetic Company. If we didn't feel that way we would not have given you the capital for your expansion in the fragrance market."

"Why don't we bring some honesty into this conversation," Matthew said loudly, tired of tiptoeing around the reason for the meeting. "You want control over the company, you want to make a shitload of cash taking it public, and then you're done with it."

"Let's not lose our heads over this," Chris said, trying to diffuse the situation, "We're all in this business to make money."

Luke snapped back. "My company is a family business and that's the way I want to keep it."

"You may not be happy about the present circumstances," Chris assured them, "But you will find yourselves much richer for it. As a public company you take limited risks and maximum profits."

"There's no way in hell I'm going to let you take over what my wife and I built together," Luke said obstinately.

"We can have our attorneys join the meeting and clarify our agreement if that's necessary," Chris said with a slight grin.

"That won't be necessary," Rebecca said, entering the conversation. "The contract states that in the event that the balloon payment is not satisfied the voting interest you have in the company will equal the percentage owned on the loan. Is that your understanding?"

"Yes, that's correct," Chris answered courteously.

"All right," Rebecca said, reaching in her handbag. "I have a cashier's check here in the amount of $3.7 million. With two-thirds of the voting power we'll handle the decisions for Clements Cosmetic Company as a family."

Chris was speechless. HLS had enough pull in the financial community to be assured that no one else would have loaned them anything without contacting them. The only thought in his head was, "Where did they get the money?"

Chris was no more surprised than Luke. He was asking himself the same question. Matthew sat in his chair chuckling to himself. He knew Rebecca had done some unorthodox finagling but he had no idea that she had done so well.

"If there's nothing further I have other things to do today," Rebecca said, standing up to leave. "What about you, Daddy?"

"Definitely, sweetheart," Luke said, following her lead.

Matthew, still chuckling, strolled out behind them.

***

The only thing Daniel was glad about lately was that 1996 was coming to a close. He started it out at the top but for crazy reasons, mostly his own fault, he had ended it on a low. He and Wendell had made plans to party at the Taj Mahal Casino in Atlantic City. On his way out he picked up the phone to call Rebecca to see what was up and wish her a Happy New Year. He knew he wouldn't be in any shape to call her in the morning.

"Where have you been, stranger?" she said instead of hello.

"Nowhere you want to hear about," he answered.

"You might be right about that," she chuckled. "Why didn't you come by for the holidays? I've been worried about you."

"I'm cool. I took a vacation, went down to Miami for a few days."

"You know you're not right. You could have called and invited me to go with you. This cold weather has been kicking my behind."

"I should have," Daniel said, thinking back on the trip. "You would have been better company."

"You should come on by my condo tonight, I'm having some friends over to bring in the New Year. It'll be fun."

"Not this time, I'm in a messed up mood."

"You know that doesn't make any difference to me. I been around all your moods and they don't bother me."

"I might stop by," he lied, knowing he wouldn't. "I really called to find out how the situation with the business is going, about the loan, and how much you need. I know my losing the title in Germany is going to kill the new campaign."

"Don't worry about it, you get your own house in order. I bought some time."

"How did you do that?" he asked, feeling relieved.

"Don't be so nosey, you don't tell me all your business."

"Okay, that's cool. I just wanted to call and wish everybody a happy new year."

"Why don't you come to dinner at Daddy's and tell them yourself."

"I'm not ready to deal with Dad yet."

"Come on, brother, it's not that serious."

"I'm still cussing myself out, I don't need any help."

"I hear you, but let's do something on the weekend."

"I'll call you."

"Take it easy," Rebecca said, feeling sorry for him.

Daniel hung up the phone, picked up his overnight and garment bags, and walked out to the limo waiting out front. He leaned back against the soft black leather and closed his eyes to relax while the car drove to Wendell's place to pick him up. In the quiet, his head was filled with flash backs of things he didn't want to think about, family, fights, and money. He turned up the stereo to drown them out. It helped some but the disappointment he carried was like a fire deep inside that was consuming him. He poured himself a glass of Hennessey to cool it down.

***

"This place is the bomb," Wendell said when they stepped into the entrance of the Taj Mahal.

"We're going first class," Daniel said. "I've got to bring 1997 in right."

He booked one of the penthouse suites and they went upstairs to drop off his bags. Daniel didn't feel like sitting in a restaurant with people staring at him so he called room service and ordered up some steaks. Wendell wasn't hungry and went in one of the bedrooms to take a nap. Daniel relaxed and watched Pulp Fiction on the TV while he ate. When he was finished he took a shower and changed into a three-piece suit. Even if he didn't fill like the greatest he was definitely going to look like it.

"Hold up a minute," Wendell said when he saw Daniel put the room key in his pocket.

"What's up?" Daniel asked, pausing at the door.

"I got to do a little something."

Daniel watched as Wendell pulled out a tiny corked bottle filled with white powder and spread it on the glass-topped coffee table.

"You said you were done with that shit," Daniel said, watching him cut it into thin lines.

"I am, man, I just got an eightball to celebrate the New Year, when this is gone, no more."

Daniel figured he wasn't in a position to judge or criticize. He had fallen short too.

"You want a drink?" he asked with a sigh.

"Yeah, man, thanks," Wendell said, somewhat distracted.

Daniel walked over to the bar and poured them both a shot. He brought the drinks over to the table and sat down on the sofa.

"You need to hold tight to your money, man" Daniel warned, wondering how much he spent on the weightless powder. "It might have to last you a while."

Wendell answered with his eyes glued on the table. "I'm straight, I told you. Plus, that thing in Germany was just a hiccup. You'll get your title back." Then in less than a second he snorted a line, paused for a few more seconds, and then snorted another. "Come on and clear your head," he said, motioning to Daniel. "One of these rails got your name on it."

Daniel hesitated, he'd smoked some weed and popped a few pills when he partied, but as a rule, nothing else. "I'm good, man. Do your thing."

"Come on, partner," Wendell coaxed, "It'll get your ass out of the dumps. They won't even be ready for us downstairs."

Daniel thought about it. What did he have to lose? It wasn't like he had a fight coming up.

"What the hell," he said, taking the rolled up $100 bill and snorting the line.

He felt the rush immediately, thrilled that the dark cloud had been blown away. His spirits were lifted instantly. He sprung off the couch like a Jack in the Box. The small amount of coke in his system had him revved up and ready for anything.

"Let's get it popping," Daniel said, already at the door.

"I'm right on your heels," Wendell howled, "I'm feeling lucky."

They strutted through the casino and stopped to play a few hands of blackjack. The table was cold so they moved on.

"This is where I need to be," Daniel exclaimed when he saw the big letters of the sign above the door welcoming him in, "The Ego Bar & Lounge."

Wendell wanted a table near the stage where he could see the scantily clad dancers doing their moves up close but Daniel wanted to sit outside the circle. He was kind of skittish and didn't like the feeling of so many people at his back. As soon as they sat down a waitress appeared.

"What can I get for you this evening?" she asked, smiling at Daniel.

He smiled back and said, "Two double shots of your best cognac."

"I'll be right back," she said, juggling her ample hips in her tight mini-skirt as she walked to the bar to get their drinks.

"Oh yeah, that's what I'm talking about," Wendell said.

When the waitress came back Daniel reached in his pocket and pulled out his credit card.

"It's on the house," she said, tilting her head to the side. "I'm a big fan."

"What's your name?" Daniel asked, putting the card back in his pocket.

"Michelle," she answered, running her tongue along her top teeth.

"It's my pleasure to make your acquaintance, Michelle," he said as he pulled out three one-hundred dollar bills and handed them to her. "That's for you, Happy New Year."

She took the bills, folded them, and slid them between her breasts. "I'll see you later."

Michelle brought them some hot wings and quesadillas and kept the drinks flowing. Daniel's blues were fading into the red, bronze, and golden colors that decorated the lounge. The sexy performance of the Angels' show had the room all fired up and when it was over a DJ started to play. That was when the club truly came alive. It was rocking from wall to wall, no holds barred.

Daniel and Wendell hit the floor bumping and grinding to the beat with whoever they came in contact with. Michelle kept her eye on him but she was on the clock and couldn't get her party on yet. Even so, she wasn't about to let that fact get between her and Daniel. When the New Year count down from '10' started she pushed her way through the thick throng of celebrators and by the time they all shouted '1' she had thrown her arms around Daniel's neck and her tongue deep into his mouth.

"Happy New Year," she said after their 30-second kiss.

"Back at you," Daniel said, amused.

"Wait for me, I get off at 1:00," she said, brushing her hand against his crotch before she went back serving drinks.

As far as hooking up with Michelle was concerned, Daniel was basically indifferent. He thought she was cute except she wasn't his type. He preferred to do the chasing but she had been running him down from the moment he walked in.

On the other hand, Michelle wasn't going to let him walk out of that club without her. This was her chance. The only reason she was working there was to meet somebody famous. She was confident that when she got up to his room and rocked his world he would be hers for life.

A half hour later Wendell was restless and ready to leave.

"I'm out of here, man," Wendell said, finishing off his drink, "Most everybody in here is coupled up."

"It's still early, where you want to go?" Daniel asked, ready to take the party elsewhere.

"You stay here, man. Don't disappoint that honey over there at the bar. She's been working to get with you all night."

They both glanced in her direction and she was looking right at them.

"I'm going back to the casino," Wendell laughed, "Maybe I'll get lucky."

Daniel sat for a while longer but he was tired of being in one place for so long. The coke still had him keyed up. He got up and was almost out the door when Michelle caught up to him, slipped her arm around his elbow, and walked out beside him.

"Sorry about making you wait," she said sweetly. "What's up for the rest of the night?"

"No plans, I came out to have some fun."

"Do you have a room here in the hotel?" she asked, hoping.

"Yeah, I do."

"I've been on my feet all evening. It would be nice to sit down and relax for a while. It's not that late."

"That's cool," Daniel said, going towards the elevator.

When Michelle saw he was in the penthouse she couldn't get off the elevator and out of her clothes fast enough. She did every freaky thing she could think of to impress Daniel. The problem was that after his world tour to more than a few countries and across the United States, he had been with more women than he could count that had done the same thing. He probably would have been more impressed by a decent conversation. After two hours of licking, rubbing, humping, sucking, and random gymnastics, Michelle was worn out. She fell over on her back to take a break.

It was Daniel's rule never to let them get too comfortable even though it was also the part that made him feel bad.

"It's time for you go," he mumbled.

"Excuse me, do you know what time it is?" she asked, wondering what his problem was.

"No, and I don't care. You have to leave," he said firmly.

Offended, Michelle sat straight up in the bed. "You mean I can't sleep here."

"That's what I'm saying. It's nothing personal. I like to sleep alone."

"I know you not trying to play me like no ho," Michelle argued indignantly.

"So you saying you're not a ho?" he asked sarcastically.

"Oh no, you got me messed up," Michelle said, jumping out of the bed and waving her hand. "Who do you think you are? You don't have no title, nigga."

"I still have my dignity, and the woman I choose to be my lady would have to have some dignity and self-respect too, not somebody crawling around naked in a hotel room."

"Then why did you fuck me?"

"You're the one who wanted to be fucked, what are you complaining about? You got what you wanted."

She curled her lip in contempt and said, "You ain't shit."

"Why, because I fucked you," he shot back, "I'm probably not."

Michelle grabbed her clothes off the floor, her handbag, and stomped into the bathroom slamming the door behind her. She made a quick call on her cell phone before she took her time getting dressed. He wasn't about to rush her.

"It's the middle of the night," she said when she finally came out of the bathroom, "Could you at least walk me to my car?"

"No problem," Daniel said, throwing on the jeans and sweater he had ridden up in.

Michelle rolled her eyes at him as they rode the elevator down in silence. He opened the door for her on the way out to the parking lot and followed her to the employee parking area. As they approached the cars, two black guys wearing jeans and hoodies got out of a dark grey Ford Taurus. The bigger one came and stood in front of them, the other holding a baseball bat had his back.

"Is this who you was talking about?" the one in front asked Michelle.

"Yeah, this is him," she said, stepping to the side.

Daniel knew somebody was going to get an ass-whipping soon; the question was whether it would be him or them.

"What's up, nigga," the one in front said, hitting one fist into his other hand. "You trying to play my cousin?"

"I don't know your cousin," Daniel said, weighing the situation.

"You walked out here with her. Michelle is family and we not gonna stand for no disrespect."

"Look, I don't know what your cousin expected but I didn't force her to do anything she didn't want to do."

"That's not what she told us. She said you called her a ho."

"We were both drunk."

The one in front pushed Daniel in his chest, then he got up in his face and said, "Yo mama is the ho."

You could say anything you wanted about Daniel but his momma was off-limits, hearing those words turned him into a bull seeing red. He charged the guy and pounded him down on the ground with punch after punch while Michelle stood a few feet away screaming. Nobody he had ever fought in the ring had received the beat down that he gave the guy who dared to besmirch his mother. The one hanging back and searching for his courage found some and jumped on Daniel's back but he threw him off like he was a mangy alley cat. Daniel was in another zone, pounding his pain into them with each blow, so much so that he didn't hear the sirens. It was finally the flashing blue lights breaking the darkness of the night that got his attention.

A big spotlight blinded him and when his eyes adjusted he was looking down the barrel of a 9-mm gloc.

"Freeze, step back and put your hands in the air," the police officer with the gun commanded.

His short sidekick shouted, "What's going on here?"

"He raped me," Michelle screamed, "They came to help me and he attacked them."

Daniel didn't move or say a word. He knew how this could go and he didn't want to cause any additional agitation. Besides, anything he said now would be a waste of breath. They were taking him in regardless.

Chapter Twenty-One

Rebecca was making a big New Year's Day breakfast for her dad and had invited the rest of the family to join them at his house. She wanted to celebrate the fact that Clements Cosmetic Company was still in their control. Grandma Gloria, Grandpa John, Matthew, and Mark were seated at the table drinking coffee. Martha was scrambling eggs while Rebecca was finishing up the pancakes, and Luke was reading the paper.

"Turn on the TV, Luke," Grandpa John said, "Let's see what's going on in the world this morning. With all them guns that fired off at midnight I know somebody got shot."

Luke walked over to get the remote from the counter and clicked on the TV. He surfed through a few channels trying to find the news. He found Headline News on channel 47 and stood there as they announced they had breaking news.

"Good morning, we have breaking news out of Atlantic City on the first day of the year. Former Heavyweight Champion of the World, Daniel Clements, was arrested in the early hours of the morning in a parking garage outside of the Taj Mahal Casino on charges of rape and assault with a deadly weapon. He is currently being held at the Atlantic County Jail with bail set at $250,000. Stay tuned for the update on that story."

"Oh Lord, what in the world is going on?" Grandma Gloria exclaimed with one hand at her throat. "I can't believe it."

"Turn to another channel, try CNN," John urged, wanting to see more of the news."

"Looks like nephew had a rough night," Mark said.

"Keep your mouth shut," Matthew said.

Luke was standing in front of the TV screen as if he were hypnotized.

"Daddy, why don't you sit down," Rebecca said, thinking he was in shock.

He still stood there motionless so Rebecca went over to guide him to the chair. He didn't respond to her gentle pull on his arm. She pulled harder and one of his legs went out from under him and he fell to the floor. His eyes looked confused and his mouth hung open as if he was about to speak.

"Daddy," Rebecca screamed, crouching under him to protect his head. "Somebody call 911."

Matthew rushed to the phone and called for an ambulance.

"It might be a heart attack," Martha said, "Is he breathing?"

Mark jumped out of his seat. "We could probably get him to the hospital quicker than waiting for them to come."

"I don't think we should move him," Gloria said, kneeling on the floor beside him.

"At least turn him on his side so he won't choke," John added.

"Can you talk, Daddy?" Rebecca asked softly but he didn't respond. "Get a pillow and blanket," she yelled.

Gloria got up and ran to the guest bedroom and pulled the pillows and comforter off the bed and ran back into the kitchen. She covered Luke while Rebecca propped him up on the pillows. It seemed like an hour even though it was only a few minutes later when they heard the siren of the EMT and saw the red lights blinking through the window. Mark was already standing with the door open when they got there and cleared the way for the gurney. Barely another minute passed before the EMTs had Luke fastened down with an oxygen mask and were wheeling him out of the door. Then the phone rang.

Rebecca saw the Atlantic City Police Department's number on

the caller ID, picked it up, looked at Matthew and said, "I need to take this."

"I'll ride with your Daddy in the ambulance," Matthew told her. "Mama and Pops can ride with Martha, and Mark can bring you to the hospital."

Rebecca nodded as they rushed out of the door. Mark picked up another receiver to listen then she brought the phone to her ear. She took a deep breath and said, "Hello."

Wendell spoke in a low voice on the other end. "Hey, is this Becca?"

"Yeah, Wendell, what's going on, I saw Daniel on the news. Why didn't he call?"

"He hooked up with some chick in the club and I don't know what went down after that. He tried to call you but there wasn't an answer. I don't have enough to make bail that's why I'm calling."

"Look, my dad got sick when he heard the news and I'm on my way to the hospital. I'll be up there as soon as I know something."

"Okay, I'll let you go. I'll be here," Wendell said, sounding hopeless.

Rebecca hung up the phone. She stared out into space and rubbed her forehead as she searched her mind for where she would get the bail money.

Mark grabbed her by the arm and pulled her out the door. "We'll deal with that later, niecey, we need to get to the hospital."

***

The Clements had sat in the waiting room for three hours without a word from the doctors. Matthew, sitting close to the door debated with himself on how much longer he would wait before he stormed into the ICU. Rebecca, close to losing her composure reluctantly accepted a drink from the bottle Mark kept tucked in the breast pocket of his coat. Gloria was close to becoming a patient herself, still refusing to eat any of the food John and Martha had brought up from the cafeteria. When the door finally opened their impatience turned to apprehension, all of them afraid to hear bad news.

A heavyset white man with thin streaks of dark hair combed over his balding head walked in with a tall black nurse in blue scrubs following two steps behind him.

"Are you folks the family of Luke Clement?" the doctor asked unemotionally.

Matthew answered, "Yes we are."

"I'm Dr. Kilpatrick and this is Roberta," he said motioning towards the nurse. "I want to give you the status on Mr. Clements. We did a CT scan and have determined the he suffered an ischemic stroke which means there was a blot clot that went to his brain. He's now on medication that we hope will dissolve the clot. We don't think there is a sizable risk of another stroke and he was brought in quickly so that's good. He's stable right now and we have him under sedation."

"Can he talk?" Rebecca asked.

"Is he paralyzed?" Gloria asked before the doctor could answer.

"We won't know the extent of any brain damage until he wakes up. At that point we can see what type of rehabilitation is necessary. In the meantime he needs rest."

"Thank you, doctor," Matthew said, extending his hand to shake. Dr. Kilpatrick shook his hand and left.

The nurse Roberta stayed for a minute. "He'll probably sleep for the rest of the day. If you all want to go home and get some food and rest I can call you if he wakes."

"I'm going to stay for a while," Matthew said, "Martha, why don't you take Mama and Pops back to the house. I'll call you if anything changes."

"I'm not no child, I don't need nobody to tell me what to do," John fussed.

"There's no need for all of us to be here, Pops," Martha said, trying to console him. "When Matt gets tired, then we'll come back and let him go get some rest."

"That's makes sense, J.C.," Gloria said, smoothing it over with John. "Let's go home."

Mark pulled Rebecca to her feet and said, "Me and Niecey gonna take a ride up to Atlantic City and see what's going on with Daniel."

"Stay in touch," Matthew said as they walked out of the door.

***

Mark merged into the traffic on I-95, moved into the passing lane and pressed down on the gas pedal, and only let it up to pay the tolls. They got to the Atlantic County Jail just before 4:00. Mark looked around in the back seat of Rebecca's car and saw her messenger bag on the back on the floor.

"You're going to need that," he said bluntly.

"Why?" Rebecca asked puzzled.

"Because the only way we're going to get in there to see Daniel is if you tell them you're his attorney. No visiting hours today."

"All right," she said, reaching over the back seat and grabbing the bag before she got out.

The charade worked without a problem and they were led to the meeting room. Daniel walked in wearing an orange jumpsuit about twenty minutes later.

"It's good to see y'all," Daniel said, sounding subdued. He pulled out a chair and sat across from them at the table. "You didn't have to come up here though."

Rebecca pursed her lips before she said, "Don't even go there, Daniel, you knew we were coming to see about you as soon as we got the news."

"Yeah we saw that crap, so what really went down?" Mark asked.

Daniel shook his head from his disappointment in himself

257

before he started to explain. "I was chilling at this club in Taj Mahal when one of the waitresses kept pushing up on me all night. On my way out she ran me down and said she wanted to go up to my room. We did the thing and then I asked her to leave. She got pissed. I guess she called for back-up to whip my ass but I wasn't having it."

Rebecca banged her hand on the table in frustration. "See there, Daniel, I told you to stop dealing with these groupies and find you somebody decent. I knew something was going to happen sooner or later, except I thought it was going to be a paternity suit and not a rape charge."

Daniel thought about Faith again. He had been thinking about her from the moment they booked him. He regretted not taking her up on her offer. He wondered what she was thinking after this, and if she would have anything to do with him. He hated that he had put himself in this position when a perfectly good woman was right there, somebody who cared about him and not his money. Trying to keep anybody from getting too close, he had slept with more women than he cared to count and he didn't give a shit about any of them. Thinking he was protecting himself he had actually put himself in a dangerous situation. Maybe he truly deserved the beat down those guys came to deliver.

"We can't worry about that now, nephew," Mark said. "We need to hire a topnotch attorney, make bail, and get you outta here."

"I'm cool, Uncle Mark," Daniel said, "I don't need a hotshot lawyer to bleed me for half of everything I got and I don't need to make bail."

"Stop tripping, you know we aren't going to let you stay in here," Rebecca said.

Daniel sat back in his chair. "It's already handled."

"What are you talking about?" Mark asked, completely confused.

"I had my arraignment this afternoon. I talked to the judge

and he offered me a deal. The management from the Taj Mahal called to vouch for me and he dismissed the rape charge. He agreed to reduce the other charges to simple assault and battery, a misdemeanor, if I took a plea. I pleaded no contest."

"You should have talked to us first," Mark said, "You could have beat the whole case with an attorney to represent you."

"Yeah, like I said, at what price," Daniel replied. "It would only get me more bad publicity and damage my reputation. There was no way I was going to trial on this bullshit."

"What did they give you?" Mark asked.

"I got a $500 fine and 60 days in county jail."

"I wish you would have waited," Mark said with regret.

"I just want it to be over," Daniel told them.

Rebecca paused to choose her words. "There's something else you need to know, Daniel. We were all having breakfast this morning at Daddy's house when the news about you getting arrested came on the TV."

Daniel put up his hand and interrupted her. "Stop, I'm sure he had a heart attack and cussed me out."

"No, that's not what happened," she said intently, "He didn't say a word. He had a stroke."

Daniel shrugged. "Stop playing, girl."

"She's not playing," Mark said, stone-faced. "He fell right there on the floor in front of the TV."

Daniel covered his face with his hands and Rebecca saw how swollen and bruised his knuckles were from the fight. She watched as he slowly began to rock back and forth. Rebecca knew he was blaming himself and the burdensome load it was on his shoulders. Deep down she blamed him a little too. Seeing his anguish, she knew the question that filled his head yet he was too afraid to ask. Rebecca knew it was cruel but she let him punish himself for another minute before she spoke.

"He's not dead," she said, putting him out of his misery.

Daniel's hands dropped into his lap. "Thank God. How is he?"

"He's stable for now, but still unconscious. We don't know any more than that."

"Damn," Daniel groaned, knowing if he would have waited and made bail he could be on his way to the hospital. "I can't even get there to see him."

"No sense in stressing about that now," Mark said. "Your time is short."

The guard came back in and told them the thirty minutes were up.

Daniel squeezed Rebecca's hand across the table before he stood up. "Stay in touch. Let me know how he's doing?"

Mark pat him on the shoulder as he walked away. "We got this out here. You take care of yourself in here."

***

Wendell drove up to Atlantic City on Saturday for regular visiting hours. Inside the visiting room he sat among the mothers to see sons, little children to see fathers, and other females to see husbands or boyfriends. Seeing Daniel come into the room with the other prisoners made him want to take a hit and a drink.

Daniel walked over and sat across from him. "Hey, man, thanks for coming up."

"No doubt, man," Wendell said, leaning forward, "I feel terrible about this shit. I shouldn't have left the club and this wouldna happened. That bitch was crazy."

"It's not your fault, it was my mistake."

"Man, coming in here brings back some memories I would rather stay forgotten. I was the one locked up waiting for somebody to come see me."

"In all my dreams and nightmares I never once thought I would be in a jail cell. Six months ago I was on top of the world."

"I know it's not much comfort but you got short time. When

you get out we can get back to training and get back on the fast track."

Daniel looked down at the floor beside him. "I don't know what I'm going to do after I get released. My Dad had a stroke behind this foolishness and it might not be worth it."

"This is just a bump in the road, my man. You're a winner. You'll be back on top in no time."

"Right now I'm not even thinking about that. I need to take care of family."

Wendell knew to back off. "I hear you, man. No pressure."

"Definitely not, I need this break to get my head straight. In the meantime I left my keys up front for you. Check on my crib for me, and I need you to pick up my things from the room at the casino and take them back to Philly."

"No problem, man, I got you."

"Thanks, man," Daniel sighed, getting up from the table. "I got to go."

"Aw 'ight, man," Wendell said, knowing the feeling.

***

Luke's condition improved over the next two weeks, although the movement in his right side was still limited and he was having trouble speaking. Dr. Kilpatrick recommended that he be transferred into a rehabilitation facility. Rebecca went to the hospital first thing that morning to make sure that his discharge and admittance at the Magee Rehabilitation Hospital would go smoothly. Matthew was already there when she got there and was helping him get dressed. It was difficult for her to see her daddy looking so frail and feeble.

"Becca, you didn't have to come by here so early," Matthew said, "You could have met us at the facility. Don't worry about your daddy, I've got him."

"I know, I wanted to be here," she said stoically.

"The best thing to do is to come over to the facility after he's settled."

"I can help get all these flowers and cards packed up," she said, wanting to help.

"Don't put too much on your plate, sweetie," Matthew said, giving her a knowing look. "Mary is on her way here to take care of that."

"Okay, then I guess I'll see you all later."

She bent down and gave her daddy a kiss on the cheek. He gave her a crooked smile and waved his left hand telling her to go. Rebecca lingered on the outside of the door leaning on it for support. With Daniel in jail and her daddy sick, it was too much. She was having that feeling that she had when her momma died. Everything in her wanted to breakdown, holler, roll around on the floor, and weep uncontrollably, except she hadn't been raised to cry. Her momma had taught her that whatever happens, you stay on your feet, you carry your behind to work, and you keep pushing. There was no time for pity parties. She straightened up, adjusted her blazer and coat, stuck out her chin, and strode out of the hospital.

Rebecca drove straight to Clements Cosmetics Company. She had work to do. Chris Crowley from HLS was tying up the phone lines demanding the balance owed on the loan. She sat there in her parking space lightheaded, wishing that she would have stopped somewhere for breakfast. For a minute she thought about pulling back out to get something to eat but that would take a while and she didn't have time to waste. She decided to ask Sherry to order her something from the deli on the corner. Just as she approached the entrance, a middle-aged white guy wearing a khaki trench coat jumped in front of her and opened the door wide.

"Thank you," she said politely.

He smiled pleasantly and said, "My pleasure, are you Rebecca Clements?"

"Yes, I am," she answered suspiciously.

In one quick motion he pulled two envelopes out of his pockets stuck them in the crook of her arm and said, "You've been served."

Rebecca wanted to curse him out but he was almost out of earshot and he was only doing a job. HLS Capital had transferred their threats into action. She put the letters in her briefcase, smiled at the receptionist in the lobby, and caught the elevator up to her daddy's office.

"Good morning," Sherry said, greeting her, "How's Mr. Clements doing?"

"Much better," Rebecca answered absentmindedly, "Would you mind ordering me a bagel and cream cheese and a large coffee from the deli?"

"Certainly, Ms. Clements, is there anything else I can get for you?"

"Yes," Rebecca answered, sitting in her daddy's big chair, "Call our attorney and have him draw up power of attorney papers for me. I need them ASAP."

A look of relief spread across Sherry's face. "I'll get that right away, Ms. Clements."

Once the door was closed, Rebecca read the summons. HLS was suing Clements Cosmetic for the past due loan. She logged onto her daddy's computer and spent the rest of the morning reviewing all the product lines of the company. The Kush Kurl Kit sales had fallen off dramatically but the Kush Perm and the Kush Kiddie Perm had taken up a lot of the slack. The skin care line was growing but they hadn't done an adequate marketing campaign to increase sales. Luke had put everything on hold while his focus was on the fragrance line. All of the packaged bottles were still in their warehouse collecting dust. The bottom line was that they weren't losing money but they were barely breaking even.

Luke had overruled her before but Rebecca was sure the next wave to ride in hair care would be hair itself. She had watched

Patti Labelle for years and hair was becoming an accessory to fashion as much as shoes and jewelry.

She made a call to Matthew on the new cell phones they bought after Luke had the stroke.

"Can you talk?" she asked after he answered in a low voice.

They had agreed not to discuss any of the issues with the company around Luke.

"Hold on a second," he said, stepping outside of Luke's room to talk. "What's going on?"

"I got served this morning. HLS is suing us for payment on the loan."

"I knew it was coming sooner or later," Matthew said, "We still owe them over $2 million and with interest it's growing."

"Hands down, they'll win the judgment and put a lien against the company's assets."

"So we lose control of the company?" he asked, dumbfounded.

"Not necessarily, they don't want to liquidate the company for payment, it's a ploy to force us to go public where they can really make a killing."

"What recourse do we have?"

"We can put it off for a while but we need to raise our revenues. I've got some ideas but I'll need power of attorney."

"How long will it take for them to drag us through the legal process?"

"Probably less than a year, maybe six to eight months.

"Have you thought about asking Daniel for the money to clear the debt?"

"It's one of the things I need to talk to him about," Rebecca said, "I'm going up to see him on the weekend."

***

Rebecca made her second drive to the Atlantic County Jail alone. She was tired of everybody in the family hovering and worrying about her. It was Daniel and Luke that they needed to focus on. The early morning ride calmed her nerves as the snow flurries blowing along the interstate melted away on the front windshield. By the time she got to the jail she had a new perspective on how to resolve the troubles that weighed heavily on the family.

Inside the visiting room she could sense the restlessness of the other visitors in the room. For all of them these minutes were the only ones that were fleeting. Once they left this room the time would slow and drudge along.

Daniel stretched his mouth into a smile when he saw her.

Rebecca smile back and asked, "So how are you making it in here, really?"

"Doing my time one day at a time, that's all I can tell you."

"Well, you don't look as bad as I thought you would."

"It's nothing to do in here but eat and kickback. It's not all bad though, I've been doing a lot of thinking and I've learned a lot about myself."

Rebecca looked surprised. "What have you found out in twenty-three days?"

"First off, I never appreciated what I had in my life. Nothing meant that much to me, my freedom, a good meal, having people around who cared about me. I thought that was the regular, nothing special. Now I can see how special it all was."

"Wow, look at you being so deep and introspective," Rebecca joked.

"I'm for real. I'm re-evaluating what's important to me in my life. I'm going to make some serious changes when I get out of here."

"Are you saying you're not going to fight anymore?"

"I don't know, I can't even think about that right now."

"Well, I need you to think about it."

"Why?"

"Because daddy spent everything he had on the fragrance line for you."

Daniel's head dropped as he sunk down in his chair. "I didn't want that."

"I know you didn't ask him to do it but he did."

"How much money do you need to set things right?"

"More than I could ask you for, and even if you gave just what we need to pay off the debt to HLS it won't put the balance sheet where we need it to be. We'd still be on the edge of a cliff."

"Then what can I do?"

"The whole fragrance campaign has a stranglehold on the company. We can't just trash it. That's why I need you to fight and win."

"Come on, Becca, look where I am," he said with outstretched arms.

"I'm not saying that only for the business, you need to do it for yourself."

"I'm not feeling that right now."

"You're the chosen one, brother. You're a winner."

"I don't know if y'all keep me sane or drive me crazy. Nobody can win all the time."

"That's not what I'm saying," Rebecca said intently, "Whether you win or not, you've got to wake up every morning with the proper frame of mind. You have to think like a champion. It's what you need to go forward after this."

"I don't know about all that. There's nothing I can do until I get out of here."

"It's like the famous words of George Clinton, 'Free your mind and your ass will follow.'"

Daniel couldn't help but laugh long and hard. It was contagious and soon Rebecca had to laugh with him.

"I love you, little sis."

"I love you too, big brother."

"So how's Dad doing?"

"Things are slow but he's making progress. It's tough on him. He has a physical therapist and a speech pathologist to help him learn to walk and talk all over again."

"I wish I could be there to help out."

"You will, and that will be worth more than the best medicine we can buy."

Then the guard announced that visiting time was ending.

"You don't need to come back up here," Daniel said, getting up. "I'm good. Next time I see you I don't want to be in here."

"That's cool, but do me a favor."

"What's that?"

"Get your jailhouse workouts going on," she said half-joking. "Isn't that what you're supposed to do in here? You got a fight to win."

Daniel smiled again as he left. "If you call doing laundry a workout I'm on it."

Chapter Twenty-Two

Five weeks later when Daniel was released a day early he didn't want any fanfare. He bought a baseball cap from a Walgreens to pull down low on his face, raised the collar on his jacket, and caught the Greyhound bus to Philly. Outside the bus station he caught a cab for the long ride out to the Main Line. He just wanted to sit at his own table and sleep in his own bed before he saw anybody. It was just after 1:00 in the afternoon when the cab dropped him off at home. He'd given Wendell his key so he used the code on the garage doors to get inside.

The smell of cigarette smoke caught Daniel off guard as soon as he opened the door leading into his foyer. That was only the first bad sign. He took long strides to his kitchen and found it was cluttered with dirty dishes and smelled like a garbage can.

"What the hell?" he asked, stunned as he walked through his house. The recreation room that he kept immaculate had ashes all over the floor and a glass of stale beer was sitting on his pool table. Trash and snack wrappers were strewn all over the sofa in his den. His house looked like a wild group of teenagers had broken in and had a ghost party. He hated to think what the rest of the house looked like. He dashed up the stairs to check out his master bedroom.

A fit of rage engulfed him like a bomb blowing up under his feet. He took a deep calming breath because his first reaction would have landed him back behind bars. Wendell was lying in his bed asleep with two naked females.

"Get y'all funky asses up," Daniel yelled with balled fists, holding himself back.

"Who, what is it?" Wendell asked still in a half-drunken stupor.

"Look who's back," one of the females said, grinning at him. The other was still knocked-out.

Daniel backed up from the bed, not sure how much longer he could control himself. This wasn't the welcome he had looked forward too. He was totally disgusted. He should have known better than to trust Wendell with his keys.

Wendell sat up, wiped his eyes, and got his senses together enough to realize that Daniel was standing there and staring him down like he wanted to fight.

"Hey, man," Wendell said, sobering up. "You should have called me and let me know they were cutting you loose. I would have picked you up."

"I gave you the keys to my crib for you to hold it down for me and you trashed it. Man, I can't believe this. You dealing with these low class hos up where I lay my head."

"I'm sorry, man. I was going to have everything cleaned before you got here."

"This is some damn disrespectful shit. You got my place smelling like a fish market."

"You right, man, my bad," Wendell said, pushing the other girl in the back.

"Why you got an attitude," the first female snapped, rolling her eyes, "You should be happy to see a woman after you been locked up"

"Shut up, bitch," Wendell hollered at her.

"You got five minutes to get the fuck out of my house," Daniel said before he stormed out of the room.

A couple of minutes later Wendell stumbled down the stairs with his two disheveled sidekicks coming behind him.

"I apologize, man. I didn't mean to disrespect your home,"

Wendell said pitifully, handing him his keys. "Sometimes I go too hard and I don't know what I'm doing. I got caught up."

Daniel opened the front door. "Just go, man. I'm done with it."

"I'm glad to see you out, man," Wendell said, walking out.

Daniel slammed the door behind them.

Too upset to stay there, he called the cleaning service to have them take care of the mess Wendell and his crew had made. Then he called Rebecca.

"When did you get home?" she asked, surprised.

"About an hour ago."

"I am so glad that drama is over and I know you are too."

"I can't even tell you how I feel."

"Give me a couple of hours and I can pick up some stuff, come by, and make you a big home cooked meal. You know everybody wants to see you."

"I need a minute before a family get-together. Plus, the house is a mess. The cleaning company will probably be here for some days. I'm thinking about staying in Chestnut Hill."

"What happened?" Rebecca asked, sensing something off in his voice.

"I don't want to talk about it," he answered, still disgusted.

"Okay, then I'll meet you at the house when I get done."

"All right, cool, I'll see you later."

Daniel grabbed his gym duffel bag and keys on the way down to his car and drove over to his Daddy's house.

***

The comfort of being home was just what Daniel needed. Rebecca made him some fried chicken, macaroni and cheese, and green beans. They laughed and talked for hours while they ate, cleaned the kitchen, and drank a bottle of wine. They reminisced on when they were kids, missing their momma, disappointing their Dad, and what would really make them happy.

"More than anything, I would really like to get the business growing again," Rebecca said apprehensively, "I feel like I can't let Momma's baby die."

"I'm not worried," he said to encourage her, "I have every confidence in you."

"What about you? Have you made any decisions about fighting again?" Rebecca asked cautiously. "You know what that would mean for the company."

"I'm considering it but my trainer is tripping. I'm going to give Earl Knight a call to arrange a meeting where we can talk about it."

"Then at least I can hope."

"Definitely, I don't think it's if I will get back in the ring, it's more of how soon. There are some other important things I have to deal with first."

"Now I'm encouraged," Rebecca kidded, fanning herself with relief.

Daniel chuckled. "I really need to spend some time with Dad before I get back to training, and there's a special lady that I would like to get to know."

"Do you mean you have learned your lesson and you are through messing with the hoochies?" she asked, teasing him.

Daniel nodded and grinned. "It took me a while but I finally graduated."

"My faith has been restored," Rebecca said, raising her arms in the air.

"Mine too," Daniel said, "Her name is Faith."

Rebecca thought back for a moment. "Wasn't she your nutritionist?"

"Yeah, she's the one."

"Good luck on that one, brother, you might have blown your chances."

"I hope not," he said sincerely.

"I'll say a prayer for you," Rebecca said, "I'm going to bed. We can go see Daddy in the morning before I go to the office."

Daniel went up to his old room shortly after her. He never thought it would feel so good to be back in his old bed again.

***

Daniel got butterflies in his stomach as he followed Rebecca through the rehab facility to Luke's room. Partly because he thought he was to blame and also he didn't know what to expect. He prayed silently that his dad wouldn't be drawn up looking weak. Rebecca pushed the door open into the dimness of the room and he walked in timidly behind her.

"Daddy, are you awake," she asked, leaning over close to his face.

"There ain't no rest in here," he answered with slightly slurred speech.

"Look who's here to see you," she said, pressing the button that raised the bed.

Even though Daniel had tried to prepare himself for what his dad's appearance might be, he was still shaken. The pure example of strength for him all his life looked fragile, as if he had been partially broken. It hurt his heart to see his dad laying there in a bed with guard rails on the side as if he were a child. This was probably the only time in Daniel's life that he would have loved for his dad to get out of himself and give him a good cussing.

Luke saw Daniel standing across the room and lifted his left arm high. "Come and see me."

It only took three long strides and Daniel was next to him.

"Hey, Dad, how are you feeling?"

"I've been better," he replied slowly. "How are you?"

"I'm much better now," Daniel said. "It's good to see you."

"It's good to see you too," Luke said, relishing the sight of his son.

Daniel leaned down on the rail of the bed to speak. "I've had some time to think and I just want to say I'm sorry for being so selfish about the decisions I've made."

Luke shook his head from side to side, short and deliberately, with disagreement. "No, I was the one who was selfish. I was only thinking of what I wanted."

"I love you, Dad."

"I'll always love you, Daniel."

"Stop it, y'all are making me tear up," Rebecca said, trying to lighten the atmosphere with humor, "Both of you are selfish."

All three of them were on the verge of crying and were grateful to have a reason to laugh. Luke looked at his children and felt joy. For weeks he had watched other patients fighting to regain their strength and independence and up until this moment he hadn't decided if he wanted to recover or not.

"Help me get out of this bed," Luke said, "I need to get on my feet."

"Wait a minute, let me get your robe," Rebecca said, going into the closet.

"Do we need to call anybody?" Daniel asked, concerned.

Luke let down the rail and swung his body to the side of the bed. "Hell no, I'm a grown man. You got your ass out of that jail and I'm going to get my ass out of here."

Rebecca helped him into his robe and slippers and brought his walker over to the side of the bed. Luke stood up. He hesitated while he tried to find his equilibrium. Then he took a small shaky step, then another, and then another. Daniel and Rebecca surely felt as proud of him as he had been of them when they were babies taking their first steps. Both of them were poised to catch him if he fell but Luke kept going until he walked to the end of the hallway and back.

"Let me get you back in the bed," Daniel said, "I know you're tired after that."

"No way, I'll sit in the chair over there by the window," Luke insisted.

"Okay, Daddy," Rebecca said, cheering him on, "That's how we do it. Show Daniel what it takes to get back in the game."

"Watch me," Luke joked, "I'll be 100 percent in no time."

Rebecca gave him a kiss on the cheek. "I hate to leave but I've got work to do."

"All right, baby girl," Luke said.

"I'll be back tomorrow," Daniel said, holding his hand out to Luke, "I've got some things to handle myself."

Luke grabbed his hand and squeezed it. "Thanks for coming by. When you get back I'll be running circles around this place."

***

Daniel drove his car down Vine Street until he got to 8th Street and then drove straight through downtown to South Street. He found a parking meter with time on it between 5th and 6th Street and took that as a positive sign. He walked down another block before he saw it, the Be Faithful Café. Daniel walked in and looked around the room. The café was filled with the busy lunch crowd as they hurried through their meals in a concert of eating utensils tapping against glass accompanied by a mass of garbled voices. Through the maze of tables, Daniel saw an unoccupied booth on his far left. He scanned the room after he sat down but he didn't see her.

The male waiter, a slim white guy dressed in black skinny jeans and a white shirt, eventually came over to where he was sitting. He smiled like he might have recognized Daniel and handed him a menu.

"Have you eaten with us before?" he asked.

"No I haven't," Daniel answered.

"We have a great selection of gourmet coffees and herbal teas to start you off with," the waiter said lively, "What would you like to drink?"

"Before I order, I was wondering if the owner, Faith Brooks, is around?"

"Sure, she's in her office. What's your name? I'll tell her you're here."

"Just tell her a friend is here to see her."

The waiter shrugged his shoulders and disappeared in the back. Faith came out a few minutes later wearing a colorful print sweater, black leggings, and a puzzled look on her face. When she saw Daniel sitting at a table in the corner by the window she stopped. Daniel stood up and mouthed the word, "please." Faith sighed, walked over to the table, sat down, and stared out of the window watching the activity on the street.

"Faith, I came here to apologize for the way I treated you when you came by the house. I was wrong and I'm sorry."

"I appreciate that but you didn't have to come all the way down here to tell me that," she said impatiently. "My number is still the same."

"I'm here for more reasons than just to apologize," Daniel said, struggling to get her attention. "I know you probably heard about the trouble I had in Atlantic City."

"Yeah I did, it was all over the news."

"I don't know what was on the news but I want to tell you personally what really happened."

Faith got agitated. "It doesn't matter to me what happened, that's your business."

"It's important to me what you think, so I want to tell you."

"You never cared what I thought before, why now?" Faith asked, wondering what was on his mind.

"When I first met you, I thought you were the kind of woman I could settle down with. You're beautiful, smart, hardworking, you have a great personality, and I enjoy your company. I kept my distance because I didn't think settling down was what I wanted."

"So that's your excuse for messing around with a different woman every night."

"It's more complicated than that, Faith. I'm not gonna lie about it, I've had my share of women, but they never meant anything to me. I don't want that in my life anymore. Going through what I went through, it's not worth it."

"I get it," she said, mocking him, "You're scared straight now."

"I'll take that. I gave you a hard time and now you're repaying me the favor."

"That's not what I'm doing," Faith said, "From everything I've seen it's obvious you weren't the person I thought you were."

Daniel was feeling less hopeful about the odds of him changing her mind but he proceeded on with his reason for coming.

"Faith, I am that guy you thought I was. All that business in Atlantic City was my fault but it wasn't what you think. I never raped anybody. She wanted to come to my room and I let her. She didn't want to leave. She got pissed and called her people to come and kick my ass. Then the cops came. I didn't want it to blow up bigger than it was so I took a plea."

"I'm glad that you can put all that behind you and move on with your life," she said when he finished. "I just don't know what you want from me."

"I want you to give me a chance to get to know you, to prove to you that I am somebody you might want to spend some of your time with."

"This is crazy. All the months that we worked together you never gave me a second thought."

"That's not true. All the time that I sat in that cell, all I could think about was you. I can't explain it. I can only tell you I missed you."

"This is crazy," she said again.

"I had feelings for you that I didn't even know about. The only thing I know is that I want to be around you."

Faith wasn't convinced. From what she had seen in her life, a guy reaches out for a woman when's he's going down, just when he's about to be swallowed in quicksand. When she pulls him up and gets him on solid ground he runs away.

"That's how you feel now," she told him, "When you get your legs under you again you might feel differently. Why don't you take some time and be by yourself for a change."

"I may have been with a few women but in truth I've always been by myself. I want something different now, something real and meaningful."

"I've been on this rollercoaster ride before, Daniel, and I refuse to get back on it. All it does is take you up and down and around in circles. It's thrilling, but in the end it makes you sick to your stomach and brings you back to the same place you started."

"I can respect how you feel. In my life whenever I think about love, I always think pain comes with it. In my mind as long as I didn't get involved with anybody I cared about I wouldn't have to worry about being hurt."

"Just for the sake of argument, where did that feeling come from?"

"My momma and Dad were crazy about each other, when she died he never got over it. Caring about somebody like that used to scare me, now after what I've gone through I'm willing to take the risk."

"I guess I can understand where you were coming from a little better after hearing that, but you were ice cold to me and that's hard for me to ignore."

Up until this moment Daniel hadn't decided if he was ready to pursue another fight. Now it was clear that if he wanted a chance with Faith he would have to fight for it. Doing that would at least keep her near him.

"All I'm asking from you today is to work with me again. I'm going to start training ASAP."

She nodded and smiled. "That I can do, I can't promise anything else."

***

Daniel made the call to Earl Knight's office to set up a meeting. Even now he thought it was unusual that Earl had an elaborate suite of offices on the eighteenth floor in the Penn Center building but always wanted to meet at Delmonico's on City Line Avenue. Daniel was nervous while he made the drive out to the restaurant. A lot was riding on this meeting, his boxing career, his family's business, and his chances with Faith.

He nodded to the maître d when he walked into the restaurant. Carl nodded back in recognition and led him to Earl's table even though Daniel knew where it was. His two ever-present security bookends were seated at the table on either side of him.

"Hey, man," Earl said, standing up and greeting him like a long-lost cousin. "Sit down. Let me take care of you; give you some good food and drinks. Guys, give us some space."

The two guards got up and moved to the table next to them.

"Thanks, man," Daniel said, sliding in the semi-circle booth beside him. "That sounds good to me."

"It's time to put that prison episode in the past and get back to business," Earl said earnestly.

Daniel extended his hand to shake. "That's exactly what I came here to talk to you about."

"I'm glad you reached out, man, I didn't know how much time you needed to get that jail smell out of your system. I don't want to rush you."

"I'm ready to get back in the gym, get my legs under me, and come out fighting. I want my championship title back. I want to wear those belts again."

"That's all I needed to hear you say. Except you got to do it right this time."

"What do you mean?" Daniel asked, puzzled.

"I mean with a proper team behind you, a topnotch trainer."

"I know Wendell has some problems but he helped me get to the title."

"That was luck and I don't like gambling with my money. He blew it on that last fight, man."

"I have to take the heat for that, I was distracted."

"His job was to resolve that but he didn't because he's a damn alcoholic and a drug addict. Having him on your team is not going to work out."

"So who do you suggest I work with?"

"Go over to Champs Gym on West Huntingdon Street. You need a clean break from your old team. When you called I touched base with Grover Teeling over there, he's good people and he'll get you straight."

"I'm down," Daniel said, raising a glass of wine, "I can't argue with a fresh start."

Earl smiled wide and clinked glasses. "Smart man, now eat. We need to get all that government food poisoning out of your system."

***

Things were looking better and better for Daniel. Going to the Champs Gym had been a good move. He was working out with his new trainers and he was feeling stronger than he had in a long time. Faith had him on a diet rich in protein and vegetables. She even delivered some of the meals herself. There was one last order of business that he had been avoiding. He knew it wouldn't be put off any longer when he noticed Wendell's car trailing him on his morning run.

Wendell pulled up beside him and shouted out the window with a bad attitude. "Hey, man, we need to talk."

Daniel stopped and dried the sweat from his face with his shirt. He knew this confrontation was coming. Wendell parked his car and got out.

Chapter Twenty-Two

"What's on your mind?" Daniel asked, even though he knew.

"I hear you back training with somebody else," Wendell said with an accusatory tone.

"That's right," Daniel said, matter-of-factly.

"Come on, man, what's the deal? Why didn't you call me?"

"After the way you trashed my house I wasn't sure if you deserved the courtesy."

"I apologized for that, man. How are you going to hold that against me and take my job?"

"Wendell, I can't use you no more. I can't have any distractions, none from you and none of my own. This is serious business for me."

"Hell, what are you talking about, it's serious business for me too."

"Keep it real, man. You know what I'm talking about."

"Look here, you got your shit together, so did I. We can get right back to where we were when you won the title."

"I can't trust you to stay straight. I can barely trust myself. When you were supposed to keep me straight you were running off in left field somewhere."

"You blaming me for that loss. I told you to cancel it and you wouldn't listen."

"It's not about that, man. That was my bad. But now I need a team that can help me get back on top of my game. Sometimes things have to change. I'm grateful for everything we did together but this is where I get off."

"So it's like that, you just gonna kick me to the curb"

"Don't try to put a guilt trip on me, man. It was a job, you got paid well. I never skimped on your money."

"I'm down, man. I need to make some cash," Wendell said, sounding desperate.

"I can float you a few dollars, that's all I can do. It's plenty of young guys out here like I was who could use a good trainer. Don't give up. You and I just have to move on."

"That's fucked up, man."

Daniel shrugged his shoulders. Wendell stomped off and got back in his car. He pushed the gas to the floor and sped down the street.

***

About a week later Earl Knight dropped by at Champs Gym. He hung back for a couple of minutes to watch Daniel working out on the double-end bag. He was pleased with what he saw. Daniel's hand speed and footwork were right where they needed to be and the accuracy of his punches was on point.

"Looking sharp, man," Earl said, moving up beside him. "You'll be ready."

Daniel stopped punching. "You got some good news for me."

"You know me, I got a deal. Boris Rabinov only has three months to defend the title."

"That's what I've been waiting to hear, man."

"We're all gonna eat, but he gets the biggest slice of pie this time. We'll make it up on the next one. The big money is with Mike Tyson and Holyfield in June."

"It doesn't matter, I just want to get back in the ring with him and show I'm the better man. I'll take on the rest one by one."

"That's what I'm talking about," Earl said on his way out. "You have your shot on July 26th."

Chapter Twenty-Three

aniel could finally see the pieces of his life coming back together again. There was just one piece that stood out to the side. That was the relationship he wanted with Faith. He had made some progress and could safely say they had officially moved into the friend zone. They enjoyed going to movies, going out to dinner, and quiet evenings at her condo playing backgammon. Over the last two months she seemed more relaxed but Daniel wanted to take their friendship to the next level. He didn't want to waste anymore time.

He called her at the café. "How's your day going?"

"Tiring, I spent half the day baking, the other half in front of the computer. Did you want me to prepare a meal for you to pick up?"

"No, I want to cook for you tonight."

"Yeah right," she laughed.

"I'm serious. I want you to come by the house. I'm cooking dinner for you."

Faith hesitated. She had the feeling this wasn't only about eating. It was the fork in the road. Daniel had made his intentions known. She liked him and was attracted to him. The problem was she wasn't sure she could trust him.

"Why don't you come to the café," she offered, "I've got a ton of food here."

"I've got some good news I want to share with you. Besides, what's the big deal? Are you afraid to eat my cooking?"

Faith laughed. "I do have some reservations."

"Sometimes you have to go out on a limb," he said with sincerity.

"Okay, okay, I'll come," she said, "What time will you be serving, sir?"

Daniel contained his excitement. "I'll look for you around eight o' clock."

When Faith hung up he started to panic. He had said all that to get her to come over and hadn't even thought about what he could make for dinner. He dialed up Rebecca to get some emergency help.

"Hey, sis, what's up?" he said after she answered.

"Same old, same old," she said, "What about you?"

"I invited Faith over to dinner tonight."

"All right then, that's nice," she said, smiling to herself. She was happy that he was done with all the hood-rats and gold-diggers. "Do your thing."

"I wanted it to be really special so I told her I was going to cook, except I don't even know what to make. Can you come by and help a brother out."

"I would but you didn't give me enough notice. I already have plans. What you need to do is call Judy B. Bakers catering and they can bring your whole meal, appetizers, entrée, and dessert. All you have to do is set the table."

"Thanks, Becca, you saved me again."

"That's what I do."

"What would I do without you?"

"Lord only knows. I'll even call them for you if you do me a favor."

"What's that?" he asked, grateful for the help.

"I'm releasing your cologne line. I need you to make an appearance at Macy's in New York next week for the launch."

"You know I'm there for you."

"Okay, now go get in the shower. You need plenty of time to

scrub your rusty behind.”

"I'm going to let that go this time since I need you to make that call."

"Look at that, you're smarter than they say you are."

Daniel laughed and hung up.

*****

Faith adjusted her little white dress before she rang the doorbell. It was formfitting with straps across the back that showed just enough skin to be both sexy and classy. She couldn't deny she was still attracted to Daniel and after his persistence and seeming sincerity she had decided to let her guard down and give him the benefit of the doubt.

Daniel answered the door wearing a casual white linen suit and a happy face. He had never seen Faith in a dress and wearing make-up. She looked stunning.

"Come on in, you look fantastic," he said, still smiling

"You look very nice yourself," she said, returning his smile.

Daniel had every intention of serving her the wonderful meal delivered from Judy B.'s, having casual conversation over a bottle of wine, and checking out the stars in the moonlight before he made his move, but with her standing there looking so good he couldn't wait. He pulled her close and kissed her. He held her tighter and made love to her mouth. He wanted her to feel all the emotions that he was feeling because for Daniel it was his first kiss, the first with someone he truly cared about.

"I expected that, but not so soon," Faith said when he finally let her go.

"It wasn't my plan but you were irresistible."

"Well let's see what else you have planned," she said, walking towards the kitchen.

Daniel took her hand and led her to the dining room. "For the many times you served me, I am going to serve you." He pulled out a chair for her. "Please, sit down."

"Thank you, I could get used to this," she said, admiring the candlelit table.

"I hope you will," he said from his heart.

The delivered food was delicious and Faith teased him about getting her there on false pretenses. He opened a bottle of wine and the rest of the evening went according to his plan. Outside in the moonlight he held her and kissed her again.

"If you stay the night I promise I'll cook breakfast for you."

She gave him the look that said don't try it.

"I'll marry you first if you want?" he added.

Faith laughed. "Don't you think you're rushing things?"

"Not at all," he said seriously, "I've already wasted a year."

He continued his request with his outstretched hand. She placed her hand in his accepting the invitation.

***

All of the Clements were pulling together for once as Daniel's scheduled fight grew closer. He was training harder, pushing past every limit, running more miles, sparring for hours, and maintaining his focus clearer than he ever had. Rebecca had expanded their hair care line into natural hair products, gentle perms, waves, and had completed the development of her synthetic and human hair line for weaves and braids. Luke had been released from the rehab facility and was back at home. After his last visit with his physical therapist and speech pathologist they had classified him as 85 percent recovered. He was keeping up his strengthening exercises and walking three miles a day on his own.

Matthew came by the house at least twice a week to check on him. On Memorial Day he came by on his way to the family holiday gathering.

"Ready to go, bro," Matthew called out, coming in with his set of keys.

Chapter Twenty-Three

"I'm in my office," Luke yelled back.

Matthew walked in and saw him sitting on the short couch in warm-ups and house slippers.

"Put your shoes on, it's time to go," Matthew urged, looking at his watch.

"I'm not going," Luke said.

"What do you mean, you're not going? Mama and Martha have been cooking since yesterday and I don't smell nothing in here."

"I'm not hungry."

"You don't have to eat but it's time you showed everybody how well you're doing. They were all worried about you."

"I don't feel like being bothered, you know it's some mess every time we're together."

"So what, that's nothing new, we're family."

"I need to take some time and do something for me."

"Something like what?"

"I want to go to the Bahamas this weekend and I want you to come with me."

"You don't have to ask me twice. I don't mind, but why the Bahamas?" Matthew asked, wondering where the idea came from.

"Because when I think about it that was the last place I remember feeling truly happy. I want to feel that way again. I want to start over. I think it would be a good place to begin."

Matthew nodded yes. He knew where his brother was coming from. He hadn't been all that happy in a long time himself.

"I'm surprised you want to take a trip right now, my brother, but I'm glad to hear it. I thought you would have beaten down the door of the office by now."

"Not yet, Becca's running things better than I ever did."

"In that case, I'll go with you if you come and eat with your family today. You don't have to stay long, just let them see you're back on your feet again."

"I probably won't get any peace until I do," Luke said, obliging him. "Give me a minute to change my clothes."

"Take your time. I'm not leaving without you."

***

Luke hadn't been back to his and Ruthie's old house in years. Stepping through the unlocked door was like taking a gut punch from the memories inside. He held the doorknob tightly while he got his bearings. The living room was basically unchanged except the furniture looked slightly more worn from the day they moved away to Chestnut Hill.

Matthew led the way through the aroma filled kitchen to the patio out back. Martha and Mary were talking and basting the chicken and ribs on the grill. Mark was drinking a beer with the cordless phone pressed between his shoulder and his ear and eating a hot dog.

"Daddy, you came," Rebecca said happily, jumping up to give him a hug."

"You look good, son," Gloria said, sitting in a lounge chair by John. "Come on and sit down."

"Hello, Mama," Luke said, taking a seat in a chair near the door. "How's everybody doing?"

"What's up, brother," Mark said and went back to his phone call.

"We doing fine," John said, "It's you we was worried about."

Martha waved through the smoke, "Don't listen to him. What do you want to eat?"

"A leg quarter and some bake beans and I'm cool," Luke answered.

"He know he better leave that pork alone or he'll stroke on out again," John said, adding his usual two-cent comment.

Mary rolled her eyes with exasperation, "Pop, why you got to keep riding his back? Let him eat in peace for a change."

"Excuse me," John said, pretending to be insulted. "I didn't know I was bothering him. Mark, get me another beer."

Gloria frowned at John giving him an evil eye. Then she turned to Luke and asked, "Where's Daniel? Is he coming by?"

"I don't know," Luke replied, "I haven't talked to him in a few days."

Rebecca chimed in, "He's all hugged up with his new lady somewhere."

"Good for him," John said, "At least he's got somebody. I can't understand why the rest of you are by yourselves. Don't y'all want somebody to grow old with?"

"I'm not by myself," Mary snapped, "Rueben doesn't come over here with me because you all never made him feel welcomed."

"Child, it tears me up that you threw your life away on that old man," Gloria said, "I wish you would have gotten you a young man and had a kid or two."

"I'm tired of y'all criticizing him," Mary complained, "He was there for me when I needed somebody."

"Uh-huh," John said, "She gonna get her chance to change some diapers, that old man's."

"Pop, you don't have the right to come down on us all the time," Matthew said, "It wasn't like you was father of the year. Maybe us being alone has something to do with the way we were raised."

"Y'all didn't get that from me," John argued in his defense, "Your mama and me been together for fifty-six years."

"Congratulations, bully for you," Matthew said, throwing up his hands, "The rest of us don't know how to let anybody get close. All we know is how to do is fend for ourselves."

Mark shook his head in frustration and popped the cap on another beer. "Why do we have to keep going down this road?"

John stood on his feet like a preacher about to give the word. "Sometimes all your mama and poppa can do for you in this life is give you some good stock to work with. I believe we did that 'cause look what you did with your life. I ain't gonna apologize 'cause I did the best I could with what I had."

There was no reply. None of them could argue with that. Matthew sat down with his head in his hands. Mark made another phone call. Mary and Martha went back to basting the meat.

"I'm kind of tired," Luke said, standing up with his food in hand, "I'll just take my plate home with me."

"You probably don't have all you strength back," Gloria said, reaching out for his plate. "I'll wrap it up for you."

"Thanks, Mama," he said, following her into the kitchen.

"I'll take you home," Rebecca said, glad to have a reason to leave.

"Your father don't mean no harm," Gloria said at the doorway, "He just has his ways."

Luke gave her a kiss on the cheek. "I know, Mama, we all do."

***

Luke looked out into the billows of clouds in the air. He hadn't been on a plane for ten years. Being so high above the earth below made him wonder what the heavens looked like and if Ruthie was looking down on him. His eyes played tricks on him and he saw her dancing in the shapes of the puffs that floated near his window.

When they landed in Nassau, it was all as beautiful as he had remembered. The tall palm trees, the fresh salt air over the blue water, and the island music played on the steel drums wherever they went. But none of it was the same without his family.

Luke walked slowly along the edge of the beach, struggling to hear Ruthie's voice above the sound of the waves rushing in. He had come to this area of the beach every evening during the week hoping and praying that she would speak to him.

Matthew walking one step behind him broke the silence. "What's on your mind, brother?"

"Thinking about these years without Ruthie, I didn't feel alive until I almost died."

"We all take our lives for granted sometimes."

"Too bad we can't turn back and do it all again."

"We all make mistakes," Matthew said to comfort him, "If you didn't make the same ones you would make different ones. Give yourself some credit, you were a good father."

"I just wanted to do right by them."

"You were trying too hard not to be the absent father that Pop was, so hard that you became rigid and controlling with Daniel. With Rebecca you were trying not to be the poor provider Pop was, you wanted to tie her hands so you could do everything for her. You were denying her the chance to earn something on her own."

"I was trying to show them the love I didn't get a chance to show their momma."

"What love are you talking about, Luke? Ruthie was happy, you meant the world to her."

"I promised her I would take care of her."

"You did, I saw it for myself."

"I didn't do enough. I didn't have enough time."

"You crying and complaining but you had more than most of us out here," Matthew said, thinking about his own family. He hadn't seen his wife or daughters for six years.

Luke sighed. "It's never enough no matter how long when you love somebody."

"I feel your pain but there's nothing you can do about it. It is what it is. Give yourself permission to be happy."

"At this point I have to, I don't have much choice."

Chapter Twenty-Four

Daniel rented two homes in Vegas, one for his team and the other for his family. They had all flown in to cheer him on in the rematch. On the evening of the fight, Gloria and John chose to watch the fight on the big screen TV. They didn't want to get out in the huge crowd. Mary and Martha went to see all the pre-fight festivities but weren't planning to watch the fight.

"I don't want to see my nephew up there getting beat on," Martha said, "We are going to the casino and play the slots until it's over."

"Martha and I will be here to clean him up when it's over," Mary said before they left.

About an hour later, Matthew, Mark, Luke, and Rebecca rode to Caesar's Palace in the provided limo and took their seats, four rows up from the ring.

Mark leaned over to whisper in Rebecca's ear. "Care to tell me who your money is on?"

Rebecca laughed, "I don't have a dime on it. If I did I would be back at the house with Grandma and Grandpop. I wouldn't have the stomach to sit here."

"I hope you made the right decision to release the cologne line," Matthew said to Rebecca. "That was a big enough gamble right there."

"Uh-uh, Daddy made that bet over a year ago. Once it was done I couldn't pull the money off the table," Rebecca replied.

"You're right about that," Matthew said, thinking back for a second.

"Relax, Uncle Matt, it doesn't matter whether he wins or loses," Rebecca said, patting him on the arm, "With all the hype for the fight going on it was the opportune time to ship it out. As a matter of fact, from the early figures the sales aren't bad at all. It seems the hip-hop fans gravitate to his bad boy image."

"I know you two are not going to sit beside me and talk business in here, my nerves are bad enough," Luke said, half-joking."

***

Daniel had the worst case of nerves that he'd ever had before a fight. His muscles twitched and jolted uncontrollably. Shadow boxing in the dressing room he tried to warm up and relax. Grover tapped him on the shoulders when he was ready to tape his hands.

"You got this," he said to boost Daniel's confidence.

"There's no such thing," Daniel said, thinking back. The first time he fought Boris, he didn't have a doubt in his mind that he would beat him. Now having lost to him, he didn't know what to think. He didn't want to think. He just wanted to act.

With his hands wrapped and his gloves on, Grover held his robe up for him to slide his arms in. He hadn't worn it since his last fight. Once it was on his shoulders he felt heavy, more than the 220 pounds at his weigh-in. He was also carrying the burden of the obligations to the family business. He jumped up and down and ran in place defying the extra load to hold him down. Grover opened the door and his new crew stood out there waiting to escort him to the ring. He walked out and they began to play his music.

Standing at the entrance, the response was noncommittal, no cheers and no jeers, just a cacophony of voices throughout the expansive room. It was like a sea of people going up to the high ceiling like a rising wave. Daniel took a step, crossed the threshold, and DJ Kool's *Let Me Clear My Throat* began to blare from huge speakers. The excitement of the fans exploded with the volume of the music. Daniel mentally plugged into the energy that flowed around him and rode it down the lengthy aisle surrounded by his entourage to the ring.

Inside the same ring where he had his first professional fight, Daniel was back in his element as he waved to the mixture of faces in the arena. The difference was night and day from the faces he saw in Germany. He took his place in the blue corner with Grover, Pepe, his assistant trainer, and Alonzo, his cut man.

Then Boris entered the stadium like a champion with James Bond's theme music playing. The taste of Hollywood was appreciated by the viewing audience. They applauded and cheered until he was positioned in the red corner.

Michael Buffer moved to the center of the ring. "Welcome, ladies and gentlemen, to Caesar's Palace in Las Vegas Nevada. Knight Promotions along with their sponsors present 12-rounds of boxing for the Heavyweight Championship of the World." He introduced the commissioners, the doctors, three judges, and the referee. "To the thousands seated here this evening and the millions around the world watching on pay-per-view, let's get ready to rumble. Introducing first, out of the blue corner wearing emerald green and white trim, with 28 professional wins, one loss, and 21 wins by knockout, straight from the City of Brotherly Love, Philadelphia, here is Daniel 'The Lionhearted' Clements. Coming out of the red corner, presenting the pride of Russia and the WBO Heavyweight Champion of the World, with 34 wins, three losses, and 16 by knockout, here is Boris Rabinov."

The referee steps between them giving the rules of the fight. "I want a clean fight, obey my commands, protect yourselves at all times, shake hands and come out fighting at the bell."

The fighters tap gloves and retreat to their corners.

Pepe puts in Daniels mouthpiece just before the bell rings. Daniel dives forward to meet Boris for the first round. They both begin in a slow pace standing flat-footed and exchange jab for jab. Each of them thinking about stamina after the first fight went the distance. Boris throws a solid right hand to Daniels chin that changes the rhythm of the fight and he counters with a left hook and a right hand to the body that makes Boris backup.

"This is not a warm-up," Grover said after the bell while Pepe pours water into his mouth. "Don't carry him. You letting him cruise."

Daniel comes back out in the second and third round dictating the pace, going in for the jab, bob and weaving back out on defense. He was landing the bulk of the punches and each one building his confidence.

"He's looking good," Mark said.

Matthew looked worried. "Boris is taking a rest, he's not hurt."

Boris comes into the fourth round head hunting with heavy shots and lands a short left hook to the side of Daniel's head. Daniel shakes it off and they match punches. Boris starts working his body with double jabs and then stepping away. Daniel lands a cross to his chin. Boris counters and both are standing toe-to-toe throwing bombs to the head of the other. Daniel stuns him with a left jab to the jaw and Boris rushes him with a head butt to the eye. The round ends with Luke, Rebecca, Matthew, and Mark stiff in their seats with balled fists.

"Keep your hands up," Grover said impatiently while Alonzo pressed the cold irons over the swelling on his eye. "Don't get lazy and don't wait on him. Take it to him."

Pepe greased Daniel's face and head with a hunk of Vaseline before he put his mouthpiece back in. The bell rang for the fifth round. Daniel comes out strong landing firm punches to the body and a left hook that knocks him into the corner. Boris is leaning on the ropes and Daniel is pounding his middle with combinations. Boris throws an intentional low blow to make Daniel back up. The referee breaks them up and gives Boris a warning. Daniel is breathing hard and Boris throws a flurry of wild punches with most of them missing. Daniel counters and is more accurate. The bell ending the round rings.

"You're not going to win this boxing, step up the pace," Grover told Daniel.

Boris comes charging out in the sixth round with his legs back under him getting off his jab first. Daniel counters with quick hands landing a combination. Boris is loading up on his punches going for a knockout. The entire ring is enclosed with cameramen resting on the edge of the canvas. Loud piercing whistles accent the roars from the crowd. Daniel is in defensive mode while Boris is holding and hitting. Daniel counters with a jab to the jaw that backs Boris up. He comes back barely missing a one punch knockout and then throws another low blow. Rebecca bows her head and covers her eyes praying for the bell to ring.

"Listen, man," Grover told Daniel back in his corner, "You can't leave this up to the judges, you got to knock him out." Pepe squeezes a towel filled with water over the top of his head and Daniel feels the individual streams running down the back of his neck. "It's hammer time," Grover tells him. Daniel nods his head.

Boris comes out slugging again but his punches don't move Daniel back. He moves to the inside firing off short jabs, digging in the middle of Boris. Boris ties him up, smothering him and holding on. The referee breaks them apart and Daniel lands a combination that knocks Boris against the ropes. He moves in with a strong right cross that connects to Boris's head. He follows with an uppercut to the chin that knocks his head all the way to his back. Daniel throws a hammer to his open throat and Boris crashes to the canvas like a heavy side of beef.

The crowd jumps to their feet with cheers and celebration. The ref goes through the motions of giving Boris the count but nobody thinks he's getting up. Daniel's corner men, Grover, Pepe, and Alonzo rush towards him and lift him up into the air. Boris' corner rush over to him as well and lift him from the floor of the ring.

Daniel was overwhelmed and relieved from the victory and cried. His tears were camouflaged among the dripping sweat on his face. His eyes searched the room until he found Faith. He waved his glove for her to come. She pushed her way through until she was ringside. Daniel fell to his knees.

"Marry me," he said intently.

"I will," she said, reaching out to him.

Epilogue

Luke created a Board of Directors for the company and Daniel agreed to serve as a member. They had their first meeting a week after New Year's. Rebecca stood at the head of the long conference table.

"It is my pleasure to announce that with the success of our Kurl hair line and the Daniel Fragrance collection the Clements Cosmetic Company is once again on solid footing," she said happily.

"We have you to thank, baby girl," Luke said, "Without you I don't want to think about what might have happened to this company."

"I second that," Matthew said, "You were a lifesaver, Becca. The loan from HLS has been paid in full."

Rebecca beamed with pride. "My motivation was to keep this a vibrant family business. My mother and father put this together with their bare hands. This will always be Clements Cosmetic Company."

Daniel began the applause. When the accolades came to an end, they covered a few more details and earnings and the meeting was adjourned.

"There is a reception being held for all employees in the lobby," Matthew added, "I think it's time we joined them."

The room emptied with the exception of Luke and Daniel.

"Son, I have to tell you how proud I am of you."

"Thanks, Dad, it feels good to hear that. I didn't mean to hurt you and I'm sorry for all the upset you went through but I couldn't stop being who I am no matter what the consequences were going to be."

"I understand, Daniel. That's what it means to be a man."

Daniel nodded in agreement.

"Can I give you one word of advice that applies to all of us in what we do?" Luke asked.

"Sure, Dad, I'm listening."

"Don't stay too long, son, there's a time to let it go and pass it on to someone else."

"I won't, I promise."

Luke patted him on the back as they went to join the others.

***

On Saturday, August 22, 1998, Luke got up to do what he always did on this day, buy flowers before his visit with Ruthie. She would have been forty-seven years old. Rebecca and Daniel met him on his way out of the door.

Rebecca wrapped him up with a hug and a kiss. "Good morning, Daddy, we're going with you today."

Luke was surprised and overwhelmed for a moment. He had always gone alone.

"Is that okay?" Daniel asked, noticing his reaction.

"Of course it's okay. I'm glad you're here."

"We can take my car," Rebecca said, waving her keys in the air.

"Do you mind if we take your momma's car?" Luke said, not wanting to break his tradition.

"No problem, if you let me drive," Rebecca said, heading to the garage.

Luke got into the front passenger side where he had ridden so many times beside Ruthie while she drove. He rolled down the window after Rebecca started the car.

"It's a beautiful morning," he said, taking in the fresh air.

"It's going to be a hot one," Rebecca said as she backed out of the driveway. "I don't see why we can't go out to eat instead of Aunt Mary wanting to do a cookout."

"She said there's going to be a solar eclipse tonight and she wants all the family there to watch it together," Daniel said. "Faith is going to meet us over there."

Rebecca pulled over and stopped the car in front of Jr. Beale Flowers on Broad Street, a couple of miles from the cemetery.

"How do you know where I buy the flowers?" Luke asked, slightly surprised.

Rebecca snickered. "Daddy, I know more than half the stuff you don't think I know."

"I'll be back in a minute," Luke said, getting out. This was something he wanted to do by himself. He came out with his crimson roses and white carnations a few minutes later.

At the entrance to Mount Peace, Rebecca parked the car on the street and the three of them walked in together. Solemnly they made their way through the garden of memorials, flowers, and gravestones until they reached the area where Ruth was buried. They stood there a few feet away reading the words on her headstone and flashing through their own sets of memories. Even almost ten years later they all hurt too much to give comfort to each other.

Daniel and Rebecca were content to go back to the car when Luke said, "Give me some time alone with your momma."

He kneeled down and placed the flowers in the vase and began to talk to her.

Sweet Ruthie, you were the girl in my dreams before we met and you will always be now that we are apart. When I first saw you I couldn't believe my eyes. I had to touch you to be sure you were real. Then when we talked and I got to know you I found you were more than I dared to dream about. You were as kind as you were beautiful, and I'm not sure why, but you loved me. All I wanted to do was keep you safe and take care of you, give you everything you could ever desire. It hurts me that I didn't do as well as I wanted to. You were everything to me, and when I lost you, for a long time I thought I didn't have anything left. Then I realized I still had Daniel and Rebecca. They turned out good. Daniel is all you on the outside and Rebecca is all you on the inside. I guess I tried to hold them too tight and Daniel got away from me. Things got bad, real low, almost underground sometimes, but we're all looking up again. Daniel is where he wants to be and Rebecca is where she wants to be. I want to be with you, Ruthie, but I guess it's not my time yet. I'll live this life as long as the Good Lord allows with an open mind and an open heart. I don't know if I'll find someone else to love before it's all said and done and that's all right because I'll always love you, sugar.

Luke kissed his fingers and rubbed them across her likeness on the headstone, rose to his feet, and walked away.

Daniel grabbed his shoulder when he got into the car. "How are you doing, Dad?"

"Better than I have been in years," Luke answered. "Thank y'all for coming with me today."

Rebecca hugged him again. "Daddy, we wanted to come."

"We love you, Dad, and we're here for you," Daniel said.

"I need that and I need you two," Luke said, shedding a tear.

"Should we head straight to the house for the cookout?" Rebecca asked cheerily, trying to tone down the intense emotions between them. "Everybody else is probably already there."

Luke laughed. "We might as well. I can't get away from my family no matter how hard I try."

The End